Book The Way

PART ONE:

RUNNING IN CORRIDORS

BY

FRANKIE FULWOOD

DEDICATION

To my leading lady – this one's for you! X
With special thanks to Pam Howes & Richard Thomas

Edited by
David Pickering

Cover design by
Jenny O'Connor

Prologue

It was running in fear that brought me here, to my little bolt hole from the troubles of the past. I don't care how big or tough you think you are, there are some things that scare all of us, and no matter how far or fast you run you can never hide from memories like mine. The lonely hours of my sleepless nights were filled with guilt and shame and haunted by that feeling that a blow was about to land—the kind of blow from a vicious crushing fist that shatters tooth and bone and leaves a man broken. Sometimes I almost wished it would finally fall and put an end to my torment, but the sunrise always brought fingers of light scratching their way into the darkness in my heart. I don't know how long I could have survived this cycle of waking with the roar of the crowd in my head and a cold sweat making me shiver as I clutched the blankets for comfort. The worst part was that the dreams didn't end when I woke. I felt I would never be able to scrub the bloodstains from either my knuckles or my soul. I was living a shambolic half-life, using my unkempt appearance and gruff manner to keep people at arm's length. I have to admit that I was just about ready to throw in the towel one final time, give up on the pain that was my life, for keeps—and then *she* came...

Chapter 1

Come on... come on... just this once... just for me... it's only a gear... you've got a box full... you stubborn pile of junk!

Just before the last bend in the road the engine started its penultimate coughing fit as I fought the steering to turn into my little plot, sweat streaming down my face, the sun blazing, and the window winder long since broken.

Then I had my first piece of good fortune for a while - the gate was open. A few more splutters and chugs and I managed to coax the old crate clear of the driveway.

Liza was weeding my little vegetable patch and came over to meet me, laughing as I hurled abuse at my old car. 'You ought to get it fixed properly instead of keeping on tinkering with it,' she said, smiling.

'How can I, love? I've just spent my last few shekels on chicken feed and a few essentials. Where's the money going to come from?'

'Why don't you get a proper job like everyone else?' she replied mischievously. Now that really annoyed me. A safe little job with a pension, a savings scheme and regular income; most of those wage slaves were no better off than

I was - all just one pay cheque away from penury. Besides, I thought, as I glanced from the alluring view across the open fields of wheat and barley to the Clee Hills in the distance and back to the perspiration beading on Liza's chest and trickling down to moisten her vest top, where she had tied it up to expose her midriff to the sun, what price can you put on a view like that? She carried on lecturing me.

'You could work part time. There are plenty of opportunities if you just go and look.'

'Sounds simple when you say it like that, love. Just hop on my bike and out-pedal the three million poor sods that actually want to sell their souls? And don't forget; now the strike's over there'll be plenty of miners joining the queue.'

'You seem to have the general idea, Frankie.'

'I haven't got a bike.' I grinned back. She ignored me and went back to her weeding - still lecturing me as she worked.

'We could use some one full-time up at the grange. It would be good money.'

Well, you just can't argue with logic like that, can you? Besides I'd been there and done that before. I decided it was high time I changed the subject; I didn't mind working with Liza on her little projects but other than that I preferred to keep out of things up at the grange.

'Can you run me into town, to pick up a few bits for the old girl, please, love?'

Liza smirked. 'The garage or the antiques centre?'

'Cheeky mare, she's built to last, not like yours. That's why you need a new one every five minutes.'

'No, Frankie. That's just because Marcus can afford it and likes to let everyone know.' She circled my wreck. It seemed to shrink under her scrutiny. 'What sort is she anyway?'

'She's a Vauxhall Viva. Well, she was until the badges fell off. Come on, a new ignition coil and she'll be as good as new.'

'She needs more than that,' Liza said, still circling.

'Maybe a set of plugs, contact breaker points, ignition leads, a condenser – oh, and an oil change - but there's plenty of life left in the old girl yet.'

Liza slid elegantly into the driver's seat of her Mercedes; her lovely tanned legs looked elegant even in shorts and old walking boots. 'Come on then. I can spare a few minutes for an old friend. By the way, who's paying for all these parts?'

'Less of the old, but it's nice of you to offer, I'll pay you back - honest.'

That's how it was for Liza and me. Halcyon days, filled with sunshine and fun. The sunshine is back, but those carefree days are gone. They went one bitter winter night and things have never been quite the same. What happened is a familiar enough tale - sex, drugs, lies, deceit, treachery and murder - but it wasn't my fault. Well, most of it wasn't anyway.

The rest of that summer went much as those that had gone before, except that I now had the pleasure of Liza's company. She was a fairly new and very welcome addition. We did my usual round of auctions, livestock sales and odd jobs and I worked on Liza's projects in her workshop. Eggs hatched, chicks grew, and my embryonic pet hen enterprise stumbled from one financial crisis to the next in a fairly predictable fashion.

It might be worth taking the time here to tell you a little about my mixed-up life. I live in the void between two different communities, my father a Romany Gypsy and my mother from the settled community that Gypsies call Gorgies. Many of them call me it too, just like most settled people call me Gypo, Pikey, Diddykoi. Racist insults – I've heard them all.

I spent half my young life in one community and half in the other. Then I grew up. Having made a mess of both lives, I gave up on people and came here. I was once asked, 'What do you consider yourself to be, Gypsy or Gorgie?' Me? I'm just what my mother called me - I'm Frankie, just Frankie; nothing more, and nothing less. And, I suppose, I was also a small - very small - smallholder.

My few acres in those days were at the western corner of a much larger farm and straddled the border of Shropshire and Staffordshire. They were roughly triangular in shape, with a fairly busy B road bordering one side. An overgrown hedge of holly, ash and hawthorn sheltered me from the traffic noise and provided some privacy on the side adjacent to the road. A hawthorn and hazel hedge, also overgrown, ran along the hypotenuse roughly parallel to a stream. This stream separated me from the rest of the farmland that surrounded Liza's home, Whitimere Grange. A bridle path ran along the stream's far bank and provided a route to the village beyond. The stream could be crossed by the few planks and stepping stones that I generously called a bridge. The shortest, eastern, side had another overgrown hedge, with the remains of a long-since collapsed dry-stone wall amongst its roots. The bridle path continued on this side and separated me from a large field that was used to grow hay - winter fodder - for the farm. At the opposite side the sharpest corner of the triangle was snipped off by a row of Scots pine trees that cast long shadows in the evening sun and prevented the eastbound traffic on the B road enjoying an open view of my land.

I had the remains of a long-since collapsed cottage, a victim of a fire in its thatched roof years before I arrived and invested my little nest egg. Rumours of foul play and hidden treasure were still rife amongst the older residents of the nearby village whenever my ruined cottage was mentioned. A cold tap provided my water at the now-freestanding Belfast sink; a functional outside loo completed the luxuries of my desirable residence. I also possessed a few shabby sheds and a couple of field shelters that all did their best to stay upright in the face of the relentless wind that blew from the south-east in the winter months. The wind made life very cold and a little harder than was comfortable.

I had given up all ambitions to rebuild the place a few years back when the previous owner of the grange, old Mr Smestow, helped me out of a financial crisis - I'll tell you about it if I get a minute - and generously took my deeds as security. He then, thoughtless old sod that he was, died; his will divided his property between a surprising number of distant relatives who rallied round the old homestead and promptly put house, land, and contents up for auction.

The only good thing to come of this, as far as I was concerned, was his insistence on me having a life interest in my little plot for a peppercorn rent. The auction left me unemployed, hence my attempts to expand my few chickens and vegetable plot into a living - though, as with everything I tried, I had little success. This was the first half of the nineteen-eighties, a long time after *The Good Life*, with Tom and Barbara's good-humoured middle-class antics glamorising the keeping of a back-yard flock and long before Hugh Fearnley-Whittingstall's *River Cottage* began the trend all over again. And so I continued to revel in the lap of poverty.

It was doing odd jobs and working on Liza's projects, made possible by my ragbag of skills and knowledge picked up from a life best described as eclectic, that kept the wolf from the door.

So there I lived in my *de-luxe* caravan - well, that's what its faded stickers said, though it hadn't seen service on the highways since I'd spent every penny I owned on buying the place and leaving my past lives, and all their problems, behind.

***

The days grew shorter and our hours in the sun turned to cosy nights under my duvet - I'm not blessed with central heating and women do tend to feel the cold, don't they? Liza spent most of her time with me, tidying up and mothering me by bringing homemade hot meals and wine from her cellar before we snuggled up. Well, she had an obligation to see that I was warm and fed - she was my new landlady after all. In truth it was her husband Marcus who was the landlord, but he was always away on business and she did love playing Lady Chatterley to my rough-handed labourer. We rubbed along together pretty well; she was gorgeous, intelligent and witty, while I was my usual charming self. We both had our problems and provided mutual support. Don't get me wrong - we weren't an item. She had her life and I had mine, but they just touched together in a few mutually convenient places; there was more to our relationship than met the eye but it was *not* what you're probably thinking.

It was a cold winter night, I remember, when I woke up shivering. We'd been doing our usual thing, listening to a local station, Better-Music-Beacon, on my little radio, singing along to the latest hits and talking nonsense until we fell asleep. When Liza was there she either had all the duvet, and spent the evenings hunting draughts to extinction, or wanted all the windows open - you just can't win with some people, can you? I woke with a hazy image of her lovely face in my mind - her hazel eyes with a sprinkling of green flecks, an impish smile playing at the corners of her delicate mouth, and her lustrous dark hair spread like a halo around her head as she reclined on the soft white pillow. My senses seemed filled by the haunting floral smell of her perfumed skin. My waking dream warmed me and I reached for her - my arm found an empty space.

I sat up, startled, to see the reason for my sudden plunge into the wintery cold. It wasn't just her absence but her failure to shut the door properly as she left. 'Inconsiderate cow,' I grumbled as I streaked to the door and pulled it noisily shut, like a moody teenager, demonstrating audibly my discontent, though she was too far away to hear it.

She'd left the radio quietly tuned to one of those odd channels only weirdos listen to - isobars and wind speeds, details of Atlantic hurricanes, all endlessly dribbling from its tiny crackling speaker. 'Wasting my bloody batteries,' I thought aloud as I turned it off. I don't know what narked me more, her not shutting the door when she left, or her not being there when I reached for her.

I crawled back into the warm patch she'd left, inhaled her lingering scent and softly sank into a lovely deep sleep... No, sorry, it wasn't quite like that. The truth is I tossed and turned, quite unable to recapture my lost slumber.

Aren't knees uncomfortable when you come to think of it? Nasty knobbly things that don't fit together properly, and don't get me started on ankles... after an hour or so I got up to start my daily grind.

I still sleep badly, but it's mostly guilt and shame that disturb my nights, and not the draughts.

Chapter 2

As a pale sun rose to reveal a morning as cold as the night it followed, I set out over the bridge and through the fields surrounding the grange with the frosty grass crunching under my feet. I approached, staying close to the house on the pretence of popping into the village, but all the time hoping to see Liza and find out why she'd left.

It's an odd old house, a huge place, basically two houses joined together. The eastern half predates the western half, which is classical early Victorian, by a couple of hundred years or more. I knew Liza favoured the older eastern half, with its courtyard surrounded on three sides by outbuildings and stables. Some of these were now workshops, which she used for her hobby business of antique furniture restoration and where she indulged her enthusiasm for craft work and ancient industry. Her activities had in the previous year expanded to casting and spinning brassware. She'd installed a traditional charcoal forge and a big old spinning lathe. While her casting was excellent, her spinning was a little hit and miss. I just don't think, despite her fitness, that she had the upper body strength it required.

I'd spent hours helping her out with her projects as I'd

picked up a few things over the years and I was always willing to learn more. This latest expansion of her seemingly inexhaustible resourcefulness had made her popular with the local heavy horse society and the steam railway. There was a fair chance she would be in there toiling away at some project or other. In fact she'd probably come up with the solution to some problem in her sleep and hared off to put it into practice.

As I walked past the open side of the courtyard, heading roughly in the direction of the village, I saw her standing in the middle of the gravel-covered expanse with Marcus. They turned towards me and, as it was obvious they'd seen me, I put on my best cheery smile and strolled, as casually as my shaking legs would allow, to greet them. Marcus was one of those natural leaders, public school then Oxford. He had a brisk military manner and a black belt in one of those pyjama-wearing oriental arts - he always seemed to be bristling with violent intentions and made me feel clumsy and uneasy. I've found violence is the first link in a chain that always ends with consequences and consequences frighten the life out of me.

'Where the hell were you until gone four this morning?' he bawled at Liza as I approached. 'I got an early flight home to surprise you and it seems that's exactly what I did.'

'I was out with a friend,' she snapped back.

'Rutting with this tramp in that mobile pigsty, was it?'

I know a real hero would have stepped in, put things straight, defended her honour, but to my shame I'm not the heroic type. I froze and stared at my feet, looking, I'm sure, guilty enough to be convicted of anything. I knew their relationship was tempestuous - she often wore her Ray-Bans to hide the evidence - but she could give as good as she got. And, speaking from personal experience, I'm not entirely sure she didn't like her pleasure spiked with a little pain, but that would just be making excuses for my cowardice. Looking back at that moment makes me sure it was pivotal in the downward slide to the desperate days that followed.

'Mind your own bloody business, Marcus,' she hissed. 'What friends I keep and who I see are for me to choose.'

'You're my wife!' he yelled, and he grabbed her shoulder as she turned to storm away.

'Get your hands off me!' she screamed, shaking with rage. 'You lost the right to touch me, or tell me what to do a long time ago. Why don't you get a plane back to your whore and leave me and my friends alone?'

He paused for a moment and turned to me with a sinister sneer. I was frozen about fifteen feet away, close enough to hear and see all, but far enough away to have a decent head start in a chase. 'Why are you still here?' he enquired with hatred in his eyes. 'Go on, bugger off.'

I stood, eyes down, shoulders dropped, shuffling my feet in the deep gravel, searching for the proverbial crack that would let the earth open and swallow me up. Liza muttered something I didn't quite hear, spitting the words through gritted teeth, something like '...not her fault it sank', whatever that meant.

He shrugged at that, smiled, and then turned and gave Liza a vicious slap across the face that knocked her to the ground.

'You'd better start behaving yourself - or do you want all your nice little friends to know your guilty secret? That wouldn't do your lady-of-the-manor act any good, would it?' Then he stormed off, his hand-stitched brogues crunching the gravel as he went. Liza sat stunned, a hand on her reddened cheek. I remained rooted to the spot.

'Bastard!' she yelled after him.

He glared over his shoulder at us. All I could feel was fear in case he came back. But he didn't, he just strolled around the front of the house and out of sight. We heard him bawling orders at a few serfs, then a car door slammed and he roared off, showering gravel in his wake.

'Liza!' I shouted as I ran to her, slumping to my knees and throwing my arms around her. She shook as she sobbed and I sobbed with her. I still don't really know why. Was it me sharing her pain and humiliation, or just my own? I'd stood there, letting my friend suffer at the hands of this bully and had done nothing. She pushed me away and got shakily to her feet. Blood trickled from her nose and her eye looked a little puffy. 'Give me your car keys, Liza. I'll go after him.'

'And do what?' she snapped back. 'Beat him to a pulp? Force him into submission and make him apologise?'

I stammered, searching for a reply.

'Forget it, Frankie.'

Then, after dusting herself down, she held her head high and walked slowly away while I stood and let her go. But that's me all over - a quitter, spineless, *lacking character* as my teachers used to say. Well then, why didn't they try harder to teach some into me? I was their tabula rasa and all I remember them doing is throwing board rubbers at me. I blame them, and the government, and... anybody, except me - it's not my fault, is it?

I left through the archway in the middle of the stables on the village side of the yard. It had massive wooden doors on each side that enclosed an open area, which divided the stable block into two halves. In each huge door was a smaller pedestrian door, which was usually left open. As I stepped through the outer door into the sunshine, I almost brained myself on the low outer edge of the archway. Then I made my way sulkily home.

I arrived back at my field to find I had company. A black Mitsubishi Shogun, with dark tinted windows and shiny chrome bits, stood menacingly in my driveway. More trouble - it just wasn't going to be my day. I walked towards it, expecting the doors to open and a couple of huge goons to get out to show me just how much worse a bad day can get when you cross a man like Marcus.

I nervously searched the pockets in my old waxed jacket as I went, trying to find something, though I have no idea what - a weapon perhaps? I usually had a few useful things in them, but I came up with nothing - just an odd glove and a few loose polo mints. So I decided to rely on my charm and my ability to scramble through a hawthorn hedge, as running in fear is a speciality of mine.

As I moved ever more slowly toward the menacing vehicle the driver's door opened and to my surprise a woman stepped out. I smiled as she shook out her long chestnut curls, their rich copper glow glinting in the pale winter sun. She stretched away the stiffness of a long drive, holding her arms high and arching her back, her long loose skirt clinging enticingly to her shapely thighs. Jenny! I broke into a trot and a smile simultaneously. She is one of the few landmarks of my fragmented life, and the only remnant of the Frankie that I was before I came here. I scooped her up and kissed her.

'When did you get back, gorgeous? I thought you were off singing and sunning yourself on the Med. Spain, wasn't it?'

'Cyprus, and I got back just now,' she replied, a pleasant hint of Gaelic in her soft voice - echoes of her childhood on the Emerald Isle - and a sparkle in her bright blue eyes.

She *is*, or as it turned out *was*, half of a singing duo that did a great range of modern songs and soft country classics, peppered with traditional folk. She'd been touring with her partner, Lydia, a posh jolly-hockey-sticks finishing school graduate who played the piano wonderfully, her ash blonde curls and pale skin a pleasant contrast to Jenny's darker looks. Despite this I had always thought them an unlikely pair. 'So what happened to bring you here then, love?' I asked.

'Digger,' she replied with a sigh. 'He's off on a contract

somewhere. New motorway junction, I think, and my trailer's locked in his yard.'

For trailer read caravan - but hers was no wreck like mine, it was a leather-upholstered, cut-glass windowed palace on wheels.

'I was wondering...' She smiled and toyed with the buttons on my shirt.

'If you could stay here?' I asked.

'Thanks. It will only be for a few days, honest.' She grabbed a bag from the back seat and threw me her keys. 'Move that for me, will you? I'm going to get some kip; I'm shagged out after the flight and the drive. Will you be joining me?'

Well, I had just had a terrible night's sleep, so I parked her car, tossed a stunted cabbage from my vegetable patch to the chickens and followed her into the caravan. Women have a way of taking over, don't they? But, after all, someone has to be in charge and I'm just not management material.

Chapter 3

I woke in darkness with Jenny dressing noisily next to the bed. 'Are you hungry?' she asked with her back to me as she bent to put her feet into her skirt, exposing her firm bottom.

'As always. Are you cooking?'

'No, you're taking me to the pub.'

'I'm broke, love, pot-less.'

'It's ok, I'll pay and I've a powerful thirst, so you can drive. Have you still got the keys?'

I nodded. She lit a couple of small candles and in their flickering light leant over me where I lay, saying 'Help me with this, will you?' She was struggling to put a gold sleeper through one of her nipples. I helped out of politeness, with my hands shaking and her laughing at my coy clumsiness. Have you noticed how a woman's breasts are always cold? As I fumbled, I had a sudden flashback to the moment Marcus hit Liza and I shuddered. My hands fell, the sleeper still clutched in my fingers.

'Are you all right, Frankie?' chimed Jenny's buttery voice. 'You look like you've seen a ghost.'

'I'm ok, just a bad memory - sorry - maybe I can have another go when my hands are a bit warmer?' I handed her the sleeper then sat on the edge of the bed and pulled my clothes on. She pocketed it and fastened her blouse as she examined her make-up in the mirror. I threw her the keys. 'Go and get the engine warmed up, while I finish getting dressed.' She looked up, about to protest. I added, 'I'll drive back,' with a smile, as I knew once she got in the pub and we started chatting and drinking it would start with a pint and end with a skin full.

The Royal Oak was a short drive from my plot. The landlord Des was a sickly, thin, wispy man with dark greasy hair slicked back from his weasel-like features. He looked as though it took every atom of strength he possessed to suck a lung full of smoke from his thin, smouldering, prison-style roll-ups. He did his best to hook the punters in, with quiz nights, competitions and guest beers and had even started a darts league and a pool team.

At the time he had big plans to reopen the long-since defunct ballroom at the back of the sprawling old place. He had already been an unsuccessful milkman and a crap plumber, so perhaps piped and bottled fluids just weren't for him.

I'd sold him a trio - a cockerel and two hens - of lovely Laced Wyandottes not long before and had built him a henhouse and run in the beer garden to attract more passing trade; children love to look at chickens. He hoped to get a supply of eggs to add a homemade appeal to his all-day breakfasts. They'd be the only things that wouldn't threaten salmonella, as long as you ordered them hard-boiled; Des wasn't the most hygienic of blokes.

He stood behind the bar smoking and scratching himself. Of course, this was all pre smoking ban - I hate fags but I would rather they'd banned him scratching and let him smoke.

'Oi... Frankie,' he called as we went in, 'them hens you sold me still ain't laying.'

'The nights are drawing in, Des, and you've been feeding them corn all day again, I'll bet? Let me come and rig up a light on a timer for you; if you stick to the layers pellets they should start any time now.'

'I'll think about it,' he answered suspiciously, adding in a secretive gruff whisper, 'Here, Frankie, what d'you know about karaoke?'

'Nothing, Des,' came my blunt reply. 'Is Ramona in?'

'She is. Why, are you looking for a trio of your own?' he said, choking on his own witticism and fag smoke. I must have looked puzzled as he went on, 'You know - a threesome.' He cackled as he leered at Jenny across the bar.

'Don't be so bloody crude in front of a lady,' I said, giving him my best watch-it-mate glare. 'We're starving, that's all, and you're a walking health hazard.'

'Cheeky fucker,' he spluttered; then he noticed my glare and mumbled, 'I'll give her a shout.'

Jenny and I sat and chatted over a couple of pints of

Guinness until Ramona was ready to take our order. 'So where's Lydia then, love?' I asked.

'Still in Cyprus,' Jenny replied with a sigh. 'We were working at a bar when it was taken over by this posh geezer and his gym addict wisp of a wife. They asked her to stay and not me.'

'And she accepted? But you've been together for years.'

'Maybe too many years.' She paused to knock back the rest of her stout in a single gulp. 'The bitch dumped me so here I am, back on your doorstep.'

'And you're very welcome,' I added with a wink as Ramona came over, giving me a forced smile and glaring daggers at Jenny. Mistrustful things, women, I've often noticed. I knew I would get it in the neck from her when we were on our own.

Ramona warmed us up a passable lasagne in the microwave and fried up a few chips to go with it, proper pub grub. Then Jenny and I both drank too much Guinness, followed by a few measures of the guest whisky - Jameson - just to keep out the cold. Afterwards we walked back to my hovel arm in arm, laughing and singing along the bridle paths, leaving the Shogun in the car park.

Next morning I went back for the car and had a bit of a spat with Ramona, who slammed the kitchen door in my face when she would usually have asked me in for breakfast. It amazes me how women can smile and do all the social niceties when they meet each other, while in truth they are born with a deep-seated mutual loathing;

they are the original misogynists. Is there an antonym for misogynist - no? Then that sort of proves my point... They look each other up and down with that *who's farted* expression and woe betide anyone who should choose the same dress. And this one for some reason had got the hump with me after my drinking and chatting the evening away with Jenny. Well, you can't win them all.

I went to visit a friend and customer of mine called Sandy, at the manor in a little village just outside Much Wenlock. She'd phoned the Oak and left a message for me; she wanted a chat and some advice on expanding her free-range egg operation to help pay for her daughter's school fees. She'd be pleading poverty, as always, despite her creaking manor house groaning under the weight of all the treasures her family had accumulated over the last twenty generations or so.

Apparently a fox had been disturbing this rural idyll and making merry with her little flock. We agreed on reinforced fencing and I was to supply a couple of dozen Black Rock hens - which I hadn't got - to make up for the losses and keep her customers satisfied. I drew the line at shooting the fox as I haven't the heart for murder and I'm not much of a hunter. I haven't the patience to lie in wait - part of my weak character, I suppose.

I also agreed to lend her my famous, or rather infamous, Rhode Island Red rooster 'Rocky' who was arrogant, violent, a serial rapist, and gorgeous with it - in short *cocky* - to ward off any unwanted visitors and sire some chicks in the New Year.

I arrived back home later that day to find a huge four-legged piebald monster with a saddle and steaming nostrils tethered to my gate and eating the heads off my winter pansies, the bloody great brute. It was only my wanton cowardice that stopped me giving the thing a slap and shooing it off. As I arrived at the caravan door Liza burst out, her eyes hidden behind dark glasses to conceal her shiner.

'Liza!' I exclaimed, with a big smile, and made ready to take her warmly in my arms. But she ignored me, mounted her monster and then thundered and snorted over the stream and into the distance. Inside I found Jenny reclining in my bed; the place had taken on a new identity, with a silky negligée hanging from the half open wardrobe door, French knickers under foot, and the aroma of lavender incense. A half-empty bottle of Merlot dripped a red stream across the table; she sat up, exposing her nakedness, and reached for her glass.

Obviously a charming scene, but not one Liza appreciated and, putting two and two together to make twenty-two, she'd stormed off in a huff; more explaining I would have to do. It looked like Marcus was not the only one in their turbulent marriage who jumped to conclusions.

'You're going to have to tidy all this up, Jen.'

'Since when did you become so house-proud? Or maybe your little friend there is spick and span on your behalf?'

'It's not like that,' I replied. 'She's my landlady and... well... my friend. She helps me a lot.'

'I bet she does,' mocked Jenny with a sexy, if sardonic, chuckle. She gave me a knowing, lopsided smile as she cupped her bare breast in her free hand and fiddled with her new sleeper. How did she get it in? After that I had to give up my argument and join her in finishing the rest of the wine. I hate my weakness sometimes.

The days passed uneventfully. Jenny came and went, building a new life for herself, booking the odd gig here and there and awaiting Digger's return. I rounded up Rocky and headed over to Sandy's for a few days, she could always be counted on for home baked treats and moral support.

Rocky was one hell of a rooster. He was around three or four years old, and could live as long as twelve, but most roosters never get past the cockerel stage without becoming top of the bill in a one-night stand called coq-au-vin. I had picked him up after an illegal cockfight organised for some of Marcus's acquaintances a couple of years ago when he first bought the farm and hall; it was this that had made me give up being an employee. Rocky had been left for dead amongst the other birds, who were being collected as food for the dogs. Bill the gardener was hosing off the bodies before tossing them to the hounds, when one started squawking and flapping - Rocky.

I took him home and nursed him back to life. He regained his plumage and strut but never his trust in anyone or anything. However, he was now more than a match for any casual predator that should try it on with Sandy's hens during the daylight hours.

In Sandy's chicken run I got on with digging trenches and

extending the fence two feet below ground to stop unwanted tunnelling, while Rocky had his wicked way with the hens. This just left me with the problem of finding some hens to make up the numbers. I decided the best place was the livestock auctions at Bridgnorth.

It's a hectic place on sale days and today was a mixed sale: heifers, steers, cull ewes, and assorted poultry. I sat most of the day watching and drinking tea slopped out of a giant aluminium teapot, pre-dosed with milk and sugar - vile stuff but it was free and it kept the chill out. I perched on the cold concrete steps watching the lots come through. Most of the front row was filled with well-upholstered and shrewd butchers who, if I didn't know better, I would have assumed had reached an agreement on the maximum bids, as everything went for more or less the same price.

The rest of the rows were made up of pensive-looking farmers, sitting on the edge of their folding chairs and watching every nod and wink of the bidding with equally shrewd eyes.

What surprised me was seeing Marcus there, and in the company of a notorious slaughter-man and horsemeat-exporter known in these parts as Black Joe. He paid peanuts for meat on-the-hoof and concentrated on the very low end of the market. Marcus was lost in conversation with him. Joe was a huge man, his waistline as impressive as his height and hands like shovels. Marcus clapped him heartily on the back as they shook hands and then turned to sneer at me. He did a good line in sneering. I remember thinking that I must try that in front of the mirror when I got home.

He lavishly outbid everyone for a huge Canadian import Aberdeen-Angus bull, and left with a smug grin highlighting his chiselled good looks. I got a dozen nice-enough Black Rocks at a reasonable price, but the bidding was fierce for everything else and I had to pay over the odds for some Light Sussex hens to make up the numbers. But as they say, you win some - you lose some, or in my case, I lose some - then I lose some more, but I was confident I could work something out with Sandy.

Chapter 4

I arrived back home to find Jenny lounging on the bed, taking her usual deep gulps of strong black coffee and chatting to Liza, who leaned against the mirrored wardrobe door as she thoughtfully sipped tea through pursed lips, still wearing her shades. I couldn't hear what was being said and as soon as I opened the door, Liza made polite excuses, gave me a forced smile, and left, walking briskly away and flatly refusing my offer of company. She left me standing alone in the cold gloom of early evening as it started to drizzle. 'What's up with her?' I thought aloud.

'Don't be too hard on her,' Jenny said as she came out to join me in the gloaming. 'She has her problems, but she's a good woman at heart.'

'She is,' I said, 'but I still feel lousy. I wish she'd talk to me.'

'Give her time,' Jenny added, putting a consoling hand on my shoulder. 'I'm sure she'll reveal all.'

'I hope so.' I covered her hand with mine and we shared a brief comforting smile before quietly retiring to the comparative warmth of my caravan.

'I've got to go soon, Frankie. Digger's back and I can collect my trailer.'

'How soon is soon?'

'In the morning,' she replied, and my heart sank a little at the thought of being completely alone, castigated by Liza, rebuffed by Ramona, and now abandoned by Jenny; even my old mate Rocky was off on his holidays.

My sadness must have shown on my face as she said, 'I'll be back soon, Frankie. I'm doing a gig up at the Oak. Des is opening up the old function room and redecorating it and I am the star of the show for the grand launch. I've put you on the guest list. I was hoping I could pitch up here for a few days if it's ok with you?'

'Sure, love,' I said. 'Why don't I come over to Digger's with you in the morning? I haven't seen him in years.'

'That'll be nice,' she said as she started undressing for bed, 'but I want to get an early start.'

She wandered around the caravan, picking up odd things here and there and tossing them into her open holdall, unabashed and resplendent in her nakedness. I sat in silent awe and planned the best way to make the most of my last night of company.

The next morning she packed her few things back into her flashy new Shogun and we headed off to Digger's yard. I actually had no wish to see him again - it had been years since the last time, but I hate saying goodbye and this way my brief reuniting with Jenny would have no definite end. It could peter out in an unemotional way with no need for heart-felt au revoirs.

We pulled into Digger's yard. It was surrounded by a high corrugated iron fence reinforced with lengths of railway line concreted into the ground and topped with barbed wire and razor wire; all tangled with discarded and rusty chain saw chains, circular saw blades, and anything else that could threaten loss of life or limb. A huge gantry of scaffolding with cameras and floodlights surmounted the gates; it looked like a post-apocalyptic science fiction version of an old Wild West fort. We got out of the car to the sound of a couple of savage-looking dogs of uncertain origin snarling and snapping lustily at the end of their chains. I was confident Jenny's trailer would be just where she'd left it and completely unmolested.

'Morning, Jenny,' Digger shouted from the doorway of his massive showman's caravan with its slide-out living-room extension. 'Is that young Frankie you've with you?'

I smiled and strolled over with Jenny.

'Don't be nervous,' she said, squeezing my hand. 'I know it's been a long time but it'll be ok.'

'Thanks,' I replied, fixing my expression into a smile to guard me against betraying anything more than the lightest of hearts at anything he had to say.

'Come on in,' Digger said, with a warm smile. As we entered he added, 'Put the kettle on Jenny, and make us a nice cuppa.' She just sighed and slumped into an armchair.

'I'll do it.' I started to rise from my chair.

'No, she can do it. She dumps her trailer here without so

much as a by-your-leave and heads off god knows where and then turns up and expects to be waited on hand and foot - go girl!' he snapped, shaking his walking stick at her, 'or I'll tan your hide!'

Jenny sighed again, then flounced moodily to the stove, grabbed the black iron kettle and headed outside for water, slamming the door behind her.

'We've a lot to talk about, Frankie,' Digger said, as soon as we were alone. 'Tell me what you've been up to since you went to ground.'

'Nothing to tell,' I quipped. 'I just keep myself to myself, that's all.'

'Come on, lad, it's about time you got back in amongst 'em. You were good, you know - could have been one of the best. It was just a tragic accident. It could have happened to anyone, son. You can't keep beating yourself up like this.'

I remember thinking, yes - but everyone didn't have you yelling at them every day, forcing them to live out your dreams; but instead I just snapped back, 'I'm not. It was years ago, another life, and I've moved on.' As I stood up and made for the door he hooked my arm with his stick.

'Frankie, come on, sit down. What's wrong?'

'Nothing. I just didn't realise I'd walked into the wrong trailer.'

'What'd you mean, lad?'

'I thought mending roads and dealing at horse fairs was your livelihood. I didn't realise you had a fucking philosophy department. You mind your business and I'll mind mine.'

Digger fell silent for a moment as he perched on the edge of his chair; his heavy hands, gnarled by a life of hard work, punching bags and opponents, handling horses, and mending roads, were leaning across the handle of his worn ash stick. His once muscular frame seemed thinner; his shirt - like mine, fraying at both collar and cuffs - was now baggy on his chest. But his eyes had lost none of their intensity; and his expression none of its intimidating edge. He looked angry for a moment, his jaw rigid, the intransigence of his younger years still visible beneath his weather-beaten features and greying hair. Suddenly his shoulders dropped and his face relaxed as if he had resolved some inner torment. He looked straight at me as he spoke, 'Ok... ok, Frankie, it's nice to see you still have some of your old spirit. Sit down and we'll change the subject.'

At that moment Jenny came in with the full kettle, dripping water on Digger's rugs. She slammed it onto the stove with a splash, the drips sizzling on the hotplate as she opened the stove door and tossed in a couple of logs.

'Come and have a look over the trailer for me, would you, Frankie? While the kettle boils.' That was my cue to escape a further grilling from Digger. I'd decided I could live without one extra cup of tea and made up my mind to eel off ASAP.

We strolled across Digger's yard, a mixture of heavy plant, trucks, horse boxes, transit vans, and four-by-fours parked in no apparent order. Behind them sat an array of trailers, a lot of which housed his workforce - his *lads* as he liked to call them. Most of his extended family occupied the others. Jenny got the usual round of jeers and well-intentioned cat-calls as she bent to polish the rear lights of her trailer - well, it was quite a work of art keeping so much sexiness confined to one size ten pair of Levi's. I got a few more deferential nods than I expected from the lads, as they stood under the shelter of the service shed. Dennis, an old friend, was taking a few of the younger ones through combinations of punches with focus pads. Meanwhile his cousin Fred was holding a punch bag to stop it swinging as an eager - though unskilled - young man pounded it with his fists. Some faces I recognised, others I didn't. They were a good bunch but not if you were embarking on an argument with Digger.

Jenny reversed expertly up to the trailer and I hitched it up and plugged in the lights then stood behind it as she tried them out. 'Full house, love,' I shouted.

'Great!' she replied. Well, there was one side light bulb out, but it had eight on each back corner, four along each side, and another four on the front, and with the chrome zigzag stripes, cut-glass windows - and being the size of a bus - I was sure people would see it coming with or without one more five-watt bulb. As I let the hand brake off and she eased it forwards, the tyres started to drag.

'Hold it, Jen!' I shouted. 'The brakes are stuck. You know better than to park it up with the hand brake on.'

'I'm sure I didn't,' she replied.

'If you say so,' I said impatiently, as I was now eager to go. She gently rocked the car in and out of reverse and first gear and the brakes un-seized with a clunk. Good, it saved me jacking it up and getting the wheels off to hammer the drums free; she left the engine ticking over while we went to inspect the interior.

Wow, Jenny's trailer was fantastic - a handmade Buccaneer, with sumptuous buttoned seats in rich ruby-red leather that had scalloped edges to match those on the cut-glass fronted display cabinets above. The cabinets were lined with mirrors that were hand cut with patterns of wild roses. The same pattern was deeply cut into the mirrors that fronted the cupboard and wardrobe doors; in fact they covered almost every flat surface in the caravan. The display cabinets would, when she had pitched up somewhere, house and display her extensive collection of antique and modern china, which included Royal Worcester, Crown Derby, John Aynsley and other choice pieces presently wrapped in tea towels and tissue paper and stored under the beds.

A wood-burning stove, finished in iridescent enamel, provided warmth on cold winter nights; its flames were reflected in the rose patterns of the cut-glass mirrors. She'd recently had a gas-powered hot air heating system installed to back up the wood-burning stove and save her the effort of chopping, or the trouble of transporting, logs.

At one end was the kitchen with cooker and fridge, but - as in all true travellers' trailers - no sink or taps; there was no toilet, shower, or other on-board water. Any water needed was carried inside in two shining stainless steel water cans or 'jacks'.

Left of the entrance door, running down one wall, was a dressing table with drawers beneath and a gap filled by a small stool upholstered to match the seats. Then there was a wardrobe, followed by the already-mentioned wood-burning stove, with cupboard space above for airing clothes. After this there was a matching wardrobe and then a horseshoe-shaped seating area that filled the front end under the big cut-glass window. Another wardrobe stood opposite the one beside the stove. The opposing wardrobe doors had a clever double fold that allowed this end to be closed off and the seating to be pulled out to convert into a king-sized bed. After this wardrobe there was another long seating area that made a comfy single bed or could be pulled out to a snug double, then a stretch of cupboard that provided room for a TV on top and glass fronted display cabinets and drawers beneath.

'Swap you,' I quipped.

'I bet you would,' she answered with a smile. 'You can always come with me for a while. I'm off dúkkerin,' she added with a cheeky wink. 'Come on, Frankie, you know you would love life on the road again.'

'No thanks, love, no fortune-telling for me, even if you are pulling my leg. I'm happy where I am, and besides, you're a mobile cliché - hoopy earrings, flowing skirts, and all this flash, you give people like us a bad name.'

'Don't be forgetting my headsquare and my crystal ball.'

I smiled. 'Thanks, but no thanks. I'll look forward to you

coming back and you're welcome to pull in with me for a while. I have room for a trailer like this anytime. Drop me off at the main road - I'll make my own way back.'

That's how we parted and my life resumed its usual humdrum routine, boring to some, but heaven to me. It was an endless round of cups of tea in cosy kitchens, talking chickens with anyone interested enough to listen, and avoiding real life at all costs. But somehow my heart wasn't in it any more. There was no Liza to share it with and, despite my frequent rambles into the village, there were no signs of her at the big house either.

Weeks passed and the weather was bitter - snow like I hadn't seen in years and lonely nights shivering in my caravan with no gas. The hens weren't laying and even my goat, Charlie, was looking more morose than a good goat should.

I still did the rounds, visiting auctions, picking up a few young birds here and there to build up some stock for the spring. There seemed to be a bit of an odd pattern emerging regarding Marcus. He was attending more auctions than I'd ever seen him at before and with some surprisingly disreputable characters - characters like the Johnson brothers, and not the ones who make the plates. They were hard hitting prize-fighters, moneylenders, and dealers in horses.

At each auction Marcus stood out by paying, publicly and loudly, over the odds for some beast or other, usually outbidding his companions with hearty good humour. Things were getting odder by the minute.

Chapter 5

With Christmas looming and the festive season getting into gear, I spent more time on my own and grew more despondent. I called in at the Oak, only to get blasted by Des. Apparently his hens had all started to cock-a-doodle-doo at sunrise every morning and he wanted his money back and other such nonsense - I tried not to laugh at his request. Well, I was a bit short.

Ramona was in a more festive mood, coquettishly pointing out the mistletoe above our heads and inviting me for breakfast. 'It's a bit late for that, isn't it, love?' I asked, dunce that I am.

'No, stupid, I meant *in the morning.*' She emphasised it with a roguish smile and a wink. I think it was fair to assume it was going be a long night and maybe I would be a bit warmer than I'd been lately. So I generously bought her a drink, and even more generously let her add it to my slate.

Next morning I lay in a stupor, exhausted from all the sleep I hadn't had and the effects of the bottle of Grand Marnier we'd sneaked from Des's stockroom, and listened to Ramona rattling pots and pans. She lived in a little bed-sit type place behind the pub kitchen. She was making one of those Anglo-Spanish breakfasts that exposed her geographical roots and kept you going until teatime; while I thought hard about recent and past events, she came in with plates and I moved to the table. I smiled at a sizeable pile of bacon, sausages, and all the trimmings, with the eggs fried in the same pan gluing the whole lot together so it slid onto the plate in one cholesterol-infused mass.

'Are you coming to the opening next week?' she asked.

'Opening?'

'Yes, the hospitality suite,' she replied.

I almost choked on a snigger and a sausage; a grand name for a converted barn, tarted up to house live acts and occasional wedding receptions.

'You're on the guest list,' she added, in her charmingly inflected English, further enhancing the beauty of her warm Spanish features. Of course, that's what the builders had been doing, and it also meant Jenny was coming back.

'Sorry, love, got to go,' I said, wolfing down another sausage and swigging my tea.

I dressed in a rush while she swore and shouted in Spanish - pointless really when I can't speak or understand a word, despite my years of modern languages at school (but that's teachers for you - useless the lot of them). I did, however, understand the shoe that hit me on the back of the head as I stalked down the path, munching a few slices of purloined toast. It must be that fiery Mediterranean temperament, I told myself, or maybe PMT? After all, women just aren't like us fair-minded, clear-thinking, even-tempered blokes, are they?

***

Jenny arrived back in style. It was a glorious evening - well, late afternoon. It'd been a clear frosty day and promised to be a lovely clear starry night. The last light of the sinking sun glinted on the polished chrome work of her Shogun and trailer as she pulled into my drive. She carefully avoided flattening Charlie, who bleated and wagged his tail excitedly. Then she reversed the huge mobile palace expertly in next to my henhouse, dwarfing my shabby bread bin and completely erasing it from public scrutiny as it cowered in the shadow of all that luxury.

I wasn't going to have much of a view of the hills while she was here, but any visitors would think I'd won the football pools, and with her around who needs crumby scenery - let's face it, when you've seen one tree you've seen them all, haven't you?

'Well, hello…' I drawled, doing my best Sean Connery impersonation as she stepped out, gorgeous as always. 'It's good to see you, love.'

'You too, Frankie,' she said as we embraced. 'Help me pitch up and I'll make you a cuppa.'

Ever the gentleman, I helped her unhitch, wind down the corner steadies, and level up. Then I attached a huge red gas cylinder to power her on-board luxury and connected the generator she had in the back of her car. She knows how to travel in style; I'll say that for her.

'Get that box off the back seat, will you? And if you fill my water jacks I'll get the kettle on.'

I passed her the box and, with the shining stainless steel cans in hand, I set off to the tap, as obedient as a border collie, but I'm a sucker for a pretty face. Did I say pretty? I meant beautiful - and hers is one of the two most beautiful I had ever seen. The other was to make a reappearance sooner than I expected.

After a brief 'rest' we opened her box and looked at her latest cassette. She always sold them in the foyer of whatever venue she was playing. Up until now they had featured both her and Lydia, but this was a fresh compilation for her new solo act. 'Wow,' I whistled as I looked at the cover. 'This must have cost a bit, love. What with studio hire, backing musicians to pay and all that - and what's this on the back, the contact number for your agent? Since when did you have an agent?'

'Since I got a secret backer,' she smirked.

That made sense. Well, all this - the refurbished trailer and the new Shogun - was surely more than a club singer could earn, no matter how gorgeous she might be.

'Anyone I know?' I asked as she bustled off to the sound of the kettle's whistle and started rattling around, clanking fine bone china with a silver spoon until the cups rang like bells in a way that makes me cringe in fear for their safety at every chime.

'If I told you, it wouldn't be a secret, would it?' She neatly changed the subject. 'Will you come to the Oak with me later? To have a look at the décor and check out the acoustics.'

'Sure, love, but you'll have to pay. I'm skint.'

'So what's new?' she added with a chuckle and we sat to drink tea. She drank hers red-hot in that asbestos-mouthed way women do and, while scalding my lips on every sip, I sat mesmerised by her beauty. I'd realised I was going to have to face Ramona at the Oak sooner or later but I would have much rather it had been later.

Jenny's first big solo gig drew alarmingly close and as the next few days passed she grew more excitable and tense. By the morning of the fateful day she was as nervous as a field mouse in the moonlight. I was nervous too, mostly because I knew the concert's end meant she would soon be leaving, and I'd got used to the warmth and company. She was sitting at her little dressing table trying out various ways of pinning up her luscious locks and I was perched on the edge of the bed watching.

'What do you want me to do then, love?'

'Put the kettle on if you like.'

'No, you lazy mare, you can do that your bloody self. I meant *tonight*. There has to be a catch. Ticket collector? Cloakroom attendant? I could even pop into the changing room to help check your bikini line in the costume changes, to make sure your side boards aren't showing?'

'Cheeky sod,' she said as I ducked impulsively. Women have been hurling shoes at me since my mother donned her first pair of Dr Scholl's clogs when I was six. 'The hot wax at the salon takes care of that, or hadn't you noticed?'

'Maybe,' I replied with a grin as she carried on.

'You don't have to do anything but enjoy yourself, though you are welcome to pop in to see me and check the quality of the salon's work if you like.' She winked. I grinned. 'I've added a case of that bottled beer you like to the rider, and extra food, so I won't leave you high and dry. You can do me a favour though.'

'Anything for you, love.'

'Come in early with me and let me choose your spot.'

'My spot?'

'Yes, it's an old show business trick, for when I do my opening number. It's to help my nerves; I need someone to focus on.'

'I get it; you want to sing love songs to me.'

'Something like that, Frankie.' She playfully pushed me backwards onto the bed, straddling my chest and opening her dressing gown. 'Here - you can check my bikini line now if you like.'

'I can't see,' I protested. 'You're pinning me down.' She laughed and shuffled further up until her knees were each side of my shoulders, my hands cupping her lovely firm buttocks. I smiled and licked my lips - and that's where I leave you to work the rest of that day out by yourselves. I'll skip to the gig.

***

We arrived early, though there were plenty of people milling around. The place held about three hundred and twenty-seven people - I say about but I mean exactly, as I'd seen a copy of the fire officer's report pinned up in the dressing-room. I hadn't realised all this was such a big deal, but I did the maths; over three hundred at the price of a point-of-lay Light Sussex pullet a head, and that was for the cheapest ticket, plus cassette sales. That's a good evening's work by anybody's standards and a good six-months' work by mine. Jenny had chosen a spot for me on a table right in front of the bar, in the dead centre of the room.

I helped her into her first costume. There were to be two breaks and costume changes and a DJ-comedian-compère warming up the audience and covering the gaps. I picked up a cassette and scanned the tracks. 'Is this going to be the playlist for tonight, love?'

'More or less - with one or two old numbers I used to do with Lydia to keep my fan base happy'.

This all seemed surreal. I knew she was a popular singer, but this was far removed from the snot-nosed cheeky fourteen-year-old who had completed my education all those years ago. I whistled again when I saw the price tag.

'Do you reckon you'll sell many?'

'I've already sold almost nine hundred since it was

produced. My agent is pushing it here and back in Cyprus.'

I whistled again, lost for words, but I really was impressed - a lot more profitable than my beloved chickens. She looked up from concentrating on her make-up and said with a smile, 'I'll autograph one for you if you like.'

I don't know why she tried so hard. She could have walked out there naked, taken a bow, and I think every bloke in the place, and a few of the women, would have considered it money well spent and gone home happy.

'Thanks, love,' I said and she took the cassette from my hands and wrote a lavish, swirly *With all my love - Jenny* on the back. 'I bet you say that to all your fans,' I said, reading it twice.

'Most of them,' she winked.

At that moment her backing band squeezed in and added to the general claustrophobia of the already cramped room. They started talking sound checks and lighting, and when the sound engineer popped his head round the door I opted out.

'Sorry, love, it's getting a bit stuffy in here. I'm off for a breath of fresh air.'

'Don't forget your place, Frankie,' she shouted after me.

I honestly didn't expect the place to be full, and there was over an hour before she went on stage. I'd already munched my share of the food, drunk a fair few of the bottles and slipped one in each of my jacket pockets for good measure, so I borrowed a reserved sign from the eatery, slapped it in the middle of my table for safety's sake, and slunk off to make my peace with the lovely Ramona.

I found her getting dressed in her little room behind the pub kitchen and received the usual dose of verbal abuse as expected. It was mostly Spanish, punctuated with the odd word I could understand - bastard, inconsiderate, that slut, and the like. She calmed down a bit when I told her I'd brought her a present; surprisingly she wasn't all that impressed with the cassette, even though it was autographed. But the beer seemed to console her so I set about showing my remorse for running out on her lovely breakfast. I arrived back at the gig a little worse for wear, with a few more buttons missing and a self-satisfied expression.

Shit, the place was heaving. They were queuing out of the door and into the car park. 'Excuse me, coming through!' I had my head down and elbows out, to make a little breathing room, as I pushed through the crowd. When I got inside it was even worse - door-to-door bodies. My table was occupied by a group of Hooray-Henry types, all tweeds and shiny shoes, and mine was the only free seat left.

I squeezed closer, trying to get there before the curtain went up, and realised with a jolt that the Hooray Henrys were Marcus and his cronies. The compère was saying his proudly-presents bit, the intro music to the first number was playing, and I wasn't in my place. At that moment the crowd stood to clap and I turned to follow their gaze. My jaw dropped as Jenny walked on stage to the opening notes of Captain and Tennille's 'Love will keep us together', strutting confidently and suggestively to the beat of the music towards the microphone, holding the hem of her long flowing skirt in one hand - revealing those gorgeous legs - with the spotlights following her. She dropped her hem, grabbed the microphone stand and threw her head back so her luxuriant curls shone in the lights, and it all began.

I was trapped by the crush of bodies as I tried to struggle forwards but the bright magnesium glare of a flashgun half-blinded me. I blinked against the blobs of bright light emblazoned on my retinas and struggled on, forcing my way through. 'Sorry - excuse me.' Jenny's voice and the music from the band boomed in my head. So much vocal power from such a small frame - awesome - no wonder she'd sold so many cassettes.

The crowd went wild and as they surged forwards I edged a few paces further, sweating with the effort and desperate not to let her down, as bloody usual. I'd almost reached my seat when I realised I was too late.

I turned to look at her through the crowd as, hand on hip, Jenny reached out her arm, pointed to our agreed spot and delivered the line that I knew was meant for me and that - deep down - I longed to hear.

Just stop, 'cause I really love you...

My head followed the line of her arm. The whole place seemed to pause for a moment when I saw who was sitting, smiling, in my seat - Liza! She stood and clapped, in a slinky mauve knitted dress that seemed to cling in all the right spots. She wasn't as curvy and well upholstered as Jenny - more of the magic size zero everyone bangs on about these days - but it suited her, fitness fanatic that she was, poised and muscular, her stilettos showing her shapely calves to their best advantage. I stood frozen to the spot. She was still wearing her shades - more domestic violence?

The song ended and the applause proper began, with Jenny now into her entertainer's stride. I didn't think she would need me any more and I decided that no matter what happened, I had to talk to Liza. The night wore on and the music was fantastic. I considered buying another cassette to replace the one I'd given Ramona, but decided against it - I could always purloin another. It would hardly be breaking Jenny's trust, as she would expect me to help myself, just as I would her; what's-mine-is-yours and all that. Anyway, I didn't have a tape player.

My opportunity came towards the end of the second interval. The comedian was fair and made me chuckle a few times. I'm crap at remembering jokes but if any come back to me I'll fill you in as I go along. Liza stood outside, talking in menacing whispers with Marcus. He threw his cigar aside and marched inside, leaving her alone. As she turned to follow him I bravely stepped out from cowering behind a transit van and collared her.

'Liza,' I almost begged, 'what's going on? Please don't keep ignoring me.'

'I can't do this,' she sobbed. 'Just leave me alone.'

I turned her to face me. 'What's with the shades?' I grabbed them from her face, and as I looked into her dazed and dilated eyes my heart sank. 'No, you're not back on that stuff; tell me it's not true, please.'

'Yes, I am.' She shook as she replied. 'And you would be too if you had to put up with him.'

'Please, Liza,' I pleaded, 'just pack a few things. Leave him and come with me.'

'And do what? He would find us and then he'd kill you. He has his interests to protect.'

'What? Making you his drugs mule between here and wherever?' I said.

'Yes.' She slumped and clung to me.

'Please, Liza! We can go away - anywhere.'

'Don't be childish, Frankie.' She sniffed back a tear. 'We tried and failed. It's over.' She visibly straightened as she intoned the last words and after dabbing her eyes she slipped her shades back on and went inside.

My mind ran over all the nights in my caravan when I'd comforted her and held her while she battled with the shivers, sweats and cramps of her addiction. I realised why I couldn't let her go. I loved her. And she was my friend - a friend who loved and was loved; nothing more and definitely nothing less. I made up my mind there and then to get that bastard Marcus - I just needed a plan.

When she had first told me her guilty secret - we all have one, don't we? - I had been horrified and had had visions of condoms full of heroin bursting in her stomach, or of him using hiding places she had and he simply hadn't to get the stuff through customs.

She'd been a recreational drug user when they met at university a long time ago and he'd used the income from his small-time dealing to bolster his embryonic business interests. When he needed to improve his cash flow he upped the scale of his drug network by using his family connections in Cyprus. He brought the stuff from the Turkish north half of the island - it was smuggled there from North Africa - and then to the Greek south, where Liza's old-school network on their yuppie yachts provided, often unwittingly, the next link in the chain. The goods were stashed during an onboard farewell party organised by their long-standing friend.

What I needed, I decided in my fury, was a way in. A cheap low-key way in, as I had no money, no passport - and a lifelong fear of flying.

Chapter 6

Next morning Jenny left on a high, in a buoyant mood, despite my failure to keep my end of the deal. She did her best to convince me that her sudden departure was not down to my unreliability. I suppose I ought to have believed her, as reliable she knows I'm not. I don't own a watch and have no natural sense of the passing of time, so it's not my fault if I'm late for things, is it? And Jenny, being my oldest friend, knows me better than anyone.

Days turned into weeks, and weeks into months, and there was still no progress with Liza. I saw her driving through the village from time to time, looking pale and gaunt, but other than that nothing happened. After a while the occasional sightings of her dried up and, as far as I was concerned, she disappeared.

My life started to warm up once more with the coming of spring. I spotted Marcus out and about at auctions. I also made a few quid selling new-born chicks to excited families and helping a few schools in the vicinity get started with their egg-hatching projects. I sometimes did school visits, taking a couple of my little bantam hens and cocky Rocky for all the little darlings to gawp at and learn of the joys of chicken ownership.

Things started to pick up the day I made one of my now infrequent visits to the Oak. It was booming. City types sprawled around the log fire on leather seats and a carvery offering a remarkable choice of meats and veg had replaced the microwave meals and fry-ups. Even Des had cleaned himself up. It looked like the new conference suite was paying off. Ramona was now manageress and had taken to dressing up a little more than she used to, in a smart skirt and blouse, very businesslike - and oh, so sexy!

Ramona made her exit through the door behind the bar, after failing to catch my eye or respond to my waves and winks all night, so I sat and brooded over a few more pints before deciding to sneak round the back to her room. She stood in the doorway as I hovered behind the trellis; she was in a clinch with a suited gent who then furtively made his way down the path. I didn't really see him and I don't have much of a memory for faces, but the back of his head looked a little greying and decidedly well-groomed – her brother, her cousin? Perhaps it was her birthday maybe? Or even his? I called; she looked up. She was clutching a huge bunch of blooms and foliage.

Her face dropped when she saw me and, after bluntly refusing to let me in, she bustled inside and came out with a carrier bag saying, 'Here - take this and get out of my sight, thoughtless pig!' Then she slammed the door in my face.

How many doors do you have to have slammed in your moói before you get used to it? The bag contained the few gifts I'd bought her - not much: a mug, a comb, a fancy boxed biro that I'd had her name engraved on, and of course Jenny's cassette. I assumed it was over. Well, at least there would be no acrimonious divorce, or custody battle, and she had conceded her half of our joint resources - and I now had two mugs - so I shrugged and tried to put my heartbreak behind me. See, that's my problem - I fall in love all too easily, only to be treated like a mug by some thoughtless bird. Oh well, I would just have to drive over to the auctions in Bridgnorth the next day to console myself.

Next morning I cranked up my old tub and rattled over to the auctions. There are no poultry sales there, just large animals and junk, sorry, I mean *antiques*. They have viewing days for the junk but I always find viewing days pointless, driving back and forth just to look at the same crap twice. Why bother? I had a brief shufti at the dross; old bikes, rusty lawn mowers, three-legged tables, wobbly chairs, and so on. I settled on chancing my few groats by bidding on a couple of boxes of assorted odds and ends. I won one for a couple of quid but got outbid on another by a stern-looking old gentleman with a baling string belt and odd shoes. Well, it takes all sorts, and I'm hardly a picture of sartorial elegance myself.

I dumped my box in the car and went into the livestock sales. I don't know why, as I'd got no money, but I did have a yearning to find a mate for Charlie, as God knows I wasn't much company and I wanted to see how much money I needed to come up with. Unusually, there were a few horses going through that day - one of their occasional specialist sales, which had attracted the usual mixture of toffs and rogues that are to be found at horse sales all over the country.

What I found interesting was that Marcus was there with the Johnson brothers and another well-dressed man I sort of recognised but couldn't quite recall where from. Things went along pretty averagely, though oddly they seemed to be selling off the beasts they had recently bought and doing it to peals of mutual laughter. They were up to something, for sure, and had been building up to it since last year - in my opinion Marcus was definitely a bad egg.

I knew the buying and selling was significant, but how did a scruff like me with no indoor plumbing, no mains electricity and no phone go about taking on a gang of these proportions with all their resources, power, and an international reputation? As you know by now, I am the easily dispirited type, and I was beginning to wonder at which point my dream of bringing Marcus to justice would end.

I headed home to sort through my box of junk and see if I'd hit the jackpot. It was little comfort, but all I had. When I arrived, things felt odd, like someone was watching me as I parked up and rounded up my flock for a ration of corn before bedtime. I lifted my box gingerly from the boot, with one hand supporting the base to save any disasters with that priceless heirloom in the bottom, and headed for the caravan, where I placed it carefully down. Then I lit the gas under the kettle and rooted around in the drawers for a mantle so I could get my one gaslight going to give a little better visibility for gloating over my treasure.

The light flickered and popped into a pale orange glow and under its light I found Liza cowering in my bed. As the mantle burned in, the light brightened and I saw her battered face looking up at me, one eye swollen almost shut and a gash in her top lip that had made it swell to a sneer, exposing a broken tooth. I sat heavily on the bed as my knees gave way with shock. She winced and a ghost of pain flitted across her already pallid completion.

I reached for my torch from the drawer and slowly drew back the duvet. She made no attempt to stop me. She was naked, except for the sparkle of the diamond studs in her ears, and her poor body was filthy, caked with mud and dried blood.

She held out a weak hand to me. I took it carefully. 'Liza, what's happened? Did he do this to you?'

She mumbled 'No' as she shook her head weakly, the effort making her wince once more.

'Then who?'

'No one.'

'What happened then? Walk into a door, did we?'

'No, I fell.'

'If you say so,' I snapped. 'I'm calling an ambulance and the police.' How, I had no idea, as I didn't have a phone.

'Leave it,' she said and then emphasised it with an imploring 'please?'

I filled a bucket with hot water and a splash of disinfectant left over from last year's lambing at the grange and added a squirt of shower gel for good measure. Then I did my best to flannel her down with a sock - a clean sock, don't worry. Her injuries weren't as bad as they seemed - mostly mud and blood from small scratches and a few deeper cuts that made her cry out as I cleaned them.

I combed out the twigs and mud from her hair with the comb Ramona had returned, and dressed her in my spare shirt, rolling up the cuffs to allow her to use her hands and to hide the fact the chickens had eaten the buttons. More missing buttons caused it to gape a little more than it should, but this was no time for modesty.

When I looked closer, her broken tooth was now just a stainless steel spike protruding from her gum where a crown had gone missing - nothing I could do about that. After a cup of hot sweet tea carefully spooned into her mouth from the mug Ramona had almost thrown at me and a couple of painkillers Jenny had left behind she was fit enough to give me a gappy smile, then she dozed for a while. Don't ask me why I did the hot sweet tea thing - it's just what you do for people who've had a shock, isn't it? And it looked like Ramona's returned gifts would be useful after all.

I cleaned up a bit, brushing the mud from the floor and throwing out the blood-tainted water as she slept, thinking of hundreds of murderous ways to wreak my revenge on the bastard who had done this to her, but failing to come up with anything feasible. But at least my plans to cover him in corn and let Rocky peck him to death, or make him walk the plank from a motorway bridge were more plausible than her 'I fell' story. I planned to interrogate her when she woke, so I settled down opposite her.

I'd slept fitfully, sitting upright, for a few hours when she woke me by gently shaking my shoulder. She seemed a little better.

'I feel so stupid, Frankie,' she said.

'Why, love?'

'It's my own fault. I did fall.'

'Of course you did,' I said with a patronising smile, again secretly planning to run Marcus through with my butter knife, or garrotte him with my bootlaces.

'No, I really did.'

'Go on then, explain. I enjoy a good yarn.'

And not expecting to believe a word of it, I sat back and listened to her tale.

Liza slept alone in her own room up at the hall, in the older part of the house. In her determination to get clean once and for all she had asked one of the staff, an Englishwoman who had joined them from their place in Cyprus, to lock her in at night so she couldn't have access to the evil stuff. But in that self-deluded way addicts have she'd been climbing out of the window and over the roof to scramble down to Marcus's study and help herself to a little 'lifter' from the sample box he kept for his clients and friends. I know what you're thinking - *unlikely,* but don't forget she was as fit as a flea, a gym junkie as well as a - I hate to say it - junkie. Riding horses, power walks, aerobics, yoga, health foods - you get the picture, and she'd been driven by her desperate craving. I think all that fitness is a wonderful thing, but I got plenty of exercise in my youth, so I'm exempt now and don't need to do any more, honest!

Now, you're probably thinking *flipping drug addicts* and *flogging's too good for 'em*, but think about it. Everyone is an addict to something; every single one of us. Maybe you just haven't worked out what your addiction is yet, but you have one. Maybe yours is self-control, self-denial, golf, or even chocolate cake, but all addictions nurture *desire*; a growing need for increased exposure to a preferred drug, for want of a better word, with an ever-increasing need to consume before gaining satisfaction. Addiction is an insatiable desire, and we've all tasted desire, haven't we?

On this particular night she'd spotted Marcus and some of his cronies through the study window - 'a pack of no-good Pikeys', she called them. Normally I would have challenged such racist stereotyping, but under the circumstances I let it go as it was out of character for her.

She'd decided to hang around outside until they'd all gone. But something they'd said had frightened her and she'd scrambled back up over the roof to find her own sash closed and latched from the inside. Then, while climbing over to the other side of the house to try and get back in through the dormer windows above the stables, she'd lost her footing, fallen into a hawthorn hedge and rolled into a drainage ditch. That was where she'd woken hours later, freezing and shaking, before making her way barefoot and naked across the fields to the one door she knew would never be closed to her. It's not all that romantic; it's just that the lock had broken years ago.

'So what was it that scared you so much, love?'

'I think,' she said, pausing to gather her thoughts and take a deep breath, 'I think they are going to kill me.'

'Surely not, love. What makes you think that?'

'They were talking about life insurance claims and a fire and rebuilding costs and I just panicked.'

Whatever it was, they were definitely up to something. I held her and shushed her as she sobbed and gently persuaded her back to sleep, telling her we could sort it all out in the morning, tomorrow's another day and all that. She slumbered, her breath softly whistling through the gap in her teeth and I, robbed of any chance of sleep, rummaged through my box of crap. There was one of those personal cassette player thingies in it, with broken earphones and no batteries, but this was back when these things cost an arm and a leg so I was feeling hopeful.

I decided I needed help, but whose? I'd no money and staying here we were a sitting duck for Marcus and his goons. Meanwhile we'd nowhere to go. I needed a friend and the only one at hand was in more desperate need than I was. I found the cassette Ramona had returned and it struck me - Jenny, who else? She would help us. I'd no idea where she was or how to get in touch, but her agent's address was on the back of the tape and that had to be the place to start.

I had the beginnings of a plan. We had at our disposal my speed machine with about three gallons of fuel in the tank and, apart from the hope of help from a friend, absolutely nothing else.

Liza was naked, I was broke, we had zilch - but we couldn't stay here. It wouldn't take much doing for them to follow her muddy tracks straight to my door as soon as the sun came up. I woke Liza, wrapped her in my duvet, and laid her gently in the back of my car.

'Where're we going, Frankie?'

'To find a friend, love,' I answered. 'To find a friend.'

We chugged and clattered down the road, stopping only to tie the exhaust silencer back on with string to stop it dragging on the floor after the rubber mounting gave up the fight. Then I pulled into an open gateway, reversed behind a hedge and threw a few branches over the car to break up its outline. I managed, despite her protests, to persuade Liza to stay put and wait for me. Why women have such a hard time trusting me I'll never know.

I stalked nervously across the field to the edge of the Oak car park just in time to see the back of *that* head on the person walking away from Ramona's door. The man, whoever he was, slipped into a shiny saloon and was soon purring away into the glow of the rising sun. Time was running out. I needed stealth and speed. I hurdled the low fence into the beer garden and carefully unpegged a choice selection of Ramona's underwear from the washing line. One or two items brought back memories and I'm sure that the lace thong should, strictly speaking, have been in my carrier bag of returned gifts. Then I grabbed her new business suit, also conveniently on the washing line, and left, pausing only to 'borrow' a couple of pasties from the milkman's fridge as he laboured up the path with a crate of semi-skimmed. I meant to pay him back, honest. I knelt beside his float, watching him scribble a note and bend to put it through the letterbox - I'm no thief, but he wouldn't miss the odd pasty, or the pint of orange juice, or the pink girls' trainers he had under his seat.

I squeezed through the hedge and ran as fast as my poor state of fitness would allow back to Liza. I threw the stuff in the car, jumped in, and, after a heart-wrenching moment when the wheels began to lose traction on the wet grass, hurtled out onto the road and headed for town.

Wolverhampton is a funny old place. If you've never been there, the first thing that strikes you is the ring road and it's bewildering signage that makes everywhere seem to be in the same direction. As you drive round and round in confusion you always seem to be looking at the back of the shops and never at the inside of the town. The whole place is dominated by huge office blocks that sit at the corners of every junction. As towns go it is pretty large - big enough for a city - and parking is a nightmare. Maybe it's the same in big towns and cities the world over, but I wouldn't know; I'm no fan of towns and cities - in fact, I'm not keen on crowds at all. They make me feel trapped and panicky. I find my best strategy in such places is to keep my head down and avoid making eye contact.

We were early, so I did another couple of laps to kill time before we settled to wait outside Jenny's agent's office. *Band Wagon Promotions*, the sign proudly proclaimed. It was a dreary-looking office above an even drearier-looking club called The Phoenix, in a drab street full of adult shops with blacked-out windows - the sort that make you nervous about stopping and asking directions for fear of being mistaken for a kerb-crawler and starting some kind of hue and cry.

I left the car parked on some single yellows next to a sign that said I couldn't park there and hoped some eagle-eyed bobby wouldn't spot that I was out of road tax, though I'd found the car ran just as well without it. With Liza in the car, its status was changed from illegally parked to waiting. I left her struggling to dress in the borrowed clothes under my duvet in the back seat.

As I dodged between the parked cars I saw the back of a familiar well-groomed head in debate with someone I couldn't quite see. I could make out cowboy boots and jeans under the sills of the jeep that was obscuring them and from the difference in height, and shoe size, I assumed it must be a woman. It struck me where I had seen that head before – it had been with Marcus at the auction and again outside Ramona's that very morning. I sensed the plot thickening. Whoever the woman was, she climbed into the jeep, slammed the door, started the engine with a roar and then floored it, making tyres squeal and hooters honk as she forced her way into the traffic. As the tinted windows slid down I caught a glimpse of the driver and, fleeting as it was, I couldn't mistake that profile - Jenny!

I was rooted to the spot. A tap on my shoulder startled me.

'Liza, what are you doing here? I told you to wait in the car.' She'd scuppered any plans I might have had of following the owner of the neatly groomed head.

'I got scared, Frankie. A policeman kept walking past and looking at the car, and at me.'

I grabbed her hand and led her into a bus shelter. She didn't fill out Ramona's clothes well and looked like a lost child, though the pink Puma trainers seemed to fit perfectly.

'Sit here, love,' I said, gently guiding her onto one of the fold-out plastic seats. 'I'll be back in two minutes.' With that I sprinted across the road, dodging the moving cars, and into Jenny's agent's office. 'Excuse me,' I said, walking straight past the receptionist and heading for a door marked *private*.

'You can't go in there, sweetheart!' the receptionist screeched as he minced over to stop me. He smelled strongly of cologne and his floral shirt was open to the waist, exposing a smooth hairless chest. I got the impression this was by choice, not because the buttons had been pecked off by chickens. 'Mr Mace will have my guts for garters if I let you in without an appointment.' He stopped me by placing a neatly manicured hand on my chest.

Now, that threw me. I'm not homophobic - I don't care what anyone does in the privacy of their own home, as long as they don't do it in the street and frighten the ponies - but homosexual men make me uneasy. I always think they're talking in euphemisms and idioms that I just don't get, and that my lack of comprehension will unwittingly trap me in some gay love tryst. For example: ages ago I knew a bloke down south - he's raving gay and was a good mate, but his partner used to put the willies up me when, every time I passed him, he would ask 'Have you been to Cockington?' while clutching his gold cigarette holder, daintily, between outstretched fingers. For those of you who don't know, Cockington is a picturesque village just outside Torbay in Devon and is well worth a visit. I've been several times, but I always said 'No' just in case I'd got the wrong end of the stick and my day's outing wasn't what he was asking about.

I mean, you can, if you're crude and have the bottle, go up to some luscious lady in a pub or club and trot out some tired line - not that I've ever done this myself - like 'get your coat love, you've pulled' or 'what side of the bed do you want me to sleep on?' or, if you're really cheeky, 'how'd you like your eggs?' and the worst that can happen is a drink in the face or a slap (unless, of course, you've done your sums wrong and she has some lovestruck lump of a bloke in tow who might have something more to add). And that's my point - if you're of *that* persuasion, how do you go about finding out if someone else is? I mean, they haven't got two heads or anything. To me they are just regular lads and lasses, but I worry that they have some secret code language I don't know to find out if you're warm or cold.

Anyway, this bloke's screeching had attracted the interest of the occupant of the private room and the door swung open. 'What's the commotion, Barry?' a sergeant major-type voice boomed.

'This gentleman would like to see you, Mr Mace, but he

doesn't have an appointment.'

It was *him* - the neatly-groomed bloke from the auction and the Oak.

'Who - me?' I stammered, my mind in a whirl. 'My mistake - I must have come in through the wrong door.' I scampered away as fast as my little legs would carry me.

I decided it was best to ditch the car, so we moved it to a dark, dank, corner of the civic hall car park, collected together our few possessions into a bin liner I found in the boot, and left. I told Liza the man had refused to help me; I didn't tell her about Jenny. All sorts of thoughts were running through my head. Surely Jenny wasn't in league with these murderous, drug-running gangsters?

Now, one coincidence you can pass off. Two is... coincidental, but Jenny's sudden improvement in financial status, and her secret backer, plus Ramona's promotion and the sudden upturn in the Oak's fortunes struck me as too many coincidences to ignore. We walked away from the car, Liza looking lost in her oversized clothes and me with the bin liner slung over my shoulder.

'Where are we going, Frankie?'

'I've no idea, love.'

At least we didn't look too out of place amongst the hundreds of students who made the pavements leading to the grotty polytechnic heave like an angler's bait box. It was all too much for me and, thinking about Jenny, even amongst such crowds, I felt, for the first time in my life, completely and utterly lost and alone. I felt responsible for Liza - and I'm not big on responsibility. Ask my old teachers; they were forever telling me so and I have lived up to their verdict on me wonderfully. I always took the things they told me quite literally, so literally in fact that I've never run with a pair of scissors yet.

Chapter 7

We headed out of town, I was aiming for the Pen road that would lead us to Himley Hall, an eighteenth century manor house that was once the home of the lords of Dudley and was, at the time of our visit, used as council offices – it would serve as a place to hide and think. We could take advantage of the seclusion of the old railway line to get there; it had long since been closed down and would keep us out of sight of Marcus and his goons. It was a good distance, but fear drove us on and we made good time.

When we arrived at the hall we hid in the storm drains at the far side of a pond until the staff locked up at dusk. Then I effected an entry, to use legal terminology, into the gatehouse that was used as the duty ranger's office. It was one of a pair that flanked the tall and ornate wrought iron gates that spanned the entrance to the drive. They were quite imposing buildings when viewed from the outside, with dressed limestone walls and pillared porticos. The grand effect, however, didn't extend beyond the front door, behind which there were just a few shabby rooms that were so small it was hard to imagine them ever being inhabited.

Once inside we swapped Liza's clothes for a better-fitting ranger's uniform and enjoyed tea and a shower, heating up my crumbling pasties on the rangers' small stove as we conspired, trying to think of a way out of this mess. Liza was all for trying to track Jenny down and I was just as keen to avoid her, but I was trying not to reveal my concerns to Liza. I needed to come up with an alternative plan. Liza filled me in a little on Marcus's activities. I asked why he was buying and selling at with no noticeable profit.

'I have no idea, Frankie, but I know they are planning to bid for some very special animals at a big sale up north in the next week or two.'

I was starting to understand what they were up to, or so I thought. I've been to enough phoney and fixed auctions to spot a scam when I see one. I wasn't convinced I was right or that I'd made the best choice, but what alternative was there? I lifted the receiver on the gatehouse phone and was pleased to hear the reassuring hum of a dial tone. That call was the one thing that I had hoped never to have to make, for fear of being dragged into a world I had long since left behind, but I spun the dial and waited as the ring tone sounded in my ear. Digger's voice croaked 'Hello?' down the other end of the line.

'It's me - Frankie. I need your help. Can someone pick me up?'

'I thought you would never ask,' he said, pausing for effect before adding, 'I'll send one of the lads straight over.'

'Better make it two,' I added, thinking of the old adage *safety in numbers.*

'Where are you?' he asked.

'I'll be at the entrance to Baggeridge Park in an hour, and I've a friend with me.'

'Ok, they'll be waiting for you,' came back Digger's hoarse voice. 'It's good to have you back, Frankie.' He chuckled and rang off.

'Come on, love, we're going,' I said, helping Liza as she rose shakily to her feet. 'Just one more walk and then you can get some proper rest, I promise.'

We made our way through the grounds. It was a lovely night; a clear sky and the moon lit our way. It was new to Liza and we even took time to marvel at the Old Hall. 'Even grander than your place,' I quipped. She smiled. We detoured through the woods and carefully crossed the stepping-stones over a stream above a little waterfall. I stopped and reminisced for a while, feeling a little sad as I felt my fingers close around Ramona's boxed pen in the bottom of my pocket. I took a deep breath and sighed as I dropped it in the water as a gesture of moving on; like a Pooh stick it floated away and I was touched with a moment's regret for my inability to relate to her emotions. I wondered if it would float all the way home to my little plot.

'What are you thinking, Frankie?'

'Nothing,' I almost snapped and then grabbed her hand. 'We'd better get a move on.'

A Ford Transit van loitered in the drive, its engine running. We could hear the thrum of the bass as music played inside. I walked cautiously over, gesturing to Liza to lag behind. I was worried that Liza wouldn't be able keep up if it wasn't them and we had to run. The side-loading door slid open and in a haze of smoke from a badly-rolled joint, Dennis stepped out.

Dennis is a big lad with a flat nose from too many punches and arms as thick as my legs. The sight of him made me feel more confident, there were two more lads in the front and Fred waiting for us in the back. 'Nice to see you, mucker,' Dennis shouted and held out his fist for the traditional travellers' 'touch-up' knuckle-to-knuckle greeting.

Dennis and Fred are cousins and great lads unless you get on the wrong side of them. Don't get me wrong - they aren't nasty or bad-tempered, but they like a scrap. Wherever there is trouble they're in it and always with a good-humoured smile, no malice or hatred. They just love a fight. 'Jump in, cuz,' he said. 'We'll have you home in a jiffy.' We climbed in and the van roared off to the sound of fiddles and bodhrán, back to Digger's yard.

'This isn't your sort of stuff is it, Den?' I said, referring to the music.

'Not really, Frank, but we're getting in the mood for the fair.'

I nodded and smiled, politely refusing as they passed the joint around. When it came to Liza she held her hand out, but stopped with a tremble and looked at me for approval. Why I don't know, but I winked at her, knowing she probably needed it after all she'd been through.

For a few minutes I thought we were being followed. 'Let the bastards come,' I mumbled, 'and we can sort it out here and now.' But the car turned off and we carried on alone. Liza was laughing with the lads and I was feeling lighter of heart than I had done since she had left me all those months ago.

We arrived at Digger's yard quite late. It wasn't that far but the lads always used a circuitous route to get there, both checking out who might be around, as they have a lot of expensive gear on site, and to throw the sheriff off the scent as, strictly speaking, it's not a residential site and too many comings and goings would soon attract unwanted attention - remote as the place was. We pulled in, the gates rattled shut behind us and were promptly barred and chained - ominous really, as from that point our sanctuary was also our prison.

We had the use of a small caravan bought to provide accommodation for sub-contractors. A few of the girls scrubbed it clean for us and Liza found it a happy medium between my hovel and the luxury of her life at the grange. She thrived over the next few days, even as her bruising came out in lurid shades of blue and purple. The stiffness in her movements started to ease and I even got to like her cheeky, gappy grin, though I would've loved to help her do something about it. She even had a selection of spare clothes acquired from generous and eager new friends.

Liza was amazing. She took everything in her stride, adjusting to the unfamiliar rituals of cleanliness among the women without a question or a murmur, separating raw and cooked food, using the toilet block and showers rather than the caravan's on-board facilities, and playing the part of a happy housewife, cooking and cleaning as if she'd been born to it.

Meal-times were a bit fraught, with me being a committed carnivore and her one of those salad-crunching nut-nibblers. To be honest, I could've easily got used to the new routine, but I was still desperately puzzled about the whole thing and really needed to find Jenny. I was also growingly aware that our sanctuary was only temporary, with each day getting me deeper indebted to Digger. And we still had no money, no transport and no clues to help me stop Marcus's nefarious scheme.

I went to see Digger and borrowed a van, leaving me yet further in his debt, and then I set off to sort out the mess we had left behind, leaving Liza with our protectors. I arrived at my plot by parking on the other side of the wooded ridge that provided the backdrop to the northerly extent of my view and then cautiously walking the last stretch.

My caravan had been wrecked. The cupboard doors had been ripped off, my mattress and cushions were outside in the rain, the windows were smashed, and the door swung crookedly from broken hinges. A few chickens, ever hopeful, were rooting through my scattered possessions; my goat Charlie was nowhere to be seen.

I was less worried about my hens, who lead a truly free-range existence as there were few predators about round there thanks to Marcus's endless hunting parties for his numerous associates, but Charlie's absence perturbed me. I had several large peck-feeders on the field designed for game birds. I simply filled each one with whatever feed pellets or grain were going cheap, pardon the pun, and left the hens to it. I'd fenced off my little vegetable plot in the hopes of keeping a few choice items for myself, but generally they got most of that as well. That day I decided to prop open the gate and let them have everything that was still growing.

There was nothing worth salvaging in the caravan except Jenny's tape. Even my auction box junk lay smashed, and my jacket and spare clothes had been trampled into the mud outside the door. I've always been a bit of a hoarder but didn't realise how much stuff I had until it was all strewn broken at my feet. I threw some corn in a bucket and rattled it as I walked the field perimeter; various hens came flapping and clucking at the sound as I scattered it in my wake. I did a rough head count and all seemed to be in order.

I also found Charlie, frightened, cowering and bleating down by the stream. I used my belt as a makeshift collar and led him back over the ridge to the van. After rubbing him down with a few handfuls of straw, to warm him, I made him comfortable in the back with bedding salvaged from the caravan. I thought it fair to assume that Marcus knew I'd been sheltering Liza and was now after us both. There was little more I could do so I took Charlie with me and headed over to Sandy's.

She was in, cheery and bustling as she prepared a lovely home-cooked meal. 'A lot of trouble to go to for one,' I joked.

'It isn't all for me, silly,' she replied, 'Michael's at home.'

She agreed to let Charlie run around with her hens for a while. Rocky had never returned from his holiday and I was sure they'd be glad to get reacquainted. Sandy's husband, Michael, popped his head around the kitchen door, I'd seen him around but we'd never been properly introduced.

'Sarah,' he called, looking straight past me. 'Will your friend be staying to dinner?'

'Yes, dear,' Sandy replied, ignoring my headshakes and gestures of refusal.

'Sarah?' I mouthed quizzically at her as he left the room, but I got no reply and had to content myself with eyeing up her lovely chubby bottom as she stood at the Aga, stirring pans.

Let me fill you in a bit on Sandy, like I said I would. You've probably registered that we were fairly long-standing friends. Despite Michael's pretensions, she was the one with the land and money, passed down from her father as he had no male heir to carry on the tradition. Sandy, being an only child, got the lot. Her father wasn't dead, just retired to where the sunshine can be a little more predictable. She had a huge rambling Tudor manor to rattle around in, but most of her life was confined to the kitchen, which was the size of a small bungalow.

We had a sort of flirty friendship with plenty of tea, cakes and cheeky banter, but little else. She had a slight, and definitely sexy, lisp. I know the old adage 'girls with lisps are better kissers' but I'd never been close enough to her to find out - well, not to form a definite opinion anyway.

Dinner was served. We had rabbit stew and dumplings followed by apple crumble and custard, a real homemade treat. Then Michael helped himself to a little port; I declined as I had my mind on the drive back. The evening wore on and we got along like a house on fire. I knew he was one of the local magistrates, having come up before them once or twice after various misunderstandings, but now he had his eye on bigger things. He'd been sitting in judgement at other courts, filling in for absentees amongst his fellow guardians of the law. I knew little else about him, though I knew he did something medical.

He was a pleasant, bespectacled, tall thin fellow, all tweeds, elbow patches and excessive nasal hair. He always seemed to be looking down at you - not in a snooty way, mind, but in a more literal way - as if his presence hovered over you.

'I heard you had a spot of bother recently, Frankie,' Michael said in a half-enquiring tone.

'Really?' I asked. 'Where'd you hear that?'

'I sent a colleague of mine over to see you. She had her mind set on a few hens, and she told me the place was wrecked and deserted.'

'Yes,' I replied. 'It was an unfortunate accident,' and I tried clumsily to change the subject.

Michel gave me a questioning look as I mumbled on before interrupting. 'Well, I must leave you. I have some paperwork to catch up on before bed - bloody NHS.' He chortled and gave me a firm handshake. 'If there is anything I can do... We even make house calls, if you can afford it.' He chortled again, winked, and then left us alone in the kitchen.

'Remind me, Sarah - he's a doctor, isn't he?' I asked.

'Sandy,' she corrected, 'and no, but close; he's a dental surgeon at the hospital - reconstructions after accidents, facial surgery and so on.'

'Really?' I said. 'How interesting.' I made a mental note to chat with him in private at the first opportunity. 'A dentist?' I repeated, and thought, that'll explain all the nose hair then.

'Why don't you stay over?' Michael shouted, popping his head round the door with a cheery smile. 'Then you can have a drink. Sarah would love a chat and I'm not much company at the moment. Busy, busy, you know how it is.'

I gave him a knowing smile and nodded affably, but the truth is I didn't have a clue.

'You could stay in the new summerhouse. Why don't you show him round, Sarah? Good night, both,' and with that he left.

Sarah - sorry, Sandy - collected a bottle of Chablis from the fridge and we sauntered into the garden and sat watching the hens as they started to roost for the night in the low fruit trees. She usually made sure they were always locked in the henhouse at night. I opened the wine with a flourish, showing my skill with a wine waiter's friend, and filled her huge chalice-like crystal glass. She drank it down greedily.

'Slow down,' I said, offering her a refill that she accepted with a nod. 'You're knocking it back a bit, aren't you, love?' I asked with a wry smile.

'I know,' she replied. 'It's Michael. He has no time for me. He's never here and when he is he just goes on about his investments and his syndicate.' She took another gulp. 'And now he would rather fob me off on you than spend time with me.'

'Did you say *syndicate*? What's all that about?' I asked, intrigued.

'Oh, he and a few associates are planning to invest heavily in buying stock to start a stud farm.'

'Is he? Where?'

'Over at the grange, next to your place,' she replied, between gulps.

Interesting, I thought, as I refilled her glass. She was a little tipsy and tearful, so I decided to join her in a drink. Liza was safe enough and I could kip in the van. I drained my glass and the troubles of recent days lifted from my shoulders as we watched the sun descend behind the distant hills.

'I'm getting a bit chilly,' Sandy said. 'Fetch us another bottle and we can retire to the summerhouse.'

I obliged and, as there were two bottles chilling nicely, I decided to bring them both. I've always noticed how the second bottle seems to go down faster than the first.

The summerhouse was lovely, made of oak logs and facing the distant hills. We sat on a huge wicker lounger, big enough to seat three in comfort and long enough to stretch out at full length. We sat staring into the growing darkness. I sensed a sort of melancholy in the air and, as marriage guidance isn't one of my strong points, I fell back on making her laugh. I recalled a crappy joke from the comedian at Jenny's gig. 'What do you call a fish with no eyes? A fshhhh.' She giggled, not rolling in the aisles, but there was a definite lightening of the mood. As I pulled the second cork she smiled and clutched my arm.

Then she asked, 'Was there anything going on between you and that woman from the grange?'

'Liza?' I replied. 'Well, yes and no, yes - we are - or at least were - very close friends. Nothing more and nothing less.'

She moved closer and leant her head on my chest.

I decided it was time for me to change tack as this was going in an unexpected direction. I didn't want to get the wrong end of the stick and embarrass us both. 'Is there a loo I can use?'

'Of course, Frankie.'

She led me into a spacious bathroom, complete with a glass-fronted shower cubicle.

'This is swanky, love.' I said with a whistle.

'Yes, and through there,' she replied, pointing to a door on the other side of the main room, 'is a sauna.'

How the other half live... She left me and as she closed the door said, 'Take a shower if you like.'

I didn't see why not, so I stripped and got under it. As I dried off, I took advantage of the bathroom's cabinet full of expensive smelly stuff, then I slipped on a towelling robe and returned to the main room.

Sandy was sitting with her legs curled underneath her bottom, her head tilted as it rested on her hand, gazing at me doe-eyed and clutching her almost empty glass. 'More wine?' she offered, while passing me her glass for a refill.

'Not for me, love. It gives me indigestion,' I lied, thinking of ways to move the conversation, and the evening, in another direction. 'That was a great shower.' I said, drying my hair briskly.

'I think I'll have one too,' she said as she stood, walked over to me, and playfully tugged at the ends of the knotted belt of my robe.

'Good idea,' I said, steering her away and into the bathroom, closing the door behind her, and thinking of making a quick exit.

'Michael has a few spirits in the mini bar,' she called through the door, the noise of the shower muffling her voice. 'Help yourself, if you like.'

'Thanks,' I shouted back and then realised I'd left my clothes in the bathroom. I couldn't run away naked, so I decided to give the bar a try. I found a bottle of cognac and two cut-glass brandy bowls. I poured myself a large one.

Women take ages in the bathroom, don't they? Makes you wonder what they get up to sometimes. By the time she came out I was feeling very relaxed and mellow.

Sandy busied around behind me, lighting the pre-prepared log fire and sorting through the cassette tapes and LPs, all in neat cases, next to the Beocenter 2200. Then she pressed play, turned the key in the lock, dropped the blinds over the French windows and turned to face me. She was silhouetted in the moonlight filtering through the blinds. As she raised her arms to smooth her wet hair away from her face, her robe fell open just as the flickering flames of the fire began to light up the room. I ran my eyes over her milky white skin and I realised why everyone called her Sandy; she obviously wasn't a natural blonde. She quickly drew her robe together, feigning coy modesty, and joined me. We sat and made small talk while imbibing the cognac and enjoying the music, until all thoughts of flight had drifted from my mind. After emptying her glass Sandy laid her head on my chest, absent-mindedly fiddling with my knotted belt.

'Why did you ask about Liza?' I asked.

'Well...' she replied in a tipsy drawl, 'I was wondering if you had room for another *friend*.' She emphasised the word pointedly.

'Who?' I asked like a clot.

'Me, stupid,' she answered, playfully slapping my thigh.

'Oh,' I said, swallowing hard. 'But we *are* friends, aren't we?'

'Yes, but I meant, *very close friends*. Nothing more and nothing less.' She lifted her head and smiled as she quoted my earlier words and kissed me tenderly on the cheek. Then she returned her head to its previous place but this time a little lower, almost to my belt, allowing me the freedom to take a hearty gulp of cognac.

'Well?' she asked again. 'Have you got room for me?'

I thought about it and sloshed a little more cognac into my glass, spilling it over my hand. I swapped the glass into my other hand and floundered, searching clumsily for something to wipe it on. Sandy raised her head and then licked the drips from my fingers.

'I'm waiting, Frankie.'

I decided, as actions speak louder than words, that it would be better to demonstrate my friendship rather than simply talk about it. So, still sipping my cognac, I lay back and watched the flames flicker on the polished pine ceiling. As Engelbert Humperdinck struck the first notes of 'The Last Waltz', I took a handful of her blonde curls and pulled her head slightly back. She let out a little sigh and then I gently pushed her face into my lap.

***

I woke up exhausted. I'd never realised she had so much energy. I had planned to slip my duds on and peel off into the ether long before cock shout, but as it turned out I'd slept through until the sun, streaming through the windows, woke me with a start as Sandy cheerfully opened the blinds. 'Good morning, darling,' she chimed, her million-watt grin more dazzling than the morning sun.

Such wanton cheerfulness worried me and made me wonder what was coming next. I braced myself for impact and dragged my weary bones into an almost vertical position, hastily hiding my modesty with the bathrobe I'd flung off in the small hours.

'I'm so happy,' she continued, humming to herself and bustling about, putting things straight. She was like something straight out of *The Sound of Music* and was frightening me more by the minute.

'I'd better be going, love.'

'Nonsense, Frankie,' she carolled. 'I have breakfast cooking.'

Now, as I've never met a calorie I didn't like, and with Sandy being such a culinary miracle worker, I decided another hour or so would make no difference. So I followed her, like the pushover I am, back into the kitchen, where I perched on a high stool at her breakfast bar, constantly rearranging my legs and tightening the rope belt on the gown to hide my... well, you know, just hide things. I munched toast and swigged excellent coffee with a faint vanilla aroma, hand-ground just for me.

A mountain of home-cured bacon, sausages and free range eggs later, I reclined by the Aga in an old leather Queen Anne period chair as she cheerfully scrubbed pots and pans in the sink.

'Things will be so wonderful now, Frankie.'

'What do you mean?' I asked nervously.

'Now that your *friend* isn't around-' I guessed she meant Liza '-you can stay here as long as you like.'

'Sorry, I can't. There's stuff I have to see to.'

'Nonsense, Frankie. Your caravan is a wreck. You can't go home.'

'The chickens?' I added hopefully.

'I've been thinking about that,' she continued, 'and I've sent Roger to round them up and bring them here. They can stay with my girls until you are straight.' Roger was a farm hand and part-time gardener.

'You really do think of everything, don't you?' I grinned, my mind racing in desperation. Now, what is it with women? Half of them want to get their hooks into you and the other half slam doors in your moói. They're just not like us emotionally stable blokes, are they? 'There is just one thing…' I stumbled for the words needed to make a decent excuse. 'I owe this bloke some money, I'm in a bit of a spot and I was wondering…'

'Oh, darling!' She rushed over and clung to me. 'Was that why they wrecked your home?'

I stood, trying my best to look humble and stoic.

'Let me help you,' she said, her voice full of concern.

'I can't,' I said, with my hand over my heart to display my earnest pride. 'It would be wrong to borrow money from you now we are...'

'Lovers...' She had a dreamy look in her eyes as she continued. 'No, it's just a loan,' she said and she grabbed a tea caddy from the shelf, her egg-sales-for-school-fees stash, which had been dipped into on my behalf several times before. She fished out a bundle of notes and pressed it into my hand. 'Will that cover it?'

'I think so, love,' I muttered bravely, with a fixed expression. 'I'll go and sort it out now.'

'You will be back for lunch, won't you?' she called as I raced up to the summerhouse for my clothes.

'Dinner, darling,' I shouted back over my shoulder as I ran.

I dressed in a rush, feeling desperately guilty about Michael. He seemed such a decent sort of chap and would have thought me a bounder and a cad. So I peeled a bank note from my wad of recent good fortune. The Duke of Wellington regarded me sternly, reminding me of Michael, and I knew I was doing the right thing when I left it on the bar to cover my share of the booze. In two minutes flat I was gunning the transit out of the driveway and back to Liza.

Chapter 8

Digger's yard was a hive of activity. Machines were being skilfully manoeuvred to the edges and the hydraulic shovels and grabs carefully interlocked in bizarre positions as if forming a defensive circle.

'Dennis, what's going on?' I shouted, struggling to make myself heard over the din of the roaring diesel engines and choking on the acrid smoke.

'We're moving out,' he replied.

'Where to?'

'To the fair, Frankie,' he called back jubilantly as he mounted the driver's seat of a dumper truck and chugged into the throng.

I found Liza in the caravan wrapping china, all borrowed, in tea towels and tablecloths and packing it away under the beds.

She'd struck up a friendship with one of Digger's grand-nieces, a girl in her early teens. I had to smile at the similarity between the two - they were both the same height and build and they shared the same bright, lively, hazel eyes and elfin good looks.

'Hey, Molly, here's a quid - go and play with your dollies and leave the grown-ups to talk.'

Molly gave me a cheeky grin. 'Why don't you go and play with your chickens, Frankie?'

Then she slipped her feet into a pair of stiletto heeled shoes discarded at the door and wobbled out, stumbling on the steps as she tried her best to imitate a catwalk swagger in her mini skirt.

'Cheeky pup, I ought to tan your arse,' I shouted after her. She looked back over her shoulder and gave me a wink. I smiled. She was a lovely kid - full of life, and sharp. She reminded me of more innocent times.

'Isn't it exciting, Frankie?' Liza was like a happy child, overflowing with enthusiasm. I sat on a bunk and watched her as she packed. 'We're going to Appleby Fair. I've always wanted to go and see the horses in the river.'

'Lovely,' I smiled, sighing inwardly as I thought of my last disastrous visit there and worrying about how I could keep her out of trouble amongst such vast crowds. 'You stick close to Molly and keep out of the horse roads.'

'She is fun, isn't she?' Liza remarked with a smile.

'No, not that Molly, love. Her mother. She's got her head screwed on, so listen to her. Fair Hill can be a dangerous place for Gorgies.' Her face dropped as I reminded her of the cultural void between us.

'I will,' she said and then asked, with imploring eyes, 'you'll be with me too, won't you?'

'Of course, love.' I hugged her.

'Did you know Marcus went to school not far from the fair? He has told me all sorts of tales.'

'Like what?' I asked, cautiously.

'Like the police fishing a dead body out of the river just after the fair. It was a young man. They say he was a fighter who had been in a bare-knuckle bout and that he'd been beaten to death for the prize money he'd won and dumped in the river.'

I hadn't been expecting that.

'Don't believe all you hear,' I snapped. 'It - it wasn't like that at all.'

Liza looked up at me, clearly startled by my abruptness. I could see her working it out. 'You were there?' she asked after a long pause, looking shocked. 'Did you see what happened?'

'Not exactly,' I replied reluctantly. 'I might tell you about it some time.' Before she could ask me any more about it I went off to find Digger.

Things were looking up, I told myself. I had money, transport and - hopefully - baby-sitters for Liza to give me the chance to try and catch up with Marcus and his cronies. I found Digger sitting on his doorstep, supervising the exodus.

'Hey, Frankie!' he beamed as I walked towards him. 'Are you coming with us?'

'I don't know yet.' I avoided his gaze. 'You're off early, aren't you? The fair's over a week away.'

'We're taking the scenic route, visiting a few friends on the way. We could all do with a holiday, Frankie - including you.'

'Do me a favour. Take Liza with you and let me catch up, will you?'

'Consider it done, Frankie.'

'Cheers - and look after her, will you?'

He nodded.

'I owe you one,' I told him and started to walk away.

'Just the one, is it, Frankie?' Digger chuckled after me, and I knew at some point he would be looking for payback for his hospitality.

But that would be *then* and I was in trouble *now*, so I decided not to tell Liza but to head off on my own and try to work out what was going on. Right now nothing made sense, but I had to try with what I had – though that wasn't much.

I decided to start with the faces I had recognised. First stop, Black Joe. Now, he had his fingers in loads of pies and, judging by his girth, he ate most of them, but he was a straightforward enough bloke when you knew him and as shrewd as any man I'd met. I decided to see if he could shed any light on things.

I headed for the sales at Leominster. It is a huge and well-organised place auctioning everything from fine art to tractors, and dealing with cars, livestock and horses on the way. Joe could often be found there, regardless of what was being sold, as he seemed to be able to make a quid out of almost anything.

When I arrived I began my enquiries by investing some of my new-found wealth in a pot of tea and a bacon butty. The café's central position would allow me to see who was coming and going without having to look around every sale area and run the risk of bumping into Marcus or anyone who would put him on my track. I also stood a fair chance of casually bumping into my quarry this way, as Black Joe was no stranger to cafés. My gamble paid off; as I sat munching and swigging my way through little Cassandra's school fees, Joe came in with a couple of blokes I didn't know, one in a flat cap with copious curls springing out of the sides, the other totally bald and hatless. *It's odd*, I thought, *how bald men don't get cold heads.*

They sat at an empty table behind me. Joe hadn't noticed me so I kept my head down and waited until I could catch him on his own. Now, I didn't mean to eavesdrop, but you can't help it, can you? You can close your eyes if you don't want to look, but you can't switch your ears off. They rattled away innocently enough, chatting about buying a car for some elderly relative.

'I told her,' said Flat Cap, 'you ought to get a Land Rover.

If we have snow you'll be stuck up there.'

'Or one of them little Suzukis,' Baldie threw in.

'They're bloody good them Suzukis - take you anywhere,' piped up Joe. From this I guessed he must have one for sale and listened as he went into detail on their virtues, then told them there would be a lovely one in next week's sale - he definitely had one then. The conversation ranged back and forth until the two blokes rose to leave, Joe didn't go with them; he said he was selling, not buying, so he would join them when a few more lots had gone through.

'Not bidding?' asked Flat Cap.

'No,' said Joe, 'I'm raising money for my new business venture.'

'What's that then?' enquired Baldie.

'Pedigree cattle. I've joined a syndicate breeding for export as there's big money to be made abroad.'

'Good luck with it, Joe,' Flat Cap said and they made their way to the salerooms.

Now I had heard *that* I didn't really want to speak to Joe, but I couldn't really leave without him seeing me. I rose and made a big fuss about sorting through my change and finding my keys, hoping Joe would think I hadn't seen him.

'Frankie,' he called, 'long time no see.'

'Wotcher Joe. How you been, mate?'

'Fair-to-middlin', Frankie. What brings you over here? No

chickens in the sale are there?' he asked with a mocking grin.

'No, mate, there's a Beswick donkey in the art sale. My auntie's trying to complete a set.'

'For some tart you're shagging more like,' he said with a hearty chuckle.

'Something like that, Joe.' I grinned. 'See ya, mate.'

I jumped into my trusty transit and left straightaway. Perhaps I should have made a show of looking at the art sale, though, as Joe's knowing eyes followed me across the yard and out of the gates.

Funny how when I am skint I can go days without really thinking about food and barely a boiled egg passing my lips - though to be honest I'm sick of bloody eggs - but when I have cash I'm constantly famished. I decided to call in on my pal June in Stourbridge next to provide me with a free snack and some headway in my investigation.

June had a lovely little flock of Pekin bantams that had the run of her garden, which overlooked the Staffs and Worcs Canal close to its intersection with the Stourbridge branch, where narrow-boats had been gliding by since 1772. June was always happy to chat poultry and usually had some homemade baking on the go. Granted it was very egg-oriented, but it was a little more imaginative than my boiled, fried, or omelette repertoire.

June was a fiery redhead, tall and slender with green eyes and, unlike Sandy, matching natural collar and cuffs.

My real interest here today, however, lay in her husband Terry - don't laugh, they really were Terry and June. Terry was into light haulage and also transported cars. He usually had a bit of inside info on all sorts of goings-on around the various auctions and trade sales.

When I called June was in the garden in the nip. They are naturists and often walk around completely starkers - hence my knowledge of her colour co-ordination. It was early June and a bright day, but I didn't think quite warm enough for nudity - maybe you get used to the cold. Terry was out, thank God, as when they are in naturist mode the company of a naked man over a cup of tea and a scone does nothing for my conversational prowess. I mean, you don't know where to look, do you? But I somehow have no issues finding somewhere to rest my weary gaze when it's just June and me.

Her nakedness is natural, and normal, and not in the least bit sexual. I sometimes get a little tempted when she is in a particularly playful mood, but we tried being more than friends once and her peccadilloes were just not to my taste. I found her liking for stilettos and fishnets in the bedroom admirable, but her requests to be bound and whipped really weren't for me. I gave it a go - it would have been rude not to - but wanton violence towards a woman, even at her forceful insistence, just isn't my cup of meat.

I began by asking where Terry was, as I'd have liked him to rescue my old crate from the dungeon we had dumped her in and return her to my place, when he had the chance. But, and this is the interesting bit, he was away working for an investment syndicate, trailing after them from auction to auction as they bought up some very expensive classic cars.

'Never mind, love,' I said, 'I'll call in some other time.'

She invited me in to see her new crystal-glass heeled shoes and said she had a bottle of vodka in the fridge if I would care to stay for a drink. I suddenly remembered an urgent appointment, made my excuses, and left. I wouldn't have wanted welts spoiling her suntan.

I pointed my van towards Wolverhampton and tried to formulate an off-the-cuff plan as I headed for the hospital. It's gone now, but back then this part of the world got its health care the traditional way at Wordsley Hospital. It was a charming old place, a converted workhouse and asylum. It's been abandoned and mostly demolished for housing in recent years in favour of a more centralised approach to health, though I doubt its original inhabitants would have mourned its passing.

I was hoping to find Michael, but how do you go about blagging your way in to see a consultant with no appointment? I could have just strolled in and asked, but I tend to take the complicated route, on this occasion fuelled by my paranoia, which had already convinced me I'd been followed here by a black Ford Granada, the same one that had followed us - in the same van - from Baggeridge Park. I ran a red light to be on the safe side, and had a go at putting it, quite literally, behind me.

I turned into the hospital grounds via the new entrance next to the maternity unit, trying to avert my gaze in case a pregnant lady caught my eye and started a trend, as I find consequences - rather like responsibilities - are things best avoided.

I swung right and parked close to the old disused entrance, reversing up to the few low bushes that blocked the redundant opening. I was a while coming up with a workable plan, as hospitals make me nervous and when I am nervous, I get edgy and often silly. It's all those long corridors - they always seem endless to me, and the echo of heels clicking on the hard floors gives me the chills. When they are crowded, it is even worse; it feels like the corridors are getting even longer - and why are they always white? Would a splash of colour have broken the bank?

I remember visiting an ailing auntie, years ago... I get disorientated in large buildings and start to get mixed up as soon as I lose sight of the outside world. I was sitting on the edge of her bed when I noticed she had one of those nurse call buttons. It was emblazoned with a rather sexist image of a nurse with a triangular skirt, an unfeasibly tiny waist, and one pointed leg. Anyway, the orange glow just kept calling my finger, and before long an angry Irish sister was barracking me. 'Those are for emergencies only,' she shrieked at me in her band-saw voice. 'Sorry, sister, my hand just slipped, sister, I won't do it again, sister.' I wasn't a natural liar, but under pressure it seemed to come as easily as blinking in the wind. She drew herself up to her full five-foot-nothing, folded her arms across her perfectly-pressed uniform and prepared for battle. 'That is what you said the last *six* times.' 'Seven,' I corrected pedantically, thinking myself very witty. 'Out - get out, this instant!' she bawled. 'You are not welcome on my ward!' All the time she was pointing sternly to the doors. I trudged out, head down and red-faced, then turned right instead of left and ended up lost in the staff canteen.

I shook my head, then pulled myself together and closed my eyes for a moment of quiet reflection before putting phase one of my plan into action. I'd found a bright yellow safety vest behind the driver's seat of the van and a hard hat stowed overhead. Using insulation tape and a few odds and ends from the junk in the back I made a fairly convincing-looking parcel.

I disembarked and walked tentatively away from the van, feeling more vulnerable with every step. The first door I came too was marked *Home Warden's Office*. Inside I was met by a pleasant motherly lady with dark curly hair, a white uniform, and Deirdre Barlow glasses. I asked where I could find Dr Jones; this was post *Raiders of the Lost Ark* and made me feel even more of a fraud than I already was.

'Which department?' she asked in her best professional voice, obviously saved for talking down to oiks like me.

'Teeth,' I replied, baring mine as if it helped the lie.

'Teeth,' she repeated with a quizzical expression. 'One moment.' She turned away with a frown, shuffled papers, and then made an internal call.

My knees were shaking. I was getting ready to run, quite sure she could see through my transparent ruse. I was standing next to a poster of a smiling new mother, her breasts defiantly bared as she held her baby proudly. The caption read: *'The way I see it, feeding a baby is what my breasts are for.'* It makes you wonder how she managed to get pregnant in the first place, stupid woman!

'We have a Mr Jones,' came her well-pronounced response at length. 'A consultant.'

'A Mr Michael Jones?' I asked.

'Yes, that's the one.' She gave me a complex set of directions involving a clock tower, gardens and car parks that made my head swim. She sensed my confusion and sighed. 'Hang on and I'll take you over.'

'Ta, love.'

I followed her across some quaint gardens and through a labyrinth of little car parks and covered walkways until she pointed me through a door and told me to ask at the desk. I nodded and smiled in thanks, took a deep breath, and forged on.

A pretty, petite, lady greeted me with a friendly smile that lit up her face; she had lavish locks of raven hair secured by a long single plait wound around her forehead. Fortunately she wore a name badge, which is a great way to get your foot in the door.

'Can I help you?' she asked.

'I hope so, Helen,' I replied, giving her my charming best. 'I'm looking for Mr Jones.'

'The consultant?' she asked.

'Yes, Helen.'

'Do you have an appointment?'

'No, a parcel.' I beamed disarmingly.

'Dangerous, is it?' She looked at my hard hat and raised her eyebrows, unconvinced.

'No, not at all, Helen.'

'So you know what's in it then?'

'No,' I said defensively, starting to panic.

'Ok,' she said, taking a deep breath. 'Who is it from?'

I was losing fast. Why are women such a suspicious lot? At that moment a door opened behind us.

'Helen, have you got those notes for me?' Michael's voice asked over my head. I turned to face him. 'Frankie? What are you doing here?'

'I came to see you, Michael.'

'You'd better come in,' he said and ushered me hurriedly inside. He glanced nervously up and down the corridor before shutting his door behind us.

There was an array of small hand tools on his desk and a gruesome model of a jawbone with a half-completed set of teeth.

'You've got some nerve coming here, Frankie, after your disgraceful behaviour.'

'I can explain.' I switched from relieved back to defensive.

'You better had. It's simply not on, your taking advantage of our hospitality like that.'

'It was her fault,' I blurted out without thinking. 'She made me do it. I was tired and-'

'That's it, blame her,' he interrupted. 'Why don't you take some responsibility, man? Sarah told me everything. You shouldn't have sneaked that woman into our home in the first place.'

'No, you're right, Michael,' I agreed, with relief, even though I was lost.

He ranted on. 'Bringing in some tart - she even stole money from us! Sarah said she's a notorious trollop, the scourge of the village. It's disgraceful. I was all for calling the police but Sarah wouldn't let me.'

'I'm very sorry, Michael.'

'Don't apologise to me, Frankie. It's Sarah you ought to apologise to. She'll be on her own a lot over the next few weeks and she doesn't need things like this to worry about.' He poked me in the chest as he raged. Ordinarily I wouldn't have been pleased with being prodded, but I decided to let it go. 'I have to go away on business and she is worried this harlot will come back,' he banged on.

I did my best to look like I was agreeing with him. 'I'll make sure she doesn't come back, I promise,' I squeezed in when he paused for breath.

'Make sure you do,' he rejoined, with a last prod. 'In fact, you ought to go and apologise personally.'

'I will. I'll go as soon as I can,' I added, wearing an expression of humble regret.

'Ok then. Let's say no more about it,' and he calmed a little.

'Thank you, Michael. I came here to apologise, so I'm glad you brought it up.'

He nodded, but seemed unconvinced by my version of the truth. 'Is it syndicate business that is taking you away?' I asked.

He looked surprised. 'Yes it is, as a matter of fact. I'm going to Cumbria with a number of other investors to a sale of bloodstock. Why?'

'Will you be away long? I was just wondering if it would be a good idea to stop over in your summerhouse for a few days. To apologise to Sandy - I mean, Sarah - and put her mind at rest. I can keep an eye on her for you, my way of making things up.'

He thought about my proposition for a moment before answering. 'Good idea, Frankie. I'll be at least a week. I'll call her and let her know you'll be popping in - you'd better not let us down again!' He prodded once more, the bastard, almost taking things too far - but I soldiered on.

'No need, Michael. I'll take flowers and surprise her.'

'So she will assume it's all your idea, Frankie?'

I looked at my feet.

'Go on then; do it your way.'

'Cheers, Michael.'

He muttered something I didn't quite hear, his back to me as he gazed thoughtfully out of the window.

'Bye then,' I said and dashed out, pausing only to help myself to a neat little case of dental tools from the desk and to try for Helen's phone number on the way back to the van.

I slumped over the wheel, exhausted, not able to make much sense out of the results of my DIY sleuthing. What was Marcus up to? Buying cows with Joe, selling them with Mr Mace and now buying horses with Michael... Were all of them syndicate members?

I could easily have slept the rest of the afternoon away but I needed fuel. I decided to drive down to the marina at Ashwood where I could fill up with 'cherry' - tax-free red marine diesel costing half the price of regular petrol. I wouldn't get into any trouble, unless I got caught. As trusting my instincts seemed to be working for me I decided to chance it and to preserve my cash as best I could.

As I eased the van forward the hard hat rolled onto the floor. I tried to grab it as it fell but my foot slipped off the clutch pedal and I stalled the engine. I retrieved the hat and looked up, only to see the dark saloon containing Marcus's hired heavies pointing straight at me, with the engine running.

They were smiling, Jerry and Johnny, the Johnson brothers - twins - adding up to four of me physically and about two thirds of me mentally. I casually restarted the engine and nodded affably as if nothing was wrong. The big saloon sprang forwards, tyres smoking, and slithered to a halt a few yards closer. The brothers gave me their best menacing stares while Jerry revved the engine. I revved my own engine and glared back, but they didn't look too scared. In fact, they laughed. Had they known how things were going to develop they might not have been so smug.

My van was a pretty new model, the pride of Digger's fleet, and though no match for their fuel-guzzling monster it was, as vans went, pretty nippy - I decided to give them a run for their money. Making the best use I could of my van's few horsepower, I revved the engine hard and slipped my foot off the clutch. The van lurched forward about ten yards, tyres squealing, and then we sat there staring, each waiting for the other to make the next move.

I checked the rear-view mirror and saw a young couple walking past behind me. The boy was a spotty lad in a tartan check Lyle and Scott golfing jumper and acid-washed jeans, clutching the hand of a cute freckled girl in matching jeans and pixie boots. They were doing that teenage slow-motion walk thing, heading innocently for the bus stop. I waited a moment then moved the van forward again, just a little, and Johnny gunned his engine in response, heading straight for me. I don't know if he would have rammed me or just stopped me getting away but I didn't wait to find out. I floored it, dumped the clutch, and a gap opened up in front of their car as my van hurtled out of their path - backwards. I bounced over the kerb and through some bushes, demolishing a steel trip rail, and then out onto the main road, where I spun the wheel to point the van towards Stourbridge. The spotty lad had grabbed his girlfriend protectively as I narrowly avoided mowing them down and he shot me an evil look. I smiled as the lad took the chance to rest his hand 'accidentally' a little lower down her back than a nice girl might otherwise have allowed.

The Johnsons, thinking better of following me down my bumpy route, swerved hard left and headed round the block heading towards the new entrance to give chase. Instead of shooting off down the road as they probably expected I would, I hurtled backwards once more, taking advantage of their few seconds of blindness as they rounded the buildings between us, bounced back over the kerb, through the flattened bushes, and onto the car park. A swift change of direction and I was shooting into the labyrinth of car parks and internal roads all hospitals seem to have.

Back then the Wordsley used to boast a few battery-powered land trains that towed huge snaking lines of panniers, transporting linen and other supplies all over the sprawling site. I did my best to dodge the one that crossed my path, swerving hard left, but I still side-swiped it, sending dirty sheets and pre-cooked meals in all directions. I fought the steering back into a straight line and headed down past the old army barrack-style wards, then I turned left onto the snaking road through the adjoining Ridge Hill Hospital's landscaped grounds. A sharp right turn at the top of the drive took me downhill to the traffic lights, where I slowed down to blend in with the traffic, and made my way unobtrusively to Ashwood Marina. Once there I filled my tank with red diesel and lay low until dark.

Digger's van was a mess. The back doors were badly dented, the driver's side panels were battered end-to-end, and the front grille was broken. Thankfully, all the lights worked and, apart from a hissing rear tyre caused by a damaged wheel rim, which I quickly changed for the spare, there appeared to be nothing to stop me continuing with my investigations.

I sat with my legs sprawled across the passenger seats and watched as the sun started to sink behind the distant trees. As I thought things through my despondency grew. I was getting nowhere fast; all I had achieved was wrecking Digger's van and getting the bad guys on my trail. All avenues seemed to lead back to Marcus and his syndicates - but what did it all mean? I didn't know then, and I am still not sure now, exactly what a syndicate even is. I was no closer to understanding any of it. It was all just a fucking jumble. Jenny had gone AWOL and the usually steadfast Liza was wrapped up in her own problems; they were the two people I loved and trusted most in the world and neither could help me – and it seemed I was incapable of helping them either...

I needed a friend. I could go back to Sandy for comfort, consolation, and home-cooked food, of course, but that would mean me having to explain my disappearance. On the other hand, I *had* supported her lies to Michael, so surely that put me in the clear? But that would only make her even more clucky and needy, and in reality I wasn't sure how much help she would be in working all this out anyway. It would just worry her sick.

So I decided my best course of action would be to head north and rejoin Digger's convoy as soon as I could.

Chapter 9

After dark, I set off towards the motorway, keeping an eye out for the black Granada, and before long I was cruising northwards at a steady fifty-five miles per hour. Any faster and I wouldn't have heard myself think as the battered van squeaked and rattled its way through the evening. By the time I started seeing signs for the Potteries I was done in; I'd been running on adrenaline all day. The clatter of the diesel engine and the wind whistling through the mangled bodywork had taken its toll. I decided to take a short detour and headed for a farm often used by road workers on contract as a base for their caravans.

Willow Brook Farm is a proper working farm, with the river Trent running through its sprawling fields. I was there once when it was in flood and watched amazed as one man changed a flat tyre on a tractor. The tyre was taller than him and must have weighed a ton but he changed the whole wheel with just a spanner and a shovel, plus experience and an ingenuity seldom found outside the farming community - except among us travellers, of course. I was relying on this when I decided to ask old George, the farmer in question, for a bit of advice.

George was out, but I was made welcome by his wife Joy

in their expansive kitchen. Joy was an adorable lady, chubby, with tight grey curls, rosy cheeks and kind eyes; she seemed to have been around forever and was old even when I was a lad. I was plied with tea and endless enquiries about my health, which I said was fine because, after all, no one ever really wants to know, do they? I polished off a marvellous pork pie, ham sandwiches - Liza would have been mortified - and a slab of stodgy cake. It seemed to give Joy great pleasure to watch me demolish the fruits of her hard work, but women appreciate men's appetites, I've often noticed.

Apparently George would be back in the morning. I declined the offer of a bed, as they do B&B and I would have been embarrassed if I didn't at least offer to pay - and I couldn't be sure she would accept anyway. So, to preserve my dwindling gelt, I chose to reverse into one of the barns and make a bed in the back of the van.

'Yer're welcome to use the shower, Frankie, and if yer bring those filthy clothes in I'll wash 'em for yer.'

'Thanks, Joy, but I haven't got any others.'

'Go an' jump in the shower and leave 'em outside the door. I'll find summat for yer. I 'ave a few things guests 'ave left behind.'

I accepted and stood in the shower. I usually wash under a cold tap outside every day, scraping my chin with a blunt razor, but lately I was getting used to showers. I stood for what seemed like ages, the water as hot as I could stand it, and felt the tension melt away. Then I opened the door and dragged in the folded pile Joy had left - a rather fetching electric-blue suit, a white t-shirt and a pair of Velcro-fastening white tennis shoes. The shirt was ok, the jacket a bit too big, so I rolled up the sleeves *Miami Vice* style. All I needed now was Liza's sunglasses, I thought, as I strolled back to the van.

The barn was half full of hay and straw and also housed a few caravans stored for weekends away. I set about making a bed in the back of my van. I had a few cushions salvaged from my caravan, a sheet, and numerous bits and bobs, including a fair mix of odd tools that were in residence when I moved in. I took a hammer and a shovel and went to work on the wooden bulkhead, removing it to make access from front to back easier. I could now go straight from bed to driving seat - a stroke of genius if ever I saw one.

I discarded the bedding and cushions. If you've ever smelt billy goat wee, you'll know why. That left me with just the quilt I'd wrapped Liza in, still in its bin liner. It wasn't going to give me much of a night's sleep on its own, so I laid a couple of straw bales side by side on the floor of the van - barley not wheat; it's a bit softer - to make a bed. I soon discovered that I needed to cover the floor in bales to stop them moving apart when I lay on them, so I upgraded to a double and then tried to get some sleep, locking the doors from the inside and leaving the ignition key in place in case I needed a quick getaway.

I had a fitful dream, with alternating images of Liza and Jenny - Jenny head back, laughing in the sunshine, and Liza shouting to me from a distance, words I couldn't hear. As I tried to move towards Liza, Jenny stayed with me, her laughter growing louder as Liza grew more distant, her shouts turning to desperate cries.

I awoke in a cold sweat in the small hours and decided it was time to move on. I went and freshened up under the tap and assessed my position. I was neither worse - nor better - off than when I had started. I really couldn't head for Fair Hill dressed like I was, I'd stand out like a cow in a car park. I needed my clothes back. I went quietly round the back of the farmhouse to the utility room and there found my clothes and shoes on the worktop, pressed and polished respectively and ready for action. Folded on top of the pile was a letter:

'I no you will need these I could not get all the stanes owt and the new buttons don't mach but I dun my best.

Joy X'

Beneath was a P.S. - she'd left me some food for the road. A tear came to my eye and, in defiance of my economy drive, I slipped into the kitchen and left one of my dwindling supply of bank notes under the teapot. Then, after helping myself to a couple of clean sheets from the utility room to justify the expense, I left.

The sun rose in a clear blue sky and it promised to be a fine morning. I made good time getting back to the motorway. I had a brief panic attack when a police car followed me for a mile or two, but then it turned off and I joined the M6 and continued to trundle northwards without hindrance. As I drove I fiddled with the radio, trying to find a station with a bit less interference than the rest - then I remembered Jenny's tape from my salvaged stuff. I slipped it into the stereo, pressed play, and my smile returned as I listened to her familiar voice belting out Pat Benatar's 'Love is a battlefield' as I drove on into the brightening day.

Just before Junction 20 I spotted roadworks up ahead - a snake of cones blocking access to the hard shoulder. As I got closer I saw a few high-vis and hard-hat clad workers leaning on their tools. With the beacons on the van roof flashing, I pulled in between the cones, using Digger's signwriting and the motorway maintenance sticker across the back doors as an excuse. I asked the men for news of Digger's gang and quickly wished I hadn't. It was as though I'd stumbled across a pub quiz team on a working holiday.

'Crash barriers on the M25, mate.'

'I think they're on the Blackpool Rail Link job.'

'I heard they were finishing the M42. It'll be open in a few months.'

The most likely clue from the many offered suggested a truck stop just a few hundred yards up the A50, off the next junction, so that was where I headed. When I got there, it turned out that I had missed them by about twenty minutes, so I set off once more at top speed. There was still about a hundred miles of motorway to cover and, assuming someone was bound to want to stop again before then, I had a fair chance of catching up.

I finally caught up with the convoy after about forty-five miles. It made a remarkable sight - a snaking line of caravans, their windows and chrome glinting, accompanied by an assortment of other vehicles. I pulled up alongside with the amber roof beacons flashing and honked the horn. A clamour of horns and flashing lights greeted me and a gap opened towards the back of the line. I pulled in, switched the beacons off and relaxed in my new-found anonymity. I had Dennis behind me, grinning from ear to ear, and the back of a horsebox in front.

We snaked on and after a few minutes a black car pulled out of the line ahead of me. The brake lights flashed as it slowed down until it drew level with me, then the tinted passenger window slid down to reveal Jenny smiling in the passenger seat. Then I glimpsed the driver in profile and mouthed a startled 'What the f-' before looking up to see the back of the horse box just inches from my bonnet. I hit the brakes and almost caused a pile-up, to a new volley of horns and hand gestures.

Liza?

I drew level with the black car again. The two of them were laughing their heads off. I suddenly felt like I'd been had. I don't know why, but my heart sank. I felt like a mug, the outsider on an inside joke. There they were in their flash motor, smirking at me and giggling, sharp minds working out all the angles, and in this particular triangle I was definitely the blunt corner. I was feeling more confused by the minute.

We pulled off and headed into Blackpool, eventually stopping in a field by a social club off the Lytham Road. There followed a period of frenetic activity, with engines revving and people waving and shouting as the whole gang pitched up. Horses whinnied and stamped as they were unloaded, eager for the fresh grass.

I slumped over the steering wheel, watching it all in a daze as Jenny's caravan arrived behind one of the horseboxes. A bang on the side of the van brought me to my senses.

'Come on, you idle bastard, Frankie!'

It was Fred. I climbed out and he passed me a sledgehammer. He was holding a couple of Transit van half-shafts in one hand and dragging long lengths of chain with the other. We walked over to the empty side of the field and hammered the shafts into the ground, about thirty feet or so apart. Then we collected more and carried on our work as the horses were unloaded and each one attached to a shaft by a length of chain for the duration of the stopover.

I stood back, leant on the hammer, and watched the animals being tethered. A collection of heavy ponies and a few horses, mostly piebald or skewbald - nice enough but nothing special, not like the thoroughbreds in Liza's stables. They were all due for sale or exchange at the fair.

As I stood lost in thought, watching the creatures test the strength of their moorings, a little tug on my sleeve attracted my attention. 'Penny for them,' Liza said gently and cuddled up to my arm. 'I've missed you, Frankie. Where have you been?'

'Nowhere special. Just tying up a few loose ends. How come you're travelling with Jenny?'

'Jealous, are you? Or frightened we've been comparing notes?'

'Maybe,' I mumbled.

Liza giggled. 'Are you blushing, Frankie?'

'No,' I snapped. 'I'm just hot, that's all. Come on, I'll let you make me a cup of tea.' We strolled back to the caravans. 'Which one are you in?' I asked as we approached the turmoil.

'I'm with Jenny; she's got plenty of room.'

'A bit of a step up from my hovel, eh?' I must have sounded a little bitter as she anxiously replied.

'No it's not that - I love your caravan. I can't wait to be back there.'

'Ok, love. Sorry,' I said, though I was thinking that it was never going to happen. 'Get in there and put Jenny's kettle on. I'll take this hammer back and catch you up.' She turned to go and I slapped her bum playfully.

'Less of that, cheeky,' came her chirpy response. 'I'm spoken for.' Then she sprinted away across the grass, her hair flowing in the breeze. She looked gorgeous and my heart leapt to see her so happy. I did the decent thing and dropped Fred's hammer - the damp grass would help keep the head tight; I was doing him a favour.

I ran after Liza, growling like a tiger, fingers hooked claw-like. She was squealing, laughing, and pretending to be scared. We arrived at Jenny's door red-faced; I scooped her up and started to tickle her. Jenny met us on the step.

'Come along, children, your tea'll be spoiled,' she scolded us mockingly - jealousy is a double-edged sword. I grabbed Jenny off the step and twirled her around until we fell in a heap on the grass next to Liza and we all lay there laughing.

We supped tea, ate biscuits and chatted the afternoon away. Jenny didn't quite explain where she had been, or what she had been doing, since I had seen her last, and she neatly dodged my questions about her agent, like a politician at the hustings. To save a stand-up row - which usually resulted in flying crockery - in front of Liza, I didn't press too hard.

'Where are you sleeping then, Frankie?' Jenny asked as she prepared for her show; it seemed that she had influenced Digger's choice of stopping places to suit her own agenda – all part of her charm I suppose.

'In the back of the van, love.'

'You can stay here. Me and Liza can share and you can have the other bed.'

'No thanks, I'm ok in my van. I like the fresh air. You women like things a bit too hot for me.'

'Fair enough,' she replied. 'But if you change your mind you're welcome.'

'And if you change yours, you're welcome at my place too,' I said as I left, adding riskily, 'either of you. I'm not fussed.' I shut the door and didn't wait for a reply as, to be honest, I was still too confused and tired for all this witty and flirtatious banter, pleasant as it was.

I strolled amongst the caravans, smiling, nodding and exchanging a few words here and there. It was a nice atmosphere - happy and playful, with excited children running and playing as all excited children do. I just wished I felt the same.

I went back to my van and parked up with the damaged side against the hedge. I'd been avoiding Digger, or maybe he was avoiding me. In some ways that was worse, as the longer I waited for the bollocking I was due for wrecking the van, the worse it would be. I sat in the front for a while, watching the kids squabbling over a lost ball among the general hustle and bustle of the camp.

I'd scrounged a large piece of carpet from Bob - a great bloke and a fantastic classical guitar player who lived out Hereford way; but more about him later. I arranged this over my straw bale bed, spread a clean sheet over that and then decided to get a bit of sleep before Jenny's show.

Chapter 10

I awoke in semi-darkness, the booming bass from the club telling me I'd missed the beginning of Jenny's show. There was a small candy-striped wash tent behind Jenny's caravan where I freshened up with cold water. Then I sauntered over to join the merriment. It wasn't your usual packed-to-the-rafters do, but more a seated-at-tables affair with a space for dancing at the front - all very civilised. Jenny would usually work through some of her more raucous numbers early in the evening and then move, through an ever-slowing tempo, to a few more intimate tunes at the end.

I clutched a pint and scanned the room for a likely candidate for a few slow numbers at the end. Molly, mother of Little Molly, caught my eye and lowered her head bashfully. Little Molly's father had run out on her before she was born and her new bloke was in prison. The way I saw it, Molly's mother was technically, if temporarily, single. She was sitting on the bench seating built against the wall on the far side of the room. I worked my way towards her, casually, without looking too obvious.

'Hey, Moll,' I intoned, smiling. 'Can I get you a drink?'

'No thanks, Frankie,' she said. 'I've got one and Fred has

put another behind the bar for me.'

I breathed a little inward sigh of relief, as I really couldn't afford to ply her with drink all night.

'You can stay and keep me company though, if you like.'

I pushed in between her and the couple next door, who moved over, grumbling a little, and I playfully put my hand on her knee as I sat. She didn't move it so I kept it there and, with a raised eyebrow, looked at her and said, 'I thought you would never ask.'

She grinned, so I pushed my luck and kissed her on the cheek. At that moment the song ended and everyone started to clap so I joined in, moving my hand and losing my advantage, but I had to applaud Jen - it was practically a duty.

A few more numbers came and went. The volume gave me an excuse to get within almost touching distance of Molly's neck as I spoke to her. At times my hand was on her shoulder, or hers on mine, as we struggled to communicate above the beat.

'It's been a long time, Frankie,' she said, looking intently into my eyes.

'Too long, Molly,' I replied.

I tripped up and down to the bar buying her Bacardi and Cokes; the odds on my investment paying off were growing shorter by the song, though admittedly my pints had turned to halves. My gap in the seating disappeared after one of these bar trips so I dragged a low stool up opposite her and we continued our flirty small-talk. The evening wore on and the tempo dropped to the slow numbers during which I would 'seal the deal' and invite Molly to sully my clean sheets. I had my hands on her thighs as I leaned forward to tell her how I loved the sparkle in her chocolate brown eyes; my lips were pressed close to her ear and her arms were draped on my shoulders. She laughed and, as I moved away, she closed her hands behind my neck and pulled my head to hers, kissing me hard on the lips. Then she playfully pushed me away with a wink and smirked.

'So you're still trawling out the same old lines then, Frankie?'

'Well, they work, don't they?' I said. 'Or at least they used to.'

She smiled and gave me a knowing look. 'Watch my seat, Frankie. I'm going to the loo.'

'Ok, Moll.' I smiled and as she sauntered away, her hips swaying slightly in her tight leather trousers, my eyes followed her ever step. Lust flashed through my mind at the site of her haunches - well she did say I was to watch her seat, didn't she?

'Daydreaming again, Frankie?'

I looked up to find Liza smiling down at me.

'Are you ever going to ask me to dance?' she said, with her head tilted at a provocative angle. She held out her hand. I took it and let her lead me to the dance floor. If you're reading this bit, Molly, I'm sorry.

We got to the dance floor in time to catch the end of Patsy Cline's 'Crazy', and then danced slow and close to Dusty Springfield's 'The look of love'.

'Where have you been?' she asked.

'Trying to work out what that no-good husband of yours is up to, love. What have you been doing?'

'Not much,' she said. 'Just hanging around with Molly and thinking about you.'

'I thought you'd been with Jenny?' I said, surprised.

'No, she only caught up with us this morning, just like you. She was waiting at the truck stop at breakfast time.'

I still wanted to know where she'd been but let it slide and held Liza a little closer, playfully nibbling her ear. One of the diamond studs that she had worn when she escaped scratched my cheek as I moved to catch her expression at my boldness. She leant forward and kissed the mark it left and I held her even tighter.

The song ended and brief applause rippled around the room. I didn't join in, as I didn't want to let go of Liza and break the spell, so we stood embracing and shuffling slightly as the next song quickly began. It was one of Jenny's signature songs. Her powerful voice shook everyone into listening, and the raw emotion of it brought a tear to my eye - 'Will you', originally by Hazel O'Connor. We shuffled in small circles gripped by each other and the emotion of the moment. My desperate race around the country had all been for nothing, or at least so I'd thought it until holding

Liza in my arms made it all seem worthwhile.

I placed my hand flat on her back, my fingers spread with my thumb at her nape, and then I slowly ran it downwards, applying a little pressure with my thumb as it ran along her spine. I continued until my thumb reached the base of her back and my splayed fingers rested on her bottom. The song carried on, *I wonder if you'll stay now...*

'Will you?' I asked. 'Stay with me tonight?'

'I can't,' she said and kissed my chest.

I looked down at her and sighed as the song faded out and the moment ended. She went back to her table by the stage looking up at Jenny and smiling while I, avoiding Molly's gaze, slipped out via the fire escape. I stopped for a moment to gather my thoughts, letting the cool night air bring me to my senses. I was an emotional wreck, my head spinning and every part of me throbbing with pent-up desire. I shook myself and headed back to my battered van.

I'd parked it a little way from the others, against a hedge that afforded me a little peace and privacy, as I knew there would be late-night story-telling and songs around a small fire, for which I just wasn't in the mood. I stripped and lay back spread-eagled to cool down for a while before crawling under my duvet and curling up for a fitful sleep. But the dream of Liza screaming while she faded into the distance woke me again - and someone was rattling the handles of the back doors.

I opened the door gingerly, expecting Liza. Now I had come to my senses I realised she'd allowed me, with good grace, to make a fool of myself. I would have to apologise. Or it could be Molly, in which case things could go either way - a bollocking or paradise. The thought of it being anyone else, friend or foe, never crossed my stupefied, lust-addled mind. When I saw it was Jenny I was more than a little surprised.

'We need to talk, Frankie.'

I nodded and hauled her into the muggy warmth of the van's interior. The sweet smell of fresh straw mixed with the traces of Liza's perfume, which still clung to my skin. As Jenny climbed onto the bales she stumbled and almost fell back out again. I grabbed her and held her close with one arm while slamming the door with the other.

'Steady on, Frankie,' she told me, 'you can let go now.'

I don't know what came over me then. I'm still a little ashamed. I was like some hungry beast. I threw her down and fumbled with her buttons. She laughed playfully as I lost my temper and tugged at her blouse, sending buttons pinging against the sides of the van.

'Calm down now, big fella,' she said as if quietening an anxious horse. I'd found my mark and with one hand on her left breast, which was cool and firm, I gently bit her right nipple. She gasped. I leant over her, my knee pushed her legs apart. 'Stop it Frankie! We really do need to talk.'

'Later,' I growled and pressed my mouth hard against hers. She parted her moist lips and her tongue met mine, spurring me on in my animalistic passions. The talking was over.

I reached down and hitched her flowing skirt up around her waist, feeling for the string of her thong. I pulled it from between her buttocks and sideways into the groove where her thigh ended and her soft curls began and pressed myself against her. She was softly murmuring, 'Don't, Frankie,' but her hands were pulling me closer.

I grabbed her wrists and threw my weight forwards, pinning her arms down, and then I looked at her face and faltered for a second, fearing I had gone too far. A smile flickered at the corners of her mouth and her wild eyes gleamed, pupils dilated by desire as she strained her neck to kiss me. She nipped my bottom lip, drawing a little blood. I knew she wanted this as much as I did and I forced myself into her. A shuddering 'yes' came from her mouth as she began to move her hips to meet mine.

Later, as I snoozed and she shivered, she woke me.

'We really do need to talk, Frankie.'

What is it with women and talking, and always at the wrong time? The first sign of emotion and they're like a United Nations delegation wanting to negotiate a treaty.

'Ok, love,' I said while playfully kissing her face and pulling her arms away from where they clutched the duvet to her breast.

'You're hopeless,' she said as I straddled her and continued my mischievous assault. 'I'm being serious, Frankie. It's about Liza.'

At that I calmed down a little, but I still kept open the

option of continuing the fun.

Someone started banging on the back doors. 'What now?' I sighed.

'You'd better see who that is, Frankie. I don't want Liza to know I'm in here.'

'Oh, fuck them. They can wait,' I said, smiling, 'I've got better things to do.'

I bent forward and started kissing her and at that moment the van doors burst open. Hands grabbed my legs and dragged me, in the blink of an eye, from warm comfort to cold pain.

I banged my head hard on the tow-bar and as I hit the floor more hands grabbed my arms. They lifted me to chest height and someone hissed, 'You're coming with us.' At this point I had no idea who it was and didn't try to work it out. I just did my best to struggle, kick, and scream, hoping to wake everyone so they would come running to the rescue.

I wrenched my right arm free and snapped my head round to see a powerfully built black man with braided hair and a gold tooth. I slammed my elbow hard into his face and he fell back. Then I kicked my legs free and we all fell down in a heap. One of the goons struggled to his feet. I kicked him in the back of the knee and brought him down again. My flailing feet kicked another in the groin and so the battle went on, with fists and feet slamming into me from all sides.

A deep voice roared, 'Hold it!' I looked up. The black

bloke had Jenny pinned against the van. He held her head back by her hair and had a knife at her throat. 'There's somebody wants a word with you, rasclat.' He paused and tugged Jenny's hair. 'Maybe you come quick, or maybe I finish what you started with the bitch 'ere, and then you can comfort her while you wait for the ambulance.'

I stood up, shaking off the hands that tried to grab me.

'Ok, I'm coming. Just let her go.'

After being hooded, with my own sheet, my wrists were tied, and I was bundled into the boot of a car. I rolled around struggling and kicking as the car bounced out of the field. Once I had worn myself out I calmed down and thought for a while. I added the black bloke to my mental hit list - I was going to get that bastard for this. I'm not normally a violent bloke, but I made it my duty to hit him as hard as I could, and as soon as the opportunity arose.

After what seemed hours the car stopped and I was dragged roughly out of the boot. Still hooded, I resisted stiffly as brutal hands guided me over some gravel, bashing me against a wall along the way. Finally I banged my head on a low doorway. Then the sheet was torn off and I blinked in the brilliant glare of halogen security lights.

'Well, what have we here?' The voice sounded familiar. 'Our neighbourhood Gypo caught with his pants down, but not with my wife for a change.'

Marcus! 'It's not like that, Marcus, we're just friends.'

'Yes, just *fucking* good friends, I've heard.' He sneered

and gave me a backhander across the face.

I reeled and thought of Liza that day in their yard. 'Untie me and try that again, you bastard!' I raged, fighting to free myself from the hands that gripped me.

He lowered his face to mine and slowly intoned, 'N-O.' Then he hit me again. I kicked out at him, my bare foot glancing off his shin. He laughed. 'Temper, temper. I'm not interested in your lame excuses. You can have the bitch. I have bigger and better things to worry about, and your sneaking around spying is getting annoying.'

'So what you going to do then, Marcus? Kill me?'

'Maybe,' he said and paused for effect. 'Eventually I might have to, if you don't play ball, but right now I have a proposition. I need labour and you need cash, so here's the deal. You work for me, help make sure things go smoothly, and I'll give you a generous cut.'

I shook my head. 'No chance,' and I spat some blood onto his brogues.

He looked down at his feet and sighed. 'Hear me out, Frankie, and if you decide it's not for you we can go back to the killing-you bit. And your little friend from the Pikey camp. I wonder how well she'll sing when we've finished with her? And then maybe I will reacquaint myself with Liza. The lads here would love a party with her; maybe with both of them. What do you think, lads?'

They all laughed, the black bloke's shoulders heaving with silent mirth. 'Maybe we can draw lots, to see who goes first with your woman.' He grinned at me.

'Good idea, Julian,' said Marcus, still sneering.

Julian? I thought - *Julian?* How did a knuckle-dragging thug like that get to be called Julian? Still, his mother must love him.

'Ok, you win,' I said. 'It's a deal.'

'That's better. Now, here are my terms. You stay away from me and my associates and mind your own business for one month from today and then you come here to work for me.'

'Where is here?'

'You have a month to work it out, Sexton Blake.' They all laughed again. 'I'll give you cash up front and leave you all alone and when this is over I will give you your deeds. And the icing on the cake is...' he indulged in a dramatic pause, '...Liza. She's all yours and I hope you're happy together.'

I nodded grudging agreement and the sheet blindfold was replaced. Then I felt a sharp pain in my neck and remembered little else but my determination to hit Julian.

***

I'm not sure exactly how much time passed before I got back to the conscious world, but it must have been hours, because it was mid-afternoon when I finally came round, battered and lying in the grass with my hands still tied behind my back. I struggled to my feet and discovered I was naked but for a black bin liner that swung from a rope tied around my waist, barely hiding my modesty. I saw that I was in a narrow lane. I walked a few yards and, after looking through gaps in the hedge, realised I was back at the camp.

I struggled across the verge, stumbling to my knees and fighting to stand again while mumbling, 'Sexton Blake - bastard, even his witticisms are out of date. At least Sexton had a sidekick; I'm in this mess on my bloody own.'

I made it to the gate and staggered in. Kids started mocking me. Little Molly was their ringleader. I don't know why, but had it been any of the other kids it would have been easier, but Molly had a way of looking straight into me and making me feel exposed. Her eyes seemed older than her years. Perhaps I was just still feeling guilty after standing her mother up so abruptly but, whatever it was, her mocking made me feel even worse than the beating I had suffered.

'Look, you can see Frankie's bum!' She pointed and the others all laughed hysterically.

And that's how I made it back into the camp, with the kids tagging along behind laughing and shouting. Bob dropped his china teacup and ran to help me.

I told you there'd be more about Bob later. Bob was a family friend. I think we were sort of related through series of marriages but I can't remember exactly how. He was a short, stocky, middle-aged man, with jet-black hair and dark skin that served as a reminder of all Romany people's Indian origins. Bob was known throughout the travelling community as an honest and competent man and was trusted and respected by all.

'Clear off!' he shouted at the kids, as he hurried over to me, swaying from the momentum of his stiff-hipped gait. 'Get home to your mothers or I'll take my stick to the lot of you!' He shook his walking stick above his head as he came. His wife Rose ran over with a throw from one of the seats in their caravan and wrapped it round my shoulders. I was shaking, despite it being mid-afternoon on a warm day. Bob pulled out a knife with a hand-carved yew handle, his speciality - he sold hand-carved things at the fair - and cut the ropes free just as a few of the lads came over to join us.

'What's in the bag, Frankie?' asked Fred, looking at the bin liner lying on the grass.

'Dunno,' I replied, shrugging my shoulders. Fred's quizzical expression asked permission to look and I nodded. The small crowd stood back as he turned the bag upside down and shook it. I was half expecting something gruesome, a severed limb or something, but then I watched too much telly as a kid. Instead, out fell rolls of bank notes, each held tight with a little coloured elastic band. The notes were a mix of denominations and the bands a mix of colours. Everyone gasped.

'Where's that lot come from?' asked Dennis.

'I think I've just joined a syndicate,' I answered through swollen and split lips.

Bob gathered up the cash and put it back in the bag. 'You'd better come inside, Frankie.'

Assisted by Rose, I followed him under a small awning he had put up on the side of his caravan. I got hot drinks and food. They had a candy-striped wash tent at the rear of the caravan, just like the one Jenny always had behind hers, and I washed myself carefully in it while Rose got my clothes from the transit van. I tentatively pulled them on, wincing at the pain. I left the shirt undone - my fingers being too clumsy to cope with the buttons - and sat dozing in a deck chair until Liza and Jenny arrived in a rush.

'Where have you been?' Liza demanded as she hurried over. 'What happened to you?'

'I'm not sure.' I answered. 'Ask her.' I nodded in Jenny's direction. 'She knows as much as me.' I was still mixed up over her involvement in all this and my bitterness showed.

'You're hurt!' Liza cried, and she dropped to her knees in front of me, inspecting my cuts and bruises.

'Leave him alone,' Jenny told her, defensive against the implied blame in my words. 'He's had worse than that - much worse, believe me.'

'Shut it, Jen,' I snapped. 'I'm in no mood for you.'

'Shut it your fucking self, ya miserable waste of space,' Jenny bellowed back. It was clearly one of our famous rows breaking out.

I closed my eyes and feigned sleep. Jenny stormed off. Liza stood trembling with indecision, like a newborn foal, then followed Jenny, walking the first few yards and then running to catch her up.

I sat and fumed. I mean, *I* was the one who was battered and bruised and Jenny was *shouting* at me for it. I suppose, realistically, the best I could have hoped for was one of those legs-akimbo-hands-on-hips apologies that always suffix 'sorry' with 'but', turning the apology into an excuse. She would accentuate each syllable with a defiant jut of her jaw, and use body language suggestive of leaning into a strong wind. I remained silent until Rose spoke.

'Messing around with women will be the death of you, Frankie,' she prophesied.

I nodded wearily and hoped for once she was wrong.

'You and Jenny have been scrapping for years. It's time you got it together or packed it in,' Bob added.

'Funny you should say that,' I mumbled, wincing at my split lip. 'Bob, have you any gold for the fair?' I asked, changing the subject.

'Yes, of course, Frankie.'

'Let's have a shufti then.'

He brought out a mixed bag of jewellery from the caravan and I sorted through it. There was some lovely stuff and some junk. I selected a nice chunk of royal lavulite set in what appeared to be white gold, with a heavy matching chain, each link engraved, and set it aside. It was old and needed a polish, but the rich purple colour of the stone warmed me. I also chose a wide thick wedding ring in twenty-two carat gold, the sort women wore in the seventies.

'Planning a proposal, Frankie?' Bob asked with a grin.

'Maybe, Bob,' I responded, as I chose a pair of earrings with multiple drops of lavulite to match the pendant - a bit showy but on the right lady breath-taking. I clumsily held Bob's loupe to my swollen eye and noted the dog's head hallmark that indicated old French platinum, but kept this to myself as I asked, 'How much, Bob?'

He suggested a price. I knocked him down and then lavishly overpaid him from my bag, telling him to treat Rose with the change when he refused to accept my offer to keep it. Then I fished a few sizeable rolls of notes from the bag and said, 'Keep this for me and give it to Moll after the fair, when I've gone and she can't give it back. It's hard with a kid on your own.'

'Certainly, Frankie.' He accepted the cash with a serious expression and a knowing nod.

'Just between us, eh, Bob?'

'Do you really need to ask, Frankie?'

I shook my head and we touched fists.

I would have given it all to her - me and money just don't seem to be easy friends and it always seems ready to leave the party before I have really gotten into my stride - but I decided to keep some of it, as I had a long road ahead and money is, as they say, power.

Rested and refreshed, I caught up with the girls and joined them for tea in Jenny's caravan. I gave a sheepish apology to Jenny for my outburst, rather than prolonging the argument indefinitely, even though it was her fault. That's the kind of forgiving and even-tempered bloke that I am. She dismissed it with a wave and offered me a biscuit from her Aynsley china biscuit barrel with its gilded edges and hand-painted fruit motif. That was a mistake; I sat and munched my way through the lot.

'I don't know where you put it all, Frankie. You're always hungry.'

'I am, love. It's all the exercise I get,' I added with a suggestive wink from my one unswollen eye.

She shook her head. 'You're incorrigible. Stop it now! I know where you're trying to lead me and I'm not following.'

While Liza fetched water for the kettle I gave Jenny a look, indicating a need for privacy.

'Ok, Frankie, I'll come and find you later.'

We drank our tea. I was manful and silent in response to Liza's renewed enquires about what had happened and told her it was nothing. I went back to my van, dosed up with pills supplied by Rose, and tried to sleep.

Jenny came later and we chatted like old friends should. Perhaps it was the chat we should have had the other night if I hadn't been so crazed and emotional. We agreed to keep Liza in the dark over the whole thing - Jenny coming to my van, the thugs dragging me off, everything.

'It's for the best,' Jenny said. 'It would only upset her and she's been through enough.'

I nodded in agreement but couldn't help thinking there was more to it.

'And we have to stop seeing each other, Frankie.'

'What do you mean?' I asked, my expression blank.

'You know,' she said, 'the *sex*.'

'The love,' I retorted.

'You know what I mean,' she replied, cradling my cheek in her hand. 'You know I love you, Frankie, but I want the chance of a proper relationship and we will never make it. We've been dancing around like this for ever and it's time to move on.'

'Ok, love,' I said, trying to hide my heavy heart. 'I'll do my best.' Then I added with a wink, 'If you will?'

She gave me a knowing smile and a peck on the cheek.

We agreed to tell Liza I had been jumped by an angry husband after I had tried it on with his wife at Jenny's gig - and the way I had been acting it wouldn't be hard to believe. In fact it wasn't a million miles from the truth.

Chapter 11

As I lay alone in my van that night, I had a change of heart and, despite what I had agreed with Jenny, resolved to face the two of them together in the morning and tell them everything I knew or suspected. Despite Jenny's misgivings, it seemed the best thing, the only thing, to do. Anyway, it would be my version of the truth and I needn't tell them anything upsetting or incriminating if I didn't want to.

I rose early from my straw bale bed feeling perky, if a bit stiff-jointed, and ambled over to see them. Liza was babbling with excitement as they prepared to leave for the fair and I decided to put off the confrontation for a while. Marcus had given me a whole month after all. I helped them pack up and hitch the trailer.

Jenny wanted to go on ahead to check out a venue for a gig that she'd planned. She could make better time alone than in convoy. I suggested they split up, so Liza came with me and Fred went with Jenny. I felt safer knowing I didn't have all my eggs in one basket. As I took my place in the slow-moving convoy Liza nodded off for a while, then woke up full of beans.

'What's it like, then?' she asked. 'The fair?'

'It's hard to explain, but you'll know soon enough.'

She pressed me for more so I gave in. 'It's like a left-over from our ancient past, a step back into history...' I droned on for a bit, throwing in a few facts - how it could be traced back to its second royal charter, granted by King James in 1685, and had now been going on for over three hundred years for certain, though no one was sure how far it really went back. It now attracted thirty thousand tourists plus Gypsies and travellers from all over Britain and Europe every year.

'You sound like a brochure, Frankie,' Liza laughed.

'Well, what do you want to hear?' I replied.

'You said you'd tell me about the lad who died, the one who was killed for his prize money.'

I hesitated but in the end reluctantly agreed. 'He wasn't robbed, love,' I started. 'He lost his fight and died in the ring. He was a top amateur from Manchester tipped for bigger things.'

'So why was he there?'

'He got in with some syndicate.' I did my best-practised sneer and thought how, phonetically at least, *syndicate* started with *sin*. 'They promised to make him rich overnight in just one fight that he couldn't lose - you know the kind of stuff.'

'So what happened?'

'He bloody lost, didn't he,' I snapped.

'Come on,' she coaxed. 'Who did he fight?'

'Do you promise not to bring it up again?'

'Of course,' she answered curtly.

'Now don't sulk - I'm serious. Do you promise?'

'Ok, Frankie, I promise.'

I sighed. 'It was Digger's nephew.'

She gasped and sat up straight.

'He grew up with his Gorgie mother while his Dad, Digger's brother, was off working God knows where. He kept getting into all sorts of bother. He was a bright lad but he just didn't seem to fit in. He would rather look after his chickens, or would play with the girls rather than with the other lads.'

'You knew him then?' Liza asked.

'I did, as well as anyone. People laughed at Digger, saying his nephew was some kind of puff. He was always in a world of his own, with his nose buried in a book when few of the other kids could read. Digger didn't like the teasing as he thought of him as the son he never had, but he'd noticed things about his nephew - how he could catch a fly in mid air, with lightning fast hands, to feed to some stray chick or other he might have in his pockets, and he was incredibly strong for his small size. So Digger, being a big fight fan, made him give up his books and chickens and dragged him round every gym and back-street trainer there was. A bloke called Simon, an ex bare-knuckle champ, finished his education.'

'So, was he a good boxer?'

'People like that don't box, love. They're real brawlers.' I held my fist up to her. 'Roma-dook.'

Liza shook her head, puzzled.

'Gypsy-fist,' I translated. 'It's a martial art all by itself. Not something to get mixed up with lightly.'

'And was he any good as a fighter, then?'

'I don't know, love. I'm no expert. What I do know is that he stepped into the ring and seemed phased by the crowd and the lights. Simon had drummed into him always to press your advantage, land a combination of at least three blows - never just throw one punch and then stand back to see if it's worked like they do in the movies. Just keep going until there is no fight left. And that's what he did. The lad from Manchester was out of his depth from the off. A bare-knuckle fight is far from the rules and rings he was used to. He stepped in, landed the first punch, knocked Digger's nephew down, and then held his hands up to celebrate.'

'And then?'

'Digger's nephew got up, didn't he. Fast as a cat, two crosses to the ribs - you could hear them crack - and, as the lad slumped, a vicious uppercut that caught him half in the neck and jaw and snapped his head back. The follow-through from the last punch landed an elbow straight in his temple. He fell, twitching and groaning, and the place went wild.' I shook my head. 'He should have left it when the lad's ribs cracked. The fight was already won.'

'So what happened then?' Liza asked, visibly shocked.

'I don't know. I cleared off, along with most of the others.'

'What about Digger's nephew?'

'He took the bag of prize money and Digger's old car and went. No one saw him again.'

'That's sad,' she said. 'Digger should have left him alone with his books and his chickens.'

'You're right. It's sad, and yes, he should have - but it's not made any better by retelling it, or by the nasty rumours people spread.'

Liza looked pensive so I flicked the radio on and changed the subject. 'We'll be turning off the motorway soon.'

Shortly afterwards we turned off at Junction 38 and onto the B6260. It's an odd junction that takes you round in a tight full circle, forcing you to take it easy.

'They won't open the Hill for a day or two yet, love.'

'So what will we do?' Liza asked, clearly impatient to see the fair.

'Camp on the fells - the open moors - under the stars and watch everyone arrive. It's my favourite part of the fair,' I replied with a grin.

We drove through Orton village. Old Joe waved at my

honking horn as he stood outside the post office.

'Who's that?' Liza asked.

'An old friend,' I replied. 'One of the best. We'll try and pop in to see him while we're here.'

Our convoy snaked on, climbing steadily up onto the fell, with cattle grids rumbling under the tyres. We were held up, close to the top, as a couple of horse-drawn caravans negotiated the steep slope. They pulled off through the gate that lets horses avoid the cattle grids - designed to keep the sheep on the fell - and we drove on. Kids waving excitedly as we passed.

Now, if ever you go up that way you will find, as the climb levels out to a plateau, that there's a little lay-by-type pull-over on the right and behind it a sudden drop into a crater-like hole left over from some ancient stone workings. It's sort of horseshoe-shaped and has a level opening set at a tangent to the road. We pulled up close to this spot and everyone busily set up for a couple of nights until the powers-that-be declared the Hill open.

We sat in the van and watched the activity. I was still feeling a bit stiff and sorry for myself, and basically lazy.

'Here, Liza, I've got you a present.' I rooted in the door pocket for my treasure, wrapped with care in a duster, and pulled out the pendant. Rose had cleaned it in warm water with a little washing-up liquid and a soft brush, making herself scarce while I'd discussed money with Bob.

'It's beautiful, Frankie. My favourite colour.'

'It's not much, but I wanted to buy you something.'

I placed it carefully around her neck, slowly closing the clasp and lingering close enough to inhale her perfume. My heart raced a little and the hairs stood up on my neck as she kissed my cheek and thanked me. I drew a deep breath and separated from her before I made a fool of myself all over again. Then I twisted the key and cranked the engine back into life. 'Come on love, I'll give you a preview.'

We pulled back onto the road and headed into Appleby, where we parked up at the top of the main drag, close to the castle, and wandered on foot down into the ancient town, steeped in history and redolent with the excitement of the fair.

A few early revellers drifted through the streets chatting and smiling. Occasional vans and cars passed with their horns honking, while friends and acquaintances shouted and waved. The odd horse clattered past, but overall it was still pretty tranquil - the quiet before the storm. A brewer's dray turned from Bridge Street and struggled up Borough Gate Hill, changing down a gear as it struggled under its load of kegs and crates.

'Stocking up,' I observed as we paused for a moment to contemplate the church.

We declined an invite to join some lads I vaguely knew for a drink and Liza popped into the chemist. I'd pressed a few notes into her hand and ignored her attempts to refuse them. Then I popped into the hardware shop next door.

We met up again a few minutes later. 'No joy,' she said

with a sigh. 'I was wondering if they had anything to cover this gap, a temporary filling or something. I feel stupid with this spike.'

'Great for eating peas though, love,' I quipped.

She thumped me playfully.

'And sweet corn.'

I dodged her second friendly blow, taking up a boxer's stance - on my toes, pushing away from her with my left foot while fending further blows off with my open hand, keeping my guard high.

We laughed and carried on onto the bridge over the river Eden, where we stood in one of the little alcoves designed long ago to let wagons pass without crushing pedestrians.

Liza leant over the wall to look into the river. I stood behind her and put my arms around her waist. She placed her hands on my arms and then leant her head back against my chest. A few lazy brown trout were keeping pace with the slow current in the clear water below. We stood in silence enjoying the moment; I kissed the back of her head and cleared my throat.

'I'm sorry about the other night at the gig, love. Things just got out of hand. I got carried away.'

'It's ok. Jenny sent me to save you from Molly's clutches and to be honest I enjoyed it.'

'How much?' I asked, tickling her sides until she giggled.

'Too much,' she answered and turned round to face me.

'Then maybe you ought to stay with me while we're here?' I said, holding her.

'No,' she replied. 'I will stay with you sometime, but not like that. I made a promise and I keep my promises.'

'Then promise we'll always be friends?' I asked.

She nodded and looked me straight in the eye. 'I promise, Frankie.'

The clatter of horses' hooves broke the spell. A rider was leading two colts over the bridge. They trotted past them then turned left and descended a wooden ramp into the water.

Liza watched, mesmerised, as the rider guided the horses out over the stretch of coarse sand that was exposed by the low water in the dry summer months and on into the deeper water, until the horses were swimming. Once back on the sand he tied their lead ropes together and set about working their hair into a lather with a bottle of fairy liquid, before plunging them once more into the deep water. As they clattered back over the bridge and past us I turned to Liza. 'All clean for sale at the fair. Come on, let's head back to the van and I'll show you Fair Hill.'

We wandered back and I wondered why, *why* she stayed so faithful to the bastard who beat her and now had her running in fear for her life. Illogical creatures, women, I mused. I decided to let it go. Thinking about it would never solve that particular rid

Chapter 12

We were strolling back to the van and as we passed the Moot Hall I glanced sideways down the High Wiend, a narrow back street between shops. As I did so I was sure I glimpsed the Black Granada I'd been avoiding for so long.

I grabbed Liza's hand. 'Come on, slow coach, race you to the top!' We ran, laughing, and arrived at the van breathless and hot. 'Better get back, love,' I said and I drove back to our camp on the fells as fast as I could, while Liza protested at missing the opportunity to see Fair Hill.

I tried to convince myself I was wrong. There are loads of black Ford Granadas, aren't there? And besides, why would they be following me now? I had a deal with Marcus, didn't I? I couldn't bring myself to believe it and came up with a more acceptable, if less plausible, answer - he'd sent his goons to make sure I honoured our agreement and that I didn't just take the money and run.

That evening on the fells was magic, like something from a fairy tale. All the kids had spent the afternoon collecting firewood, so we had more than enough to last all night. We soon had a nice blaze going, fire irons around the edge and food sizzling, sparks rising into the dusk. There was drinking, a few odd bursts of singing, and everyone felt good. A group of Irish travellers pulled in pretty close. If you read the text books they would have you believe that Irish travellers and Romany people go for each others' throats at sight, as if they were the opposite sides in a Wild West family feud. Admittedly, it was fairly unusual for us to get along, but it wasn't impossible. Digger's gang was a bit of a mix of people from different backgrounds anyhow, and Jenny herself was originally from an Irish travelling family. There were even a few 'mules' like me, neither fish nor fowl - but does it really matter? When, it comes down to it, people are just people, aren't they?

Anyway, a couple of young men from their camp came over asking for firewood. They started being a bit bolshy when they were refused. I think things could have gone either way, but Digger sorted it out by inviting them to join us. We all sat on the grass, under the stars, sharing their bottles of potcheen and swapping tall tales.

As the night wore on a few more serious attempts at music broke out. Bob collected his guitar and - accompanied by a fiddle, a bodhrán, and a trio of tin whistles - ploughed through a few old folk songs. Jenny danced instead of entertaining everyone for a change.

I still felt a bit sore, so I sat back and watched Jenny and Liza, their eyes sparkling in the firelight, laughing and cavorting. Sipping and smiling, I promised myself I would sort all this out and when it was over do my utmost to get my life back to normal - deep down, though, I knew we had all come too far ever to go back to the way we were.

Later, I stood shakily after imbibing a little more than I

could handle and wandered out of the circle of light and into the flickering shadows that danced around the caravans. And there it was, parked on the road, in the lee of a row of Scots pines… the Black Granada. It had to be them. I worked my way back round the fire until it was between me and the road, confident that the occupants would be focused on the revelling. Jenny and Liza were now the centre of attention as they twirled and jumped to the music, enough to hold anyone's gaze.

I made my way, low and slow, across the fell, taking frequent stops as in the darkness it is movement you notice first rather than colours or shapes. The flickering shadows helped to camouflage my outline and at every whoop of excitement, as the tempo speeded up, I darted on a little further, making the most of the distraction.

I reached a dry-stone wall, backed by few scrubby trees twisted and bent by the winter winds, and jumped over. When I reached the road I sprinted across, into the row of pines, and padded, hidden in their deep shadow, up to the car. I got close enough to touch it and still went unseen. The noise from the camp was fading into the background. It was them all right, the Brothers Grimm, sitting and plotting in the darkness. They had a pair of field glasses and were taking it in turns watching the show.

'He's a jammy bastard, that Frankie,' I heard Johnny say. 'Look at them two. Fucking gorgeous the pair of 'em.'

'Give us another look then,' said his equally eloquent brother as he grabbed the glasses. 'He gets 'em both and I would be happy with just the one.'

'Which one?' cut in Johnny.

'Either, I don't care - I even fancy yours.'

They both laughed like drains.

'Well, Marcus says we can have them when it's over, as long as we clean up our own mess.'

Does he now? I thought, *and here he is not trusting me, treacherous bastard.*

'Bags the Gypo with the chubby arse and big tits. I'd love to make them wobble,' said Johnny, chuckling. 'A good slapping would do her good.'

'I'll take that skinny posh bitch then. She won't sound like she's got a plum in her mouth when she's pinned over the bonnet with this up her tight little arse,' said Jerry, grabbing his groin. There was another burst of laughter.

Now, you know how there is a point beyond which you just can't put up with things any more, when a line has been crossed? Well, I'd reached that point. These two idiots were already on my mental hit list, but standing there listening to them plot rape and murder was too much for even my placid peace-loving character. Their place on my list had changed - they were now at the front of the queue.

I thought about grabbing a stone from the wall and slinging it through the windscreen. Then I could batter at least one of them before they realised what was going on and leg it. But I was just too incensed for a rational plan and my feet just carried me forward. I leant against the car roof, my face in the open driver's door window.

'Good evening, ladies,' I grinned. 'Not coming to the party? You'll get a warm welcome.'

The two men were quick to recover from my surprise appearance. 'Fuck off, Frankie, or we'll do you here and now.'

'Johnny you're such a charmer.' I smiled, then added with a snarl, 'Come on then, brains, get out and fucking try it.'

I opened the door and held out my hand in invitation. Johnny placed his right foot on the ground and leant on the steering wheel to ease his massive bulk out from behind it. Just when I was sure he was committed to shifting all his weight to his right leg, I slammed the door on his shin and then, with my welcoming left hand clenched into a fist, I punched him in the face, twice. Jerry was fumbling in the glove box and in a moment had pulled out a gun. Remember when I said how running in fear was a speciality of mine? Well, the sight of that gun was my cue - I was off through the trees like a startled rabbit, scraping myself on branches, running into a trunk, falling into a ditch and losing a shoe, as the first shots rang out, whistling over my head.

I'd run what must have been a mile away from the camp when I ran into a low branch and knocked myself to the ground. The impact seemed to bring on a moment of clarity and I realised that I was no longer being pursued, so I slowly returned to the camp by a long circuitous route. I arrived battered and knackered, my day ending with me even more bruised than when it began.

I stumbled to my van. I'd learnt my lesson on the parking thing and had squeezed it in amongst the caravans where I had the benefit of company. The throng had now thinned out and an old chap I didn't know - I assumed he was one of the Irish travellers - was playing a squeezebox and grinding out a few slow laments. Jenny and Liza were still dancing but slowly now. Liza's hands were on Jenny's shoulders and Jenny's on Liza's hips as Jenny talked her through the steps of a dance in slow motion.

I decided against spoiling everything by stumbling out of the darkness like some ghoulish, blood-stained, apparition, setting everyone screaming, so I crawled into my van and locked the doors. It probably sounds stupid, looking back, but I had the best night's sleep since this whole crazy escapade began.

I woke feeling quite chirpy, until I tried to stand and sudden pain brought the night's adventures crashing back into my brain as I stumbled out into the blinding sunshine.

'What time do you call this?' asked Dennis sarcastically, without really looking at me, as he led two horses back towards the trucks.

'What the fuck happened to you, Frankie?' Fred said as he registered the state I was in. I had one shoe, a sleeve ripped from my shirt, the seat of my trousers in tatters, and cuts and scratches all over; I even had mud and twigs in my hair. I shrugged, trying to remain buoyant.

'I drank too much potcheen and fell in the crater,' I told them. They laughed.

'You're a rare one, Frankie,' said Fred as he took a lead rope from Dennis. 'Shall we send your *ladies* to clean you up?' They chuckled some more.

'No.' I said 'I'm all right.'

'Are you sure?' Fred retorted mockingly.

'I'll be fine. I'm going back in to sleep it off.'

They went away, shaking their heads. I returned to my bed, a mass of aches and pains.

Someone banging on the van side woke me a little later. I sat up with a start, adrenaline overriding the pain as I braced myself for another attack. Then I realised it was Jenny and Liza and I surrendered to the agony once more. They helped me out, sat me in a folding chair, and washed me down like a helpless baby. Dressed in my suit and trainers I felt better - well no, I felt a complete knob to be honest.

Dennis came by again. 'Which one are you then, Frankie? Crockett or Tubbs?'

'Fuck off, Den.' It was the wittiest my battered brain could manage.

'We're off. The Hill's open,' he called back as he walked away, grinning, to busy himself with packing up.

'Great,' I said, searching for my keys in the remnants of my tattered trousers.

'You can't drive in that state,' said Jenny as she handed

me two pills and a bottle of Pepsi. See - women are good like that; they always have handbags full of useful stuff, Kleenex, painkillers, pens...

'I'll be fine, love. I can drive,' I said while drinking from the bottle and finding my keys.

'You'll do no such thing,' said Jenny, snatching them from me. 'I'll drive the van and you and Liza can bring my car. See you on the Hill.'

She jumped in my van and screamed - well, no, chugged - away leaving me standing with a pile of filthy, ripped clothing and an odd shoe at my feet. I gathered them up and threw them into the remains of last night's fire. While watching them smoulder I thought, *Where will this all end?* I felt way out of my depth and I was going to have to ask for Digger's help again sooner or later.

A horn sounded and Liza pulled up behind me. 'Get in, Frankie - we're off, and I don't want to miss a minute of it.'

I slumped in the passenger seat as she shot off after Jenny. The turbo diesel engine roared as she accelerated and the all-terrain tyres rumbled as we joined the tarmac, grit and mud spitting from their deep treads and rattling under the arches. I just sat in silence. She had Jenny's tape playing and was singing along to Dolly Parton's song 'Jolene', and in a pretty passable voice. 'I cannot compete with you...' She blushed as she realised I was listening to her.

'You can, love.'

'What?' she asked.

'Compete. You're as beautiful as anyone, more beautiful than most.'

'Pack it in, Frankie. I'm not falling for your flannel.'

She was also the smartest person I'd ever met and her intelligence didn't stop with just ideas - it extended right through to the skill in her fingertips and on into everything she put her hands to. But I didn't tell her that. I like to think I'm pretty clever and I didn't want to lose my advantage. I skipped to the next track saying, 'Come on then, love, sing me another.' And that's how we arrived in Appleby, both singing along to Pat Benatar's 'We belong together', competing to outdo each other on the tricky bits; I lost without even trying.

We followed my van, Jenny at its wheel, down Borough Gate Hill and into the tail-end of the throng waiting to get onto the Hill. A crush of people and a chain of vehicles competed, inch by inch, to get over the bridge. It's the only crowded place I can stand, as crowds like that usually make me run a mile. Liza edged through the traffic excitedly, craning her neck out of the window, eager to take it all in.

'Look at all their gold,' she gasped in wonder as a group of women headed towards us on the passenger-side pavement. The women had flowing dark hair and long skirts; a very traditional look.

'The Gypsy look would suit you, love,' I said.

'I couldn't.'

'You could,' I said. 'Jenny would help you out and I have a few touches I can add myself.'

'Really?' she said.

I winked and touched the side of my nose secretively. 'Wait and see,' I said, with a deliberate air of mystery.

'I hate surprises, Frankie.'

'Well, I love them, so you'll have to wait.'

The queue snaked on, horses clattering past on both sides to add to the hubbub. We turned left off the bridge, along The Sands and on into Battlebarrow. Ahead we saw a line of brightly painted bow-top wagons and Reading wagons with lantern roofs and wooden sides, collectively called Vardos. Some had horses still sweating between the shafts, while others had been there long enough for the horse's tired limbs to have cooled enough for them to join those being washed in the river.

'Wow!' Liza was enthralled.

'I bet you'd love to be in there with them, wouldn't you?' I said, gesturing to the people and horses in the water. She nodded. The cool, hard Liza who had faced Marcus in their courtyard seemed worlds away from this eager young woman with childlike excitement in her eyes. 'We'll have to see what we can do,' I told her, with a smile.

The line snaked on. We saw a police check point as we turned under the railway bridge. 'What are they doing?' Liza asked.

'Looking for someone, or something,' I replied. 'Or maybe just advising Gorgies to be careful on the Hill.'

'Will they stop us?' She looked worried.

'Probably, love. I would arrest me just for wearing this suit.' I pointed and told her to pull into a side road called Belgravia, where we parked up and finished the journey on foot. 'We can come back for the car later, when it's quietened down a bit.'

I took her hand and led her through the crowds. We walked up onto the Hill and saw our lot arguing as they reversed caravans into place and pushed vans out of the soft ground. I pulled Liza sideways through a gap in the hedge into the market field.

'Let's have a nosey round. Let them buggers do the donkey work.'

After all, I had no horses to sell, no caravan to pitch up, no responsibilities at all - and that's how I liked it. How I could have been so deluded, with things the way they were, is anybody's guess. I bought Liza a veggie burger at a mobile nosh bar - a huge fairground-style thing with neon lights and shining stainless counters. Then we came to a spit roast and I grabbed myself a chunk of steaming, dripping venison, carved straight off a whole deer as it spun over hot coals. I gnawed it greedily. The girl who served me refused my cash with a wave.

'Why didn't you pay?' Liza asked.

'Because I'm famous at the fair. I'm something of a

celebrity.'

'Really?' she asked, her face a picture of genuine interest.

'Of course, love,' I added with a grin. 'And besides, she *is* my cousin. See you later, Julie,' I called as we walked away. She smiled and waved back.

Liza just nibbled at her meat-free meal and then threw half of it away. She never had much of an appetite. Was it her lack of appetite that made her avoid meat? Or was it the lack of meat that ruined her appetite? Whatever it was, she seemed to do very well on it. She took my arm and we strolled on, with me still gnawing my chunk of flesh.

There are stalls at the fair selling everything for the country-man - or woman - as well as household goods: china, traditional carved flowers and pegs, horse tack and carriages - all sorts. I finished my meal and grabbed us a couple of overpriced tins of beer. Normally I would argue every penny, as there are two sets of prices and my suit was giving me a Gorgie look and a bad deal, but it wasn't my money - so stuff it. We sipped warm beer as we went into the lane to watch the harness racing.

Chapter 13

A few trolley men on sulky carts were putting their trotters through their paces for the benefit of prospective purchasers. For the benefit of those innocent of the technicalities of the sport, in harness racing the trolley man must drive his animal as fast as possible - sounds obvious, right? But there's a snag - the horse *must not* gallop. Like every sport, it's more complicated than just that one rule, but you get the basic idea.

There wasn't a lot going on as it was still pretty quiet that early in the fair, but we lingered a while, sitting on the grass verge and watching the preparations. Back then there were no safety rails to stop an excited or frightened animal careering onto the verge and into the spectators. A few promising-looking combinations thundered past.

We watched until we were hungry again - in my case about ten minutes - and then decided to head back to the caravans to see what plans Jenny had for dinner. We stopped at the market field on the way and Liza helped me choose two new shirts from a country clothing stall. I also bought new trousers, underwear and a nice tweed trilby hat for good measure. She was exasperated at my lack of adventurousness clothing-wise, but I like to stick to all natural fibres - cotton and wool - as textures of things are important to me. So she would have to make do with me in my checked shirts and plain black trousers for a while longer. A few stalls down I lashed out on a well-made pair of brown leather dealer boots, and my outfit was complete. Lastly we bought a bunch of hand-carved chrysanthemums before heading on to find Jenny.

Generators hummed in the background as we approached and Jenny's caravan was filled with the smell of cooking. She'd made some vegetable lash-up, though I think the term she used was goulash. I ate it, grumbling and thinking that just because Liza lived on a lettuce leaf and a breath of fresh air didn't mean I had to. I accepted seconds gratefully, however, and asked if she had a sausage she could slip in there to make up for the missing cholesterol. My quip fell on stony ground, so I munched on through the green stuff and swigged enough wine to make up the balance of calories.

'Jenny, Liza would like you to give her a makeover for the fair,' I said.

'Would you, now?' Jenny looked at Liza with an enigmatic smile.

'Well, I had thought...' Liza mumbled shyly. The sun had brought her freckles out and she looked very young.

'It would be my pleasure,' beamed Jenny.

I left them to it and rose to check out my new gear in the mirror.

'Don't worry, Frankie, you're not losing your looks,' said Jenny. 'You're still plug-ugly.' They both laughed.

'I love you too, ladies,' I said. 'And to think I brought you flowers.'

I left to collect Jenny's car, which I parked up next to my van, then spent a little time rummaging through my loot. When I returned to Jenny's caravan I found Liza sitting on a stool, bedecked in a long flowing skirt and tight broderie-anglaise blouse, which showed more cleavage than usual. She was also wearing a hand-decorated waistcoat, in a rich purple colour, with coins and tiny mirrors worked into the design. Jenny was just finishing the look by adding a few pre-Raphaelite curls, which were her trademark, to Liza's usually sleek straight hair. Liza stood up as I entered and spun around.

'What do you think, Frankie?'

'All right,' I said gruffly. It sounded like damning with faint praise, but I was sort of in two minds: A - I wanted to scoop her up and kiss her right there; B - she had a style of her own and I was slightly uneasy at the transformation. But I thought her changed appearance might throw the goons off her scent and that had to be good. With a bashful smile I drew the lavulite earrings from my pocket and helped her swap them for her diamond studs.

'One last thing,' I added. I pushed her back into a chair, propping up the cushions to support her head and then settling her in a semi-reclined position. Then, with a flourish, I rolled out the tiny tool kit I had filched from Michael's desk.

'I'm going to make you a new tooth, love.'

Liza looked a little surprised, but smiled and obediently opened her mouth for me. Jenny stepped between us, facing Liza.

'You're not going to let this ham-fisted lummox loose on your teeth, are you, you stupid woman?'

'Why not?' Liza said. 'There's no one I trust more - and besides, he is good with his hands.' She giggled.

'Well, I can't watch.' Jenny flounced out and slammed the door, then flounced back in again. 'I think I'd better stay for when it all goes tits-up.'

'Sit down and shut up then, or it will,' I snapped.

Jenny sat with a sulk on the stool and beamed loathing at me as I worked.

The thick twenty-two carat gold ring I'd got from Bob cut easily with Michael's miniature cutters and I opened it out with the pliers. Then, with the tiny hammer, I tapped it into a straight bar across the top of Jenny's stove. Its natural flattened D-shaped cross-section saved me a lot of work as it produced an almost tooth-shaped profile. I offered it up to the gap and, after eying up the form, honed it roughly to shape with the tiny files before drilling an oversized hole that sat a little loosely over the stainless peg.

'Don't just sit there on your chubby arse looking pretty,' I told Jenny. 'Get me some baking soda.'

She got up and huffed at me, mumbling something about

152

'chubby'. I was surprised she hadn't thrown a plate at me; I assumed the restraint was for Liza's sake. 'I've got none.' She flopped back on her stool.

'Then go and bloody *get* some,' I demanded and off she went.

'You owe me,' she growled through gritted teeth when she returned a few minutes later. 'I had to ask Molly and I'm not doing it again.'

The tension rising between us was making my nape hair prickle, as I knew where it usually led. God, she was gorgeous when she was angry. Passion tingled in the air like electricity.

I snipped the gold to length and shaped its tip into a passable biting edge, then I sat and polished it up with the metal polish Jenny kept for the stainless steel crazy bands on the outside of her trailer. Finally I cleaned it with freshly boiled water and let it dry in the heat the boiling water left behind. I was quite pleased with the result. I asked Jenny to get me two sheets of moistened kitchen roll. After tearing a hole in one, I used it to cover Liza's face and lips. The other I kept pretty wet and pushed into her mouth, asking her to press it behind her teeth with her tongue and bite down. This was to save her from any unnecessary contact with the fumes from my home-made dental adhesive-cum-filler - maybe a bit overcautious, but better safe than sorry.

'You're a fucking lunatic, Frankie,' Jenny hissed. 'If you hurt her I'll-'

'Shut it, Jen.' I collected a tiny amount of the spilled soda from where Jenny had slammed it down and careful filled the tiny hole I'd drilled in the gold. Then I took a tube of superglue from my pocket, bought from the hardware shop in Appleby. Jenny made a move as if to stop me but I warned her off with a sharp look. I dripped a tiny glob of glue onto the powder in the hole, waited a few seconds for it to soak in and then pressed the gold onto the little spike, checking its alignment and holding it for as long as Liza felt comfortable. A few minutes later she was smiling at herself in the mirror.

'A gold tooth… a gold tooth,' she kept repeating. She looked both pleased and a little shocked.

'We can get it sorted out properly when we get the chance, love,' I added.

Jenny stood behind Liza, her hands on her shoulders and joined her gaze into the mirror.

Liza squeezed Jenny's fingers and said. 'What do you think?'

'Better than I expected,' replied Jenny reluctantly. 'No, it's pretty good actually.' She hugged Liza playfully. The tension in the atmosphere dissolved. I sighed as Jenny bent to throw the screwed-up paper towels into the stove, her gorgeous bottom inches from my hands. I knew she wouldn't need to work her anger out on me in the van later - well, you can't win them all, can you? I bade them both goodnight and left.

Later I called for Fred and Dennis and we set off for the Crown and Cushion in Appleby, where we settled in for a few drinks. There was a card school going on. Dennis joined in while Fred and I sat drinking and catching up. A bit of a scuffle broke out as we were leaving; one of the players was resentful at losing most of his money so early on in the fair. Once in the street a police van cruised slowly past. Its presence cooled things down and we made our way back to the Hill.

I was a bit tired-and-emotional after a pint or three and decided to call in at Jenny's caravan in search of some comfort and company. I stood outside and broke into an appalling rendition of 'I just called to say I love you', in the hope that this would bring delight to those within. No joy; the place remained in darkness. But I'm not for falling at the first fence, so I pressed on. I increased the volume for 'Every breath you take' and as I moved on to 'I'm your man' Jenny relented and opened the door, wrapped in a rather small towel.

'What d'you want now? Móttoméngro! Dínilo!'

'I forgot my hat, love. I'll just pop in and get it.'

'No you bloody won't. I'll fetch it.' She turned. I stepped into the doorway and grabbed the bottom of her towel, half pulling it down and revealing her bare bottom. 'Fuck off, Frankie!' she hissed as she covered herself.

My hat was lying where I'd left it amongst the scatter cushions on the seat that made the single bed. She flattened it against my chest as she pushed me out.

'We are trying to get some sleep. Leave us alone, will you!' She pushed me again and I fell backwards off the step as she slammed the door shut behind me.

Charming, I thought, as I sat on the grass. I usually gave her a round of applause when she sang - so ungrateful, the pair of them! I stood and dusted myself down then leant on the bonnet of Jenny's car. Muted voices sounded from behind her drawn blinds.

A few people wandered past, all going in the same direction. I paid little heed until a group - I would have said bevy but it's not *PC* these days - of young women wobbled by in high heels, mini-skirts and heavy make-up. They were giggling, chatting, and passing round a bottle of Johnnie Walker. I suddenly developed a dry throat and hurried to catch them up. I scrounged a swallow of whisky and exchanged some light-hearted banter with them about skirt lengths.

'Where are you off to then, ladies?' I asked.

'To the fight, of course,' said a cheeky, round-faced girl with a turned-up nose and fluorescent pink boob tube.

Bare-knuckle fights are not really my scene, so I made my excuses. I don't think they were too heartbroken when I parted company with them.

I wandered on, getting a bit fed up, and was on the verge of going back to my van, when I spotted two familiar figures. They also appeared to be heading for the fight, one of them leaning heavily on a stick. The Brothers Grimm again. I spotted their black Ford Granada among some parked vehicles nearby and sneaked over to it to try the doors. Locked - well, what did I expect? The pair ahead of me halted to speak to someone through the partly open window of another car. I could hear their voices but wasn't close enough to make out what they were saying, so I sneaked a little closer, keeping low and in the shadows.

My heart pounded when Johnny turned and pointed my way with his stick. But they were looking back up towards the caravans on the hill; Jenny's was prominent in the foreground. I stole a little closer to the vehicle and, though I couldn't see the driver, recognised it at once as Marcus's car. I didn't wait to hear any more but sneaked back through the darkness to the Granada. Along the way I found a smooth flat stone and, when the roar of an excited crowd rose a little distance away, I used it to smash the side window. It took just a moment to grab the gun from the glove box, then I was legging it back to my van.

I sat in my van, as nervous as a cat, with the radio on low. Adrenaline and fear had both sobered and woken me, just when a good night's sleep would have done me the world of good. I wrapped the gun in the white T shirt Joy had given me. It was a stubby revolver like the guns in American cop shows. I stuffed it under the driver's seat next to the black bin liner full of cash. I had no idea why I had taken it or what I was going to do with it; was it even loaded? It had just seemed a good idea to deprive its owners of it - if nothing else it would make it harder for them to cause me harm. I finally managed to sleep and snored on into the late morning, only waking when Jenny roused me with food.

'I don't know why I bother with you sometimes, Frankie,' she said. 'What was all that about last night?'

I shrugged my shoulders apologetically and accepted the bacon sandwich and tea that she offered with a sheepish smile.

'What're you two doing today then, love?' I asked.

'Not much. We're going with Digger's lads to see the racing in the lane and to look at a few horses being sold. Want to join us?'

I shook my head. 'No ta, love. I'll just hang around here. I haven't slept well for days and I need the rest.'

'Don't go sleeping all day and then keep decent ladies up until all hours when you're not tired tonight, will you?'

She left. I felt groggy after my fitful sleep. I was past nervous, past confused; just sort of numb. You know when I said hospitals overwhelm me and make me silly? Well, I felt like that - past caring and ready for anything life threw at me. The only thing that kept me partially grounded was my concern for Liza and Jenny. It had by now become almost instinctive and needed no rational input from me.

Eventually I started up the van and drove back up onto the fells. There I walked into the trees where I had been chased a few nights before, taking the gun with me, just for fun. I closed my eyes while I pointed it towards the ground and squeezed the trigger. It frightened the life out of me when it went off with a bang. It also frightened sheep and birds for miles around and made me feel like eyes were on me from every direction.

The noise rang in my ears for ages and ruled out any idea

I might have had about a shoot-out with the syndicate. I bundled the gun back under the seat and headed into town. I found an empty space in one of the diagonal bays by the town's few shops and, deciding a bit of tranquillity would do me good, walked under the arched gateway into St Lawrence's church, where I sat in a pew and reflected for a while.

Divine consolation didn't seem to be forthcoming, so after a few minutes I put some coins in the collection box and strolled through the churchyard and out onto the western bank of the Eden. There I sat on the grass under the shade of an oak and watched the horses in the water. Liza and Jenny were there, I saw. Fred was taking a horse into the water, with Liza sitting behind him, holding tightly round his waist and smiling broadly.

As they turned round to go back Liza spotted me and waved frantically, with the result that she almost fell off, but she recovered herself and held on even tighter. I laughed. She dismounted on the far bank and met up with Jenny, her wet skirt clinging to her legs. They linked arms and walked briskly over the bridge towards me, waving to catch my attention; I wandered onto the pavement and met them halfway across.

'We have to talk,' said Jenny. 'In private - it's important.'

Here we go again, I thought, as we headed back for the church and sat ourselves down on the flagstone floor, leaning against the huge oak doors in the cool of the interior. Jenny filled me in. They had been to the sales; Marcus had been there and he'd bought several horses, but only cheap nags no one else seemed interested in.

'Did he see either of you?' I asked, trying to keep the desperation out of my voice.

'No,' said Liza, 'and if he did, he didn't say anything. Maybe he didn't recognise me.'

'Maybe not,' I said, 'but I want you both to stick close to me.'

'Don't be so flaming dramatic,' said Jenny. 'I'm off. See you back at the caravan.' She rose and began to walk away. I scowled - she was growing more distant by the day.

'Do you mind if I stay here with Frankie for a while?' Liza asked.

'Suit yourself,' Jenny answered over her shoulder. She opened the door and stepped outside.

'What's up, Frankie?' Liza asked, looking at me. 'Feeling left out? Or maybe you're a little jealous?'

'Something like that, love.'

Liza put her hand on my cheek. 'I'll make it up to you some time, Frankie, I promise.'

We left the church and made our way back up through the town. I stopped outside the newsagents, where the deliveryman was changing the flyer on the *Evening Mail* 'A' board. *Armed robbery*, it read, *police target horse fair*. I went inside and bought a copy. As we headed back to the van I asked Liza if she fancied popping over to see old Joe in

Orton; she nodded consent and sat reading the paper as we wound our way across the fells.

We found Joe hard at it, as usual, in a pen of hurdles in the small field opposite his front door. He had a small portion of his vast flock of sheep rounded up. We drove in and parked up amongst a few tents, walkers stopping off en route along the Pennine Way. We leant on the wall and watched as Joe trimmed hooves, working expertly with the shears.

'How do, Frankie, lad,' he said, straightening from his work and limping over to us. 'Who's this you've brought to see us then?'

'This is my good friend Liza.'

'She's a bit of all-reet, Frankie,' he said, stooping to kiss her cheek.

'Liza, meet Joe,' I said, completing the introductions.

'Come inside,' he said. 'I'll get Sheila to put the kettle on.'

Shelia produced a plate of her homemade cakes and took Liza on a tour of the house. They were usually busy with guests but didn't accept B&B bookings during the fair; it gave them time to pop into Appleby to join in the festivities.

'Have they caught yon robber then?' Joe asked.

I shook my head, puzzled.

'It's in all the papers,' he went on, evidently surprised at my ignorance.

'Oh, that,' I answered. 'I've bought a copy to read about it but I haven't had a chance yet.'

'I was at a sale in Penrith,' said Joe. 'Some fellas from a syndicate down your way sold some 'osses and then got robbed in the transport café in Tebay. Funny thing is,' he continued, 'I don't know why they sold 'em anyway- silly sods.'

My ears pricked up at this. 'Really, Joe?'

'Aye. They bought them from a racing trainer at the harness racing in Kirkby Stephen not long back, then sold them on for virtually the same price. Why buy them in the first place? Some businessmen, eh? Some fella in a transit van held them up. He had a gun and made off with a black bin bag full of cash.'

I choked on my tea, slopping it into the saucer and then over my trousers. I put the cup down, spilling more on the tablecloth.

Sheila bustled in. 'Clumsy bugger, Frankie! As if I haven't enough washing to do.' She dabbed at me and the tablecloth with a dishcloth before getting me a fresh cup.

'You all right, lad?' asked Joe.

'Fine, ta,' I said. 'It just went down the wrong road.'

He chuckled and slapped my back. 'So what brings you and yon lovely lass up our way, then? Have you come with the Gypos?' I nodded. 'Will you be staying over here?'

'Hadn't planned to, Joe.'

'You're welcome to, Frankie. You can pitch up out back and plug in the barn. I've got a new toilet block now,' he added proudly. 'If you're in time you can help crotch them ewes - I'll pay, no bother. I'm getting too owd to do it on me own. I just wamble about the owd place now.'

'I might take you up on that, Joe,' I replied. 'But we have to rush; we've left Jenny on her own.'

'You still with her then, Frankie?' Sheila asked. 'I thought you two'd thrown the towel in years ago.'

'So did I,' I quipped and with smiles, kissed cheeks from Sheila, and a hearty handshake from Joe, we left.

Chapter 14

We sped back over the fells.

'Have you heard about the robbery?' Liza asked.

'Yes, love.'

'The police are searching the fair for the robber. Perhaps that was what the police were doing the other day,' she speculated.

'Maybe.'

'He had a gun,' she continued, looking at the newspaper, 'and a big bag of cash.'

'Reach under my seat and tell me what you find,' I told her.

She frowned, then leant down and groped under the seat. In a moment she had pulled out the shirt and unwrapped the gun. I glanced sideways to see her looking down at it as it lay in her lap. Her face had paled.

'And that,' I said, nodding to the bag she'd left on the floor, 'is the cash.'

'Frankie! You didn't?'

'Of course fucking not,' I snapped, and then just as

quickly added, 'I'm sorry, love, but we're all in real danger. You need to help me to persuade Jenny to come away with us. I'll tell you everything when we're on the road.'

Liza nodded agreement and hurriedly rewrapped the gun.

As we climbed to the highest point of the fells and rattled over a cattle grid I saw the black Granada standing in a lay-by on the left.

'Shit.'

'What is it, Frankie?'

'Hang on,' I warned her. As the Granada pulled out behind us, its tyres smoking, I changed down a gear and floored it. The van's engine screamed but we made little headway. The Granada was closing on us fast.

We thundered on towards the town. I suppose I was hoping to come across friendly faces or a crowd to give us witnesses to whatever was about to happen. I thrashed the van on while Liza sat frozen, hanging on to the seat. The fear of the past weeks was coming home to her in a rush.

The van was struggling now, spluttering clouds of bluish smoke and losing power, but I couldn't stop. We sped down Borough Gate, but the tail end of a traffic jam blocked our path.

'Shit, shit, shit!' I thumped the steering wheel.

Then things got worse still. A police car pulled out of the castle gates, siren blaring and blue lights flashing. I drove on, trying to find a route round the jam. Once past the Moot Hall I hit the brakes, slid the van around the back of the building, and swerved hard right into the High Weind. The police car driver didn't react in time and had to slam on the brakes. But that road was blocked by traffic too. That was it - we were done for. The black saloon pulled in behind us.

'Brace yourself!' I yelled at Liza. She hung onto the door handle and pressed her feet against the floor.

'All right, you bastards!' I shouted as I peered over my shoulder, 'I'm coming!' Then I slammed the van into reverse, bang into the front of their car.

The door on my side had been jammed shut by the impact so I transferred quickly to the middle passenger seat next to Liza, who was still frozen with fear.

'Come on!' I shouted at her. 'Get out - get out, you stupid cow!'

I struggled to undo her belt. By now Jerry had run up to the van and was reaching in through the driver's window, trying to grab me. He couldn't reach, so clutched at the keys instead. I swivelled round on the middle passenger seat and drew up my legs level with the steering wheel, then kicked out through the open window. Both my feet hit him in the face. The blow knocked him backwards and he slumped in the narrow gap between the van and a brick wall. I opened the passenger side door and half pushed, half threw, Liza out onto the tarmac. Then I grabbed the bin liner of cash, jumped down, and dragged her to her feet. She reached back into the van and grabbed her handbag.

'Come on!' I screamed again and dragged her off through the crowds.

The black Granada was smoking, threatening to burst into flames, and that kept the police at bay as we made our way on foot back to the Hill and Jenny. Liza was stumbling and sobbing as I dragged her along, swearing and shouting at her and urging her on. It was, paradoxically, not unlike the moment we started on this journey - with me dragging a dazed and confused Liza through unfamiliar streets, and with a bin liner over my shoulder.

'What the fuck have you done to her?' Jenny shouted, rushing to meet us.

'Nothing, love!' I gasped. 'Let's get her inside and I'll explain.'

We held Liza between us, her arms over our shoulders and ours around her waist. Once inside the caravan, Jenny cleaned up her grazed knees and wiped her face tenderly, all the time whispering gently.

'It will all be all right, my darling, don't worry.' She kissed Liza's forehead and then just hugged her and rocked her gently. Gradually the sobbing stopped and the shaking calmed.

'I'm ok now, I think,' Liza whispered at length, with a flicker of a nervous smile, cuffing away a tear and sniffing. 'It was just a shock, that's all.'

'What was?' Jenny asked.

'We had a bit of an accident, love,' I said quickly. 'The van is... I mean has... sort of... broken down.' I was trying to play things down as best I could, until Liza blurted out her version.

'Some gangsters chased us - and the police - and then Frankie rammed them - and then he threw me out of the van - and-'

Jenny exploded. 'Tell me what's going on right now, Frankie - or I swear you'll fucking regret it!'

'All right, love, calm down. But we need to get out of here first. Come on, I'll help you pack.'

In five minutes flat we were on the road in Jenny's Shogun, heading north up the B6261 and onto the M6 at Junction 9. I lay across the back seats and Jenny and Liza sat in the front. We took the slip road off at Junction 38 and headed back towards Joe and Sheila's place, passing the café and petrol station at Tebay - the site of the alleged robbery.

Joe and Sheila made us welcome. Jenny told Sheila I had accidentally dropped Liza while showing off and lifting her high in the air, dancing in the street outside the Crown and Cushion. Sheila called me a *clumsy bugger*, again, and clucked over both women like a mother hen.

Joe helped me pitch up the caravan, conveniently out of sight between the barns and the back of the house, and safe from prying eyes. Jenny drove back into Tebay, filled up the car with diesel and bought what food she could at the petrol station. Then she dashed around the few shops in Orton village to build up our supplies before returning to the caravan.

Sheila had made a delicious mutton casserole in the farmhouse and we ate heartily, washing it down with lashings of home-brewed wine. At least, I did. Jenny just nibbled at hers, looking a bit pensive, while Liza made do with a vegetable broth Sheila made just for her.

I didn't feel too guilty as I munched, despite Jenny's admonishment and Liza's shocked and sorry state. After all, I didn't get us into this bloody mess, did I? And it was me who was taking all the flack, wasn't it? Me who had got kidnapped, battered and shot at, me whose home had been wrecked, me who had chased half way around the country, me the police were after... I'd sacrificed all my principles for Liza - and what thanks did I get?

Then it dawned on me, slowly, that Jenny was probably the most generous and loyal of us all. She had just dropped everything to help us, and had taken Liza into her home and her heart without a question. She owed me no favours - so why, I wondered, didn't she just dump us and go? Then I remembered her long absence and the man I'd seen both at Ramona's and with Marcus – the man who had turned out to be Jenny's agent, Mr Mace. I felt less indebted and a little more resentful, which of course eased my guilt enough for rhubarb crumble and custard.

Later we tried to relax in Jenny's caravan. None of us felt particularly chatty and there was a definite atmosphere. I'm no good with uncomfortable silences, reading minds to work out what I'm supposed to say or do, despite what women always seem to think. I had been waiting for Jenny to demand and answer to the '. . . you'll fucking regret it!' question she's asked earlier, but she didn't. I was getting fidgety so I just came out with it. 'Jenny, when you went AWOL all those weeks, where were you?'

'Who - me?' She laughed nervously and blushed. 'Away on business.'

'Your agent was busy while you were away,' I pressed her. 'Was it all on your behalf?'

She looked at me quizzically, as if deciding whether to fill me in or chuck me out for my cheek. 'I don't have to explain myself to you or anyone.' She spat the words at me. 'My life is my fucking affair, ok?'

I nodded agreement. A row would get us nowhere, though I smiled inwardly at her choice of words. A 'fucking affair' was a pretty apt summary of my relationship with her.

'But seeing as how you have asked so nicely,' she continued, hands on hips, bristling, 'I was showcasing new talent for a big European tour this autumn and winter.'

She turned and flounced away, her point made.

'Sorry, Jen,' I murmured. She turned to look back at me questioningly. 'Sorry I doubted you. All this has made me a bit edgy, that's all.'

'It's ok,' she replied with a sigh. 'I've been wanting to talk to you about it for ages.'

'Really, love?' I was all ears.

'The thing is,' she continued, holding her hands together and looking down slightly to avoid eye contact, 'it's Liza.'

The two of them met each other's gaze.

'Yes?' I asked.

'*She* is coming with *me*,' Jenny intoned flatly. I waited for more, but nothing more came. Now, I've never been the most urbane of blokes but that really *did* leave me lost for words. I struggled to find the right thing to say. If I wasn't careful, I was going to lose them both. 'It will be so exciting...' Jenny started babbling on about all the fun they would have. I watched her lips move but could take nothing in.

Liza's singing and the dance tuition Jenny had given her suddenly acquired a new significance in my dim brain. *So that's what-*

Then I returned abruptly to earth, with a bump, at the sound of a single word - *syndicate*.

'What was that, love?' I said.

'We have a syndicate backing us,' she repeated. 'Wealthy businessmen who are investing big in clubs and hotels all over the place.'

Bile rose in my throat and the room spun around me. I dashed outside and the custard made an unexpected reappearance. I was in a cold sweat.

Liza followed me out, looking bewildered. 'Are you all right, Frankie?'

'It's all been too much for me,' I told her. 'Listen. I've changed my mind. We have to move on tonight. We can't stay this close - the police will be widening their search. Go back in and I'll join you in a minute.'

I washed my face under the outside tap and splashed cold water over my head and neck as I took in several deep breaths. It was all coming together, and it was more serious than I had imagined...

The girls thought better of arguing with me about moving on. We agreed to get some sleep and to move out in the early hours, so we packed and hitched up the caravan. That done, I lay back on the double bed and closed my eyes.

'And what do you think you're doing?' Jenny asked.

'Getting some sleep?'

'Not there you're not.' I moved to the single. 'Nor there - out!' She marched me to the door.

'Where then, love?'

'The car.' She threw me a blanket and shut the door.

I curled up on the back seat, but I couldn't sleep. I tried everything. As there were so many about, I even tried counting sheep, but it didn't work. Eventually I got up and showered in Joe's new toilet block, using the towel roll from the machine on the wall in the toilet to dry off.

When I got back the girls were already getting under way, rattling kettle and cups while talking in whispers. I gulped a cup of tea and slunk back into my kennel, tail between my legs, feeling a bit sorry for myself at the lack of attention, and left them to complete the final preparations.

We moved out into the darkened lanes, back through Orton and Tebay and onto the motorway. The movement of the car and the music quickly soothed me to sleep. I dreamed about Jenny, Liza, Jenny and Liza, and... the rest is my dream, ok? In my head, and that's where it's staying. I woke slowly and comfortably, feeling the bright sun warming my face and glowing through my eyelids. I kept them closed and re-arranged myself on the seat, shading my eyes with the blanket. I wasn't in the mood for idle talk, so I lay back and let someone else make all the decisions. Liza noticed me stir.

'Is he awake, Jen?'

Jenny leaned over from the passenger seat and tugged my blanket. 'No, sleeping like a baby.'

I sensed the warmth in her voice as she rubbed the back of my head gently and I decided to stay put.

'Like a baby,' Liza repeated and laughed. I heard the indicators *tick-tick* as she changed lanes.

'You're doing well towing this,' Jenny said.

'It's no different to a horse trailer really,' Liza replied, adding with another laugh, 'just much, much bigger.'

She could do anything that one - so clever it was scary. It made me wonder why she'd been so passive all this time. I began to suspect she too had a few secrets.

'He'll wake up soon, screaming and wanting to be fed,' Jenny joked.

'As long as I don't have to change his nappy,' said Liza, and they both giggled.

'He's ok though really, isn't he?' Jenny said, leaning back and rubbing my head again.

'One of the best,' Liza added, 'even if he is in a dream world most of the time.'

I felt a bit smug at that and decided to stay put and listen.

'He's like an overexcited puppy, always wanting a bit of attention, trying so hard to be liked.' Jenny sighed as she took her hand from my head. 'And getting it all wrong most of the time.' She sighed again and turned to face the road as Liza changed the subject.

'What's with that Molly?' Liza asked. 'She looks daggers at me all the time.'

'Don't worry about it,' replied Jenny. 'She looks at me like that too. I remember the first time was at a wedding - she caught the bouquet, I caught her eye, and that was it; she never looked at me the same way again.'

'Were you trying to catch it too?' Liza asked.

'Was I fuck - I threw it.'

'Really?' Liza's reply was high-pitched. 'You're married?'

'Yes. Surprised?'

'A little. Who to? Anyone I know?'

'Yon soft lad in the back,' Jenny replied, mimicking old Joe's northern accent.

Liza fell silent.

'Does it bother you, Liza?'

'I had no idea.'

'Didn't the rows give us away?' asked Jenny. 'Or the moods and tantrums?'

I thought, *That's it Jenny, carry on - confession is good for the soul.*

'He can be a bit juvenile, can't he?' said Liza, and they both laughed together again. *Juvenile, me? Bloody cheek.* I clutched my blanket tighter and Liza carried on. 'I didn't think he was the marrying sort. He does like the ladies, doesn't he?'

'He's not,' answered Jenny. 'The marrying sort, I mean - and yes, he does. That was part of the problem. He had an on-off thing with that Molly before we were married and it stayed on when it should have been off.'

'Is that why you split?' asked Liza with eager interest.

'That and other things. Settling down with a man just wasn't really my thing.'

'I guessed that bit,' said Liza in a low voice.

'So it gave us both a way out.'

'Are you divorced?'

'No, just split.'

'So you're still married then?'

'Yep!' Jenny said, rather pointedly.

A horn sounded, honking into the distance as we drove past. 'Sorry,' said Liza, her attention obviously wandering.

'We'll pull in soon and swap places,' Jenny told her.

I took this as my cue to wake up. 'What time is it?' I said. 'I'm starving.'

Jenny smirked knowingly at Liza.

'And I'm busting for the loo.'

They looked at each other and laughed.

We stopped at the services just after Junction 15, close to Stafford, and I got mugged for coffee and pastries, which Liza barely touched, so I finished hers for her. I used a little of the money I had left from Sandy's caddy as we had decided it would be best not to dip into the robbery loot unless we had to.

When we got back in the car Jenny refused to let me drive as she had seen the state of Digger's transit and had heard of its demise.

'My whole life is riding on these wheels,' she said, 'and I'm not having you wreck it all just because something spooks you.'

I shrugged and slept the hours away in the back seat. Jenny drove and we cruised southwards to the M5. We stopped again at Frankley services, close to Junction 3 and Birmingham. This time we pulled into the truck spaces to brew up. That way fewer people saw us - and we avoided paying the extortionate prices.

A wiry man with a litter-picking stick told us we couldn't have the cooker on, or make tea, so we drank up and carried on. This time Liza took the reins. Our last break was at Gordano services close to Junction 19. By then Liza was feeling the strain of recent events, as well as the long drive. She found the islands leading us off the motorway to the services difficult to negotiate, so Jenny took the baton and we pressed on. We passed a hoard of miserable-looking hitchhikers stranded at the M5 South sign as we pulled back onto the motorway. As we drove we shared crisps and a bottle of fizz. When I grumbled at the lack of calories, they both swore at me, so I kept my head down and went back to sleep.

Chapter 15

We carried on until the motorway faded into the A38 and shortly afterwards took the fork to Torbay. I sat up, feeling more confident of anonymity, and directed Jenny to a pub in Blagdon. It was about four miles or so inland, in the gentle hills and quiet lanes behind Paignton - an impressive Victorian building, with holiday apartments and a few spaces for touring caravans. I remembered it from a rather optimistic holiday I'd shared with Jenny; it seemed like a lifetime ago.

I thought the owner was going to have a coronary on the spot when we pulled in, so I mentally rehearsed my CPR and crossed my fingers. He went white then ran over to us, his head changing through various shades from pink to purple as he waved his arms and ranted.

'You can't stop here! The council won't allow it. We aren't allowed commercial travellers...' We recognised the usual racist clap-trap, but we knew what his problem really was - it was just *us*.

Jenny stepped out and leaned with one hand on the car roof, stretching, arching her back, and smiling mischievously. 'I'm so stiff,' she said, rubbing her arms to stimulate the circulation. Then she slid her hands down her legs, starting at her thighs, back straight, until she could grip her ankles, pressing her right hip against our tormentor's groin. She always was flexible... I could tell you more but I'd best crack on. She straightened up with a sigh and smiled. 'I'm sorry, did I bump into you? Aren't I clumsy?'

Liza stepped out and shared Jenny's concern for the man's welfare, straightening his shirt and rubbing his shoulders. The bloke did a mental u-turn so fast I could smell tyre smoke. He shut up and ushered us to a pleasant spot shaded by the branches of towering pine trees. As we set up our camp Jenny moaned about sap and needles, saying they would drop onto her paintwork. Women are bloody fussy, aren't they? At Jenny's prompting the owner remembered us having stayed there before, and he left us to it after we promised to join him for a drink in the bar later.

The few happy campers already on the site ushered the smaller children into their caravans, in case we stole them. Then, gradually, after picking up the courage to reappear, they nodded and gestured to one another and chatted in muted tones. They quickly turned the other way when we looked at them. A sudden concern about being robbed in the night was breaking out everywhere.

Jenny left it to me to prepare food, as I hadn't done any of the driving. The pair of them took a nap on the big bed and closed the doors, shutting me out so my clattering of pans wouldn't disturb them. I rustled up a gourmet meal from next to nothing. It's surprising how creative I can be. I had a bit of a dither when I couldn't find the tin opener -

that could have scuppered my entire menu - but it soon passed; and after finding Jenny's emergency stash of tins in the bottom of a cupboard I was off.

Usually when people open tins instead of doing some proper cooking I think it's just plain lazy, but when I resort to it, it is merely expedient - and besides, I'm an expert. In no time I had a kind of vegetable - risotto? - made mostly with baked beans and potatoes in a low oven. I considered carefully the meat content before putting the hot dog sausages in - *honest*. If Liza didn't like them she could always bung them on my plate. After all, it was me slaving in the kitchen while she was snoozing so it would be rude if she complained, wouldn't it? I left the utensils to drain to save getting the tea towel damp. It would make it easier for Jenny to put the stuff away later as I wasn't sure where it all went. My job done, I slipped over to the Inn to see if they had a bottle of wine to accompany the meal.

There I met a charming Maltese lady called Melita, who was organising tables for the open mic night that evening. She was pleasantly plump and had a cheerful Mediterranean charm that reminded me of Ramona. She was dressed in a tight black pencil skirt and a tailored red blouse that gaped a little between the buttons, showing lovely olive skin beneath and a little of the lacy bra that struggled to contain her ample bosom.

She told me she sang and played the harmonica and that she was performing a few songs that evening. She also said the event was a bit hit-and-miss, sometimes attracting a few performance poets from Totnes or hippy types who churned out folk songs. It sounded a bit of a drag but I promised to come and see her sing later and smiled at her twice, just to make sure she smiled back, before I left.

When I got back, Liza and Jenny were awake and setting up the table.

'Smells good,' Jenny said.

'You'll love it, ladies,' I said, plonking the bottle of Shiraz I'd forgotten to pay for on the table that Jenny had just finished laying. The table was mounted on a single leg that slotted into a metal-lined hole in the floor and could be moved to a couple of different positions. The enclosed double bed had been packed away and we were going to eat seated at the front of the caravan in the horseshoe-shaped seating area.

I retrieved the casserole dish from the oven, burned my thumb, and set it in the middle of the table. Then I assumed my position in the middle, with a gorgeous dining companion at either side. They were in a chatty mood; the sleep had done them good. Jenny had a sublime smile and Liza looked a little dreamy but the vibes were good. Or they were until I took the lid off the casserole dish. Jenny's face dropped.

'What is it?' she asked with a worried look.

I bought a little time by pulling the cork from the wine with a pop. 'It's a kind of chasseur, sort of Cajun-type dish.' I grinned. 'It's very traditional,' I added with a knowing nod and serious expression.

Liza poked around in the dish with a fork. 'Are those

sausages?'

'Yes, but from vegetarian pigs that died of natural causes.'

'We aren't eating that!' Jenny fumed. 'Come on, Liza, we're eating out.'

'Ladies!' I protested. 'I can dredge the sausages out.'

'No, we're off, aren't we, Liza?' insisted Jenny. Liza nodded. 'And don't expect us back until late - clean up when you've finished.'

They left without as much as an au revoir, jumping in the car and shooting off down the drive. I popped the casserole dish back in the oven, my appetite temporarily at a low-ebb, re-corked the wine, and strolled back to the Inn. Melita was still there, laying tablecloths and smoothing them down.

'Can I help?' I asked her, favouring her with my best smile.

'Sure,' she replied in a sultry tone. 'You can help me stick these' - she held up candles - 'into those.' She pointed at a case of empty wine bottles. 'I have been trying for more than one hour.'

Her English could do with a little work, but I was sure I could spare her a few minutes for tuition.

'Certainly,' I said, and mucked in.

She'd been trying to shave the ends with a kitchen knife

and had powdery wax residue on her skirt, as well as a cut index finger. We went to the kitchen together for a jug of hot water and a plaster from the first aid box. I covered her wounded digit and gave it a playful kiss. Then I warmed the ends of the candles in the hot water so they could be squeezed into the bottles. Working together, we chatted and flirted an hour or so away.

'Are you coming later?' she asked.

'Of course,' I said. 'I wouldn't miss hearing you sing for the world.' I took her hand again on the pretext of examining her injured finger, but instead kissed it, bowing low, and laying it on as thick as I could manage.

'Thank you.' She smiled back, coyly. 'I have to run now. I'm hungry and I need to change my clothes.'

'Would you care to share my dinner?' I offered graciously. 'You can change in my caravan too, if it saves you time.'

'Thank you,' she said. 'Geoff is a bit - you know. He comes in and tries to look at my boobs.'

I shook my head and assumed a stern face. 'Disgraceful!' Then I held out my arm and she took it with a smile.

We retired to *my* caravan. It's a cracker - I'll have to describe it to you sometime. I lifted the table into its back-up spot in front of the single bed and opened the doors of both wardrobes so they created a private space. 'You can change in there,' I told her. She gave the skirts in the wardrobes a questioning look, so I explained that my mother sometimes used the caravan. She seemed to accept that and stepped behind the doors. I bustled away in the kitchen, livening up my casserole with a good glug of the Shiraz and stirred in a few chunks of cheese.

'It's ready when you are,' I called.

'Thank you.' She stepped out in a little pink wrap-around silky thing - and nothing else. I made a mental note to resist manfully any temptation that crossed my path.

'I'll take a shower after dinner and then get ready.' She spoke slowly, her eyes flashing around the caravan and taking things in, the way women do. I should have hidden a few of the scatter cushions to convince her it was mine.

'We've got a couple of hours yet,' I said. 'No need to rush.' I offered her a drop of wine. She was impressed with the meal. I told her all about how it was prepared in a time-honoured way to a secret recipe and was a traditional Romany feast. She didn't eat too enthusiastically, but as you know I can be enthusiastic enough for two so it balanced out well enough. Then she showered while I, as I'd promised myself, manfully resisted the temptation to wash up and stashed it all in the oven.

Melita returned from the shower block, slightly damp, her silky thing sticking to her a little as she fought the rising hem to protect her modesty - no wonder Geoff kept his eye on her. We sat looking at each other in our opposite corners and finished the wine. She told me of her life on Malta and her wish to be a star. Her singing voice, I gathered, was a gift passed down through the generations. I listened intently, showing the same polite interest she had shown in my cooking. I don't know how it happened, but we spent the last minutes before she needed to get dressed snogging like love-struck teenagers in a bus stop; I indulged in the odd grope here and there and she playfully fought me off.

All too soon she had to go and get ready. I sat in the caravan and pondered. My blanket was in the car, so technically I was homeless. I put the big bed together, sliding the base out from under the front seats and then dropping the back of the seat down to form the mattress. After a little nap, I went over to the Inn to watch the acts. Never one to mix the hop and the grape, I ordered another bottle of Shiraz and sat with it in a quiet corner, watching the punters roll in.

The night wore on, with the acts ranging from middle-of-the-road to bloody awful. Soon it was time for the delectable Melita's spot. She arrived on stage to a round of vigorous applause. As it died out she told us all how she was going to entertain us with some traditional Maltese folk songs. I smiled and clapped again, winking suggestively at her when I caught her eye, and wondering what she looked like naked. Well, they say it helps a performer's nerves to imagine the audience naked, don't they? And I was a nervous audience.

My God, though I clapped vigorously at the end of each song, she was awful. I can't remember ever hearing such a row - if I had, I'm sure I would have remembered. She wasn't so much tone-deaf as tone-dumb. After about twenty minutes or so of this auditory abuse she stopped quite abruptly, bowed stiffly, and stepped off the stage.

I stood and applauded, slapping my hands together until they hurt, while whistling enthusiastically. Enough of the meagre crowd joined in to make it convincing and she came over to my table, all smiles.

'Did you like it, Frankie?'

'Loved it.'

'Which bit did you like best?'

I thought, *The end - I applauded because you'd stopped, silly cow*, but that's not what I said of course. 'The third song. It was... moving?'

'It was about my grandmother.'

'Lovely!'

I plied her with wine. We finished my bottle and then, with a third bottle she'd bought and the candle from our table, we retired arm-in-arm to my caravan for a nightcap. She chatted as we walked – God, women can talk sometimes, can't they? I was eager to hurry things up a bit, in case the girls came back. She wanted to change out of her stage clothes and as the bed was already made up she changed there right in front of me by the light of the candle. As I watched I tried to block out the sound of her chatter and played a mental soundtrack to myself - a little Lionel Richie, though poor Lionel was losing, drowned out by the more recent memory of Melita's gruesome caterwauling.

Melita's peasant plumpness warmed me, however. As she stooped to remove her stage make-up, rubbing vigorously with some creamy stuff from a pot, I admired her, both in the cut glass mirrors and from behind, and tried to weigh her up. Now, some women like tenderness and some prefer a more forceful approach. There are all sorts - submissive, dominant, liking to take the lead, or preferring to be led – and I love them all; I have no favourites. But I do, perhaps, have a *least* favourite and that's the sort who lies there expecting their mere presence to be enough of a contribution. The *lie-back-and-think-of-England* sort usually put me right off and as often as not I find myself getting dressed again faster than I helped them to undress.

'Melita,' I asked her, 'you do know why I asked you back, don't you?'

'Of course,' she said in her charming accent. 'Sex, no?'

'Sex, yes,' I replied.

She stepped out of her thong; it was barely visibly anyway, being so well hidden in the cleavage of her plentiful buttocks. She bent forwards, hands spread flat on the dressing table, her heels turning outwards as she stood on tiptoes.

'So what are you waiting for?' She looked round at me with an impish grin. I thought I'd just figured her out as one of the quiet ones - but no, this was a type that was new to me. It takes all sorts, doesn't it?

I stood but as I did so I realised I felt nothing, nothing at all, despite my careful engineering of the whole thing. This wasn't what I wanted; it felt cold, callous even. For whatever reason, my head was filled with remorse. I'd rather not dwell upon the next couple of minutes. I rushed through getting her dressed and then hurried her out, apologising profusely. She seemed confused and embarrassed but was too startled, I think, to protest.

After she had gone, I slumped on the bed. Was it the thought of losing Jenny and Liza that'd made me realise what a serious thing love is? Or maybe I was finally growing up? Or even, and perhaps this was the conclusion I was hoping for, I was coming down with something? Whichever I chose to believe, the whole project with poor Melita had been ill conceived - pardon the pun.

I gave in to the pressing weight of temptation and filled the kettle to do the washing-up. I cleaned up, dried up, and packed everything away. I was on my hands and knees with the dustpan and brush when the car pulled up and Jenny and Liza bowled in, laughing.

'Had a pleasant evening, ladies?' I asked.

'Great,' Jenny replied. 'We've been to the Spinning Wheel in Paignton. Good food and a great band.'

'Why are you back so early?'

'We felt a bit guilty about leaving you on your own,' said Liza.

'I fancy a drink,' Jenny added, with a gleam in her lovely eyes.

'I've got a bottle here,' I offered.

'No, let's go to the Inn,' she replied, with a wink. 'I feel like having some fun!'

Chapter 16

We returned to the Inn, I was dreading the prospect of seeing Melita again so soon after the debacle in the caravan. Thankfully, she was nowhere in sight and I gradually relaxed, sipping slowly at the wine - I'd sort of gone off that too. The acts were thinning out now; the present one was a musical trio playing Irish folk songs. There was a fiddle (excellent), a tin whistle (very good), and a banjo (middle-of-the-road); the overall effect was passable, even if the vocals were a bit on the ropy side. When they played 'The Irish rover' we brightened up and thumped on the tables as we sang along. Then Jenny sloped off and spoke to the fiddle player between songs.

'What's she up to?' I asked Liza.

'Search me,' she replied with open hands and a shrug.

'I might take you up on that,' I told her, with a wink. She smiled; it was how we did things - I flirted, she fended me off, and, apart from me getting carried away every now and then, it worked for us.

Jenny came back, looking pleased. 'Come on, Liza, we're on next.' And before Liza had time to object she'd grabbed her hand and led her briskly to the stage.

The two of them harmonised to 'When Irish eyes are smiling' and it was the best song I'd heard all night. But I couldn't help thinking they'd need a lot more practice if Liza was going to replace Lydia. Liza rejoined me at the table while, predictably enough, Jenny turned off the microphone; her voice was more than enough for the smallish venue. She worked through the rest of her playlist to rapturous applause from a captive audience of holidaymakers and a few locals, who were getting some decent entertainment for once.

That was pretty much the pattern for the days to come - eating, drinking, dancing; fun all the way really. I was even given the odd night's parole and allowed to sleep on the single bed. Despite the good humour and lack of problems I had a growing sense of unease. I knew this couldn't last forever and sooner or later we would have to leave.

Geoff, the owner-cum-landlord, was a pretty likeable bloke if you could get past the odd lecherous look (but be honest, tell me a bloke who doesn't do the same, at least to a small degree). He had a small flock of Faverolle chickens, an ancient French breed with five toes rather than the usual four, which gives them a strange raptor-like gait. I helped him out a bit with them by borrowing tools from his shed and making new nest boxes and perches. I was hoping to improve their laying, and a new broody coop would provide the possibility of a few chicks. As I worked I brooded myself on the threats that had been made against Liza and Jenny. I kept getting flashbacks of the knife at Jenny's throat, the brutal slap Marcus had given Liza - not to mention those he had given me - and then there was Julian and my unfulfilled promise to hit him. My resolve hardened. In addition, the time limit to accept Marcus's offer, not that I had any faith in it, was running out.

Geoff had a salmon Faverolle rooster who took a dislike to me, unusual for this amenable breed. No matter how many times I tried to calm him down he just kept attacking me. I tried every trick I knew, like getting him to focus his fight on my right hand then pinning him down with my left. I tried spraying him with a water pistol. I even tried ignoring him and letting him attack me; this resulted in a hole in my new trousers. A method I have used successfully with bad-tempered roosters is holding a sheet of thin plywood or cardboard, about two feet square, between them and you. They don't seem to see you, and quickly lose interest - but you can't work like that, can you? In the end I put a tea chest over him, plunging him into darkness and sleep so I could get on.

It's funny really, but cockerels don't show any fear when their fighting switch is thrown. It's as if fear and self-preservation just aren't on their list of instincts. They just attack any perceived threat in an unemotional, cold, almost ritualistic way, using the same technique over and over until they win or die trying. I was starting to feel a bit like that myself - cold, hard and determined to end this once-and-for-all. There was no point delaying the inevitable. The police would have found the freshly fired gun, with my prints on it, wrapped in my t-shirt, in my - well, no Digger's - van. All I would do by staying here longer was let Marcus and his goons get away with whatever it was they were planning. I decided to break it to the girls that night over supper.

As this was to be our penultimate day together, if I had my way, I took a roll of notes from the robbery loot, snapping the blue band as I pulled it off. I fanned the notes out on the table to check they weren't consecutively numbered, then I strolled over to the Inn and got Geoff to book me a taxi. Jenny and Liza were washing the car in wet vests and shorts. A row of happy campers, the husbands mostly, had decided that it was too hot to stay indoors and were out lounging and pretending not to glance from behind sunglasses and newspapers as a playful water fight broke out.

'Come on, ladies,' I told them, 'we're going out.'

'Where?' asked Liza.

'I've got things to do,' said Jenny.

So I uttered the magic word 'shopping'. They were changed and ready for the taxi before the onlookers had time to make excuses to their wives.

We spent the afternoon in Torquay. The girls went off on their own, buying dresses, shoes and stuff. Women shopping drive me mad so I did my own thing. I bought a new jacket, in dark green waxed cotton with plenty of pockets and zips, and a pair of smallish folding binoculars that slipped nicely into one of my voluminous new inside pockets. I felt good; my whole wardrobe had now been replaced. I even bought a couple of packets of polo mints to give my pockets the familiar feel of my old jacket, which I'd lost when my caravan was wrecked.

The girls were at it for flipping hours. We'd arranged to

meet for coffee and I assumed that would mark the end of it. I slurped mine and they shared a pot of fancy tea as I ate all the cakes to save them feeling guilty, the way women always do, about the calories. It turned out this was only half-time. I sighed and sulkily agreed to meet them later on the beach, at the foot of the bridge that crosses over the Torbay road.

I arrived early and sat on a bench, snug in my new jacket and playing with my new binoculars. But there were no birds, ships or anything else of interest in range so, after scanning a few windows and distant car number plates to test the focus wheel, I pocketed them. Then, with my hat down over my eyes, I nodded off. I was woken a while later by the girls, laughing and happy and clutching numerous bags.

We went home to change. I sat in the bar and waited for the girls, nibbling peanuts and conscious of Melita's eyes boring into my back. I tried to apologise to her but she was having none of it. They're like that though, aren't they? Not natural forgivers like us blokes.

Later we made our way by taxi to the Inn on the Green, where they had a cabaret singer, and we could have supper served at our table. I'd showered, shaved and risked my best pair of trousers and shirt; I'd even cleaned my boots. I opened the taxi door with a bow and tried to be at my charming best. We arrived to a pretty full house, all seated, with a few early shufflers on the floor as the Brian Ferry wannabe singer, with slicked back hair, padded shoulders and shiny suit, did his thing. It was a mostly middle-aged-plus crowd mixed with a few younger couples, all looking pretty straight-laced. We caused a bit of a stir as we arrived and were shown to the table I had reserved by phone. The girls looked glamorous enough to be in the show, while I looked scruffy enough to be doing the dishes - I do try, but elegance just isn't my natural state.

It was a great night. I danced with both of the girls in turn, much to the surprise of astonished neighbours at other tables. As we chatted and drank we played up to it a little, being flirtatious, holding hands across the table and even sharing the occasional kiss. Gossip rippled round the room and, to be honest, I felt like a dog with two... two... bones? I sat as smug as a Tory MP as we revelled in the attention of the other diners.

The girls both looked stunning, with their hair scraped back and immaculate make-up, including voluptuous red lipstick. They wore matching, tight-fitting dresses in cherry red, with a little gold thread sparkle to create a look right out of 'Addicted to love', which was the big music video of that summer. I loved the dresses and the way they clung alluringly in all the right paces, with gold chain belts to accentuate their slim waists and matching stockings and stilettos to show off their shapely calves. What more could a man possibly ask for? I was truly replete. I guessed I'd just financed costumes for the new stage show, but I was happy and so were they, so what harm could their dreaming and scheming do?

Jenny, true to form, asked permission to sing while the cabaret artiste took his break. Then she trotted out a few belters for Liza and me to dance to. The first was Blondie's 'Atomic' and the second - just to tantalise all those who were getting hot under the collar about our ménage à trois - was Tina Turner's 'What's love got to do with it?' I took advantage of the fun we were having to be lavishly over-familiar with both of them. I'm no dancer really, but as I twirled Liza round the floor I made a show of feeling her bottom and running my hands over her hips.

'You ought to stop that,' she smirked at me.

'Why?' I challenged.

'You're only winding yourself up. You know it's not going anywhere, don't you?'

'That's where you're wrong, love. I can dream whatever I like.'

She slapped my shoulder playfully and we finished our dancing to Jenny's last number, Toni Tennille's 'Do it to me one more time', a favourite of Jenny's that had narrowly missed being on her tape. Then we went back to our table, laughing and breathless. I was content; it was a true last supper. Jenny collected Liza from the table and I sat and imbibed single malt as the girls danced together. The singer announced with cheese, smarm, and a showbiz grin, 'a song for those ladies in red' then ground his way through George Michael's 'Careless whisper'. The girls went into overdrive, carrying on in outrageous style, running their hands over each other and mimicking passionate kisses to wind up the murmuring audience. It seemed so polished I assumed it was part of their new act. I sat and thoroughly enjoyed it, thinking that if this was how it was going to be, maybe Liza would be able to replace Lydia after all.

At last they returned to the table and, reluctantly, I decided it was time to spoil the mood. 'I'm leaving tomorrow,' I told them both. 'I'm going back to sort all this out. I can't ask you both to keep running and hiding.'

Liza tried to argue but Jenny had more experience of my resolve and didn't try to change my mind. 'We're coming with you,' she informed me. 'Don't argue with me. We're coming and that's that. We've come this far together and I'm not deserting you now.'

Liza squeezed my hand and Jenny's and nodded agreement.

It was getting late. I noticed that the doormen were changing shifts with the night security staff and my malt-infused mind took in a flash of a profile not unlike Julian's. I assumed it must be the whisky playing tricks with me; anyway, we were leaving in the morning. We had one last dance together as the other punters filed out and then we went to wait for our taxi. We waited, and waited, and waited. The lights were turned out behind us and the doors were locked. Still we waited.

'I did book one, honest,' I said, getting my self-defence in first - something that later was to prove a good strategy. I tried flagging down a taxi or two, but they all take office bookings only now, don't they? Anyway, they just ignored me.

I gave the girls my new jacket to keep them warm. Now, if I had been with either one of them I would have gallantly draped it around her shoulders - but what can you do with two? They did their best to share it, cuddling together against the evening chill, which was made worse by the contrast after the warm club and the exertion of dancing.

'Wait here, ladies,' I told them. 'Back in two minutes, I promise.' I wrenched a hairpin from Liza's locks, causing a squeal of protest from her. She rubbed her head and mumbled abuse.

'You'd fucking better be!' Jenny called after me, charming as ever.

I headed down to the Spinning Wheel and turned right. It was all over there too - lights, band, everything - except, that is, for a bloke who was defensively locked in his car outside the main entrance while a rather cute girl with a head of bubbly blond curls screamed abuse at him in an Australian accent and kicked the shit out of his motor. She was going on about the lipstick on his collar not matching hers. She registered my presence and gave me an ugly look.

'And what the fuck do you think you're looking at?' she screamed at me.

I dropped my gaze as she turned her attention back to her row; all that energy in such a petite frame - *interesting*. I walked on with a smile. Then I turned left and ploughed on, eventually finding my quarry in a little car park off Kernou Road, a neat little red-and-white Citroën Deux Chevaux. 'Hello, dolly,' I drawled as I glanced around furtively and made my way over.

Those little Citroëns were a piece of piss to steal, pardon my French. You pull out the edge of the canvas roof in the middle, where a metal strip fits through a slot to hold the whole thing taut. Then you pull the roof outwards as hard as you can and lift; this gives enough slack to reach your arm in and pop the window latch. You then pull the three round plugs off the back of the ignition switch and, if you've been clever enough to bring a paperclip or a hairpin with you, you're away. You join the live and return together, then touch the end of the clip on the terminal of the starter motor wire. You pull the choke out, hold the accelerator flat to the floor, and finally put the choke half-way back in once the engine's running.

This one, being one of the last made, had a steering lock, so I turned it until it latched. Then I stood outside and braced my foot on the steering wheel's one spoke, kicked out hard, and heard it crack.

Within minutes the three of us were bowling back to the caravan. Those little cars handled beautifully on winding country roads, which was just as well really considering my driving. I dropped the girls off and dumped the car in a gateway a little further down the road. I gave it a final pat on the roof, and a 'thank you', then I went back to get some well-earned rest.

The three of us said little more to each other that night but just lay down together on the bed. I had an arm around each of them as I lay in the middle and that was how we stayed for a long time, until I woke up moaning some time in the early hours because my arm had gone to sleep. It sort of spoilt the moment, so I moved to the single bed.

The following morning would find us once again preparing for the road, but this time we would be heading back towards home. I was ahead of the deadline Marcus had set but I had planned a sort of pre-emptive strike. As I lay in the single bed I modified my mental plans to include all three of us - well, up to a point, because despite all this *all for one and one for all* camaraderie there was no way I was going to let the girls get themselves into any danger. After all, I had done all right on my own so far, hadn't I?

We packed up fairly early after hearing a police car not far away going *nee-nah nee-nah*; nowadays, of course, they all do that American *wah-wah* thing that grates on your nerves. The sound woke me and I couldn't get back to sleep again after that, so I started the packing-up process while the girls were still snoring in oblivion. They were still asleep when I heard a car engine coming to a halt somewhere outside, prompting me to peek out of a window. A police Mini, almost the same shade as a Crested-Cream-Legbar egg, had pulled into the drive; it looked quaint even back then. An adolescent bobby was quizzing a pyjama-clad Geoff, who was shaking his head with a perplexed expression and pointing northwards.

'Cheers, Geoff,' I said to myself. The bobby thanked him earnestly and returned to his duty, upholding the law against all manner of rogues. And maybe I'm one of them - but you know what they say, we are *loveable*. Aren't we?

Chapter 17

The return journey went much the same as the first. We stopped at Taunton Deane services just after Junction 26. Apparently it's close to the site of some ancient bloodshed, hence the cannon and other weaponry on display at the entrance - it struck me as a little ominous, considering our destination.

Looking at the price list inside, I felt like the victim of an armed robbery rather than the perpetrator - but I was onto them this time. I ordered two pots of tea and a pot of hot water. It was a bit early for lunch, but we'd missed breakfast so I also ordered two meals. Liza had a vegetarian lasagne and Jenny a ploughman's lunch with plenty of rabbit food (which I don't consider suitable sustenance for a real ploughman - I mean, driving heavy horses all day on nothing more than a chunk of cheddar and a few leaves - bloody ridiculous, if you ask me). I also bought a big bread roll.

I chose a table as far from the counter as possible and we sat down. The girls immediately tucked in.

'Is that all you're having, Frankie?' asked Jenny.

'Are you ok?' inquired Liza.

I fished a Cumberland ring sausage, some chips and some butter portions out of the voluminous pockets of my new jacket. I topped these off with a purloined teabag for my pot of hot water, for which I'd had to pay, incidentally. It's amazing how easily these things slip into your pockets.

'Ladies, I know, before you say it - it's not even my money,' I replied, 'but it's a matter of principle. These places are bloody terrible. They have a monopoly and they abuse it. It's not as if some greasy Joe can park his mobile nosh bar on the hard shoulder, is it? Somebody ought to do something about it.'

The girls exchanged knowing looks but said nothing. And besides, I thought as I scoffed, I had a good idea whose money it really was.

We trundled on, taking it easy so as not to attract attention - though how a thirty-foot long crystal-and-chrome palace on wheels pulled by a huge four-wheel drive could go unnoticed is anyone's guess.

I half-sat, half-lay, somewhere between the blissful fantasy of my dreams and the cold reality of wakefulness. I was on the back seat again and reminiscing, thinking about the day I first met Liza. It wasn't all that long ago really - a few short years compared to the almost lifetime of friendship I had shared with Jenny. It was not long after old Mr Smestow's house and land was auctioned. I had gone along for curiosity's sake, carelessly disregarding its effect on the proverbial cat. And that was where I first saw Marcus. Our eyes met momentarily as he nodded his winning bid. I had no reason to like, or dislike, him then and so reserved judgement, ignoring the gossip and speculation of the locals. The weeks slipped by while the house was rewired, redecorated, and new heating was put in; nothing much happened. I popped in and out, helping myself to the odd bundle of old copper wire or lead pipe and weighing it in at the scrap yard - just enough to keep me in food and drink, you understand.

Then one day, out of the blue, a long low sports car trundled down the bridle path. My hedge was pretty sparse in places so I had a good view. The driver stopped and openly inspected me and mine through a pair of opera glasses. I waved and smiled. At that the engine roared as the driver tried to speed away; rather optimistically as it turned out, due to the fact that the driver was on a muddy track in a convertible. As the car spun itself into a rut I wandered over to see if I could either help, or mock, depending upon how the mood took me. And that was when I first laid eyes upon the most beautiful, intelligent, and plain irritating woman I'd ever met.

She refused my offer of help with a curt 'I can manage, thanks.' Then she climbed out of the car without opening the door. She was wearing those Lycra leggings, skin tight, that come to just below her knee, a matching Lycra crop top, and Reebok trainers. Her hair was tied back in a tight ponytail and her expression was hard to read behind wrap-around designer sun specs.

She stood facing me, proud and defiant. 'Goodbye,' she said, meaning 'get lost, scruff', and opened the boot. I was interested to see how things progressed, as her size six - UK not US - body (tanned, toned, epilated, exfoliated, manicured, perfectly muscled, every inch a work of art) hefted the spare wheel and the jack out into daylight. *This'll never work*, I was thinking, as she placed the wheel under the car and used it as a jacking point to stop the jack sinking into the soft ground.

'Great idea, love,' I said as she jacked the first wheel out of the mud.

'Well, if you're going to stand their leching at me you might as well help!' she snapped.

Bloody cheek! It was me who had offered to help in the first place, silly cow. I couldn't really argue about the *lech* bit, though, as it was lust at first sight.

I collected a few stones from under my hedge, remnants of a dry stonewall that had melted back into the landscape aeons ago, and filled the hole left by the wheel, which was now hanging in the air. She lowered the wheel onto the stones and moved the jack round to the other side. It was a hot day and I watched the beads of perspiration that gathered on her lightly oiled back and ran down... *clunk!* She stood up and slammed the jack handle down.

'This might work better if you could tear your eyes away from my backside for a minute.'

'Ok then - moody mare - I'll be in my caravan if you want me.' I left her to it, without looking back.

And want me she did. She had come to warn me about pilfering scrap metal from the house. I had been duly warned, though of course I denied it vigorously as a matter of principle. From that day on we bumped into each other regularly and every time the sparks flew, but eventually we started to rub along. She had all the ideas and I helped her make them real. Until one day when I was ranting at her as usual, over some mistake we couldn't agree who was responsible for, she started to laugh, and then I did too. We stopped rubbing each other up the wrong way from that day, though sadly we never really progressed to rubbing each other up the right way - not for lack of trying on my part.

It was all so different to my relationship with Jenny, which had started with easy friendship and eager passion in our early teens and over the years had worked its inexorable way up to force ten rows and mutual antagonism...

'Frankie, wake up! We're stopping for a break,' Liza said, ruffling my hair.

I opened my eyes. We stopped again, this time at Strensham services, after which we left the motorway at Junction 7. Jenny reluctantly agreed to let me drive so we swapped places in a lay-by close to Stourport-on-Severn and I took us on the last stretch, about twenty-five miles north-west. We pulled onto the car park of The Feathers at the tail-end of lunchtime. I reversed the caravan carefully into the far corner of the car park, under the shadow of a few ash trees. Then we went inside for a drink and to explain to the landlord that we were only breaking a journey, before he called the police.

I hatched a quick plot to leave Jenny there in charge of

the car and caravan, which she agreed to after I offered the alternative of looking after them myself - just to create the illusion of choice. Then I walked over the crossroads with Liza, slipping her a roll of bank notes as we went.

The gates were open and the flag was at full mast, so there was no need for excessive formality. I rapped the aged oak doors and waited; after a few calls and barks from inside they swung open with an ominous creak.

'Liza,' I whispered hurriedly, leaving her no time to argue as a hesitant bespectacled face appeared, 'just agree with me and follow my lead.'

'Yes?' the bespectacled face enquired.

'Michael,' I said, beaming and shaking his hand before pushing past into the hall; I gave Liza a stick-with-me gesture. 'Is Sandy in?'

'She's in the kitchen.'

'Thanks, Michael.'

We pressed on without waiting for the luxury of an invitation and making the most of the element of surprise. We burst into the kitchen with Michael tagging along behind.

'Sandy,' I trilled, putting my arms around her and kissing her on the cheeks. 'Lovely to see you.' The way I said it made it seem as if she was the visitor and me the visited. Sandy looked nonplussed and floundered for a moment until Michael caught up. Then she quickly recovered.

'Frankie - I hope you've come to apologise. Michael told me he had seen you and had given you a stern reprimand.'

'Yes.' I nodded agreement. 'A heartfelt apology - it was my fault entirely. Though I had my reasons. Please let's all sit down and I can explain.' Brontë-speak was always the dish of the day at Sandy's family seat.

Sandy's eyes fell on Liza, who looked a little more tousled than Sandy had seen her before.

'Let me introduce the village trollop,' I intoned, and presented Liza to Sandy.

The penny dropped and recognition showed on Sandy's face. She had no love for Liza, just because she was another woman and therefore an automatic rival, but she did respect her county set status.

'Liza, how lovely,' Sandy drawled with a million-dollar false smile, courtesy of Michael's fiddling the NHS books, no doubt.

The two women touched cheeks in that pseudo-kissing ritual they do and we all sat down. Sandy brought over tea things and a biscuit barrel, a combination that always works for me.

I sipped at my cup, then turned to Liza. 'Liza, we've forgotten to return the money we borrowed from Sandy.'

Liza picked up the thread quickly, drew the roll from her pocket and placed it on the table.

'Liza had some trouble at home,' I explained, ad-libbing

faster than a legal-aid lawyer. 'We needed some cash in a rush and knew you wouldn't mind. After I saw Michael I assumed you didn't get the note. Maybe a draught blew it into the Aga?'

'That must be it,' Sandy said apologetically as she picked up the roll. 'Look, Michael, they've repaid the loan.'

There were smiles all round, some of them false, but I think Sandy's was genuine enough this time. Michael tore his eyes away from Liza's cleavage long enough to look down at the roll of notes and his face fell. I guessed it was at the sight of the coloured elastic band, the sort an orthodontist might use to correct a malocclusion. He flushed, then cleared his throat and mumbled nervously.

'Thank you, both.'

We finished our tea and I decided my best tactic was to separate them. I asked if Liza could freshen up, as we had driven a long way to see them; Sandy obliged and led Liza off to show her the facilities.

'Shocked?' I asked Michael, once we were alone.

'Should I be?' he countered.

I emptied rolls of notes from my pockets onto the table. 'Your syndicate contribution, I assume?'

He reached for the rolls but I quickly gathered them up and stuffed them back in my pockets. 'I have it all, just not here.'

'I don't know what you mean,' he replied, feigning

indignation.

'Don't worry,' I told him, 'I'll not grass you up for cooking the books.' I added a cheeky wink for good measure.

'Now, look here!' He raised his voice and sat upright in his chair. 'You can't just walk in here making accusations like that.' He accentuated every syllable by prodding my chest with a long bony finger. I knew I should have put a stop to that last time. I grabbed his finger and twisted it until the back of his hand lay flat on the tablecloth. He squirmed with pain, so I gave it another tweak to make my point as I hissed through clenched teeth.

'Poke me again and I'll break it, ok?'

He nodded so I let go.

'Now that's sorted, would you care for more tea, Michael?'

He nodded again as I refilled the cups and quickly summed things up for him. 'Your syndicate members are a bunch of crooks, and you're in it up to your neck. I'm going to sort it all out, so if you want to come out of this mess in one piece you have to do exactly as I say, understand?'

He nodded once more, but this time sheepishly. Sandy bustled back in, smiling. 'She's rather charming once you get to know her, isn't she?'

'Yes,' I replied with a smile. 'She certainly is.'

'Not sure about the gold tooth, mind,' Sandy added.

'I was rather hoping Michael could help out there,' I replied, giving him a meaningful look. Sandy was already off rattling pans in the oven.

'Of course,' Michael said, with an attempt at hearty good humour. Then he leaned towards me and whispered. 'Ok, anything you say. Just don't tell Sandy.'

'Don't you mean Sarah?' I whispered back, with a smirk.

Chapter 18

Having settled things with Michael, I invited Sandy to show me how my hens and Charlie the goat were settling in. We left the kitchen and made our way outside. Michael did nothing to stop us going. Once in the fresh air, Sandy stormed off in a huff. I trotted up behind her, imploring her to listen. She headed for the summerhouse and flounced in, stamping her feet like an angry child.

'What the hell do you think you're playing at, Frankie?' she hissed, glaring daggers at me.

I moved closer, palms spread in surrender and honesty. 'Sandy... darling...' I tried to hold her.

'Don't *darling* me, you inconsiderate pig!' she yelled and then slapped me. 'After we... and I...' She started to sob, so I threw my arms around her and kissed her - first consolingly on the forehead and within seconds hot and hard on the lips. I locked the doors and drew the blinds.

'What about Michael?' she whispered, with obvious trepidation.

'Don't worry about Michael,' I said. 'That's why I brought Liza - to distract him. I was desperate to see you.' I clutched her hands.

'Were you, darling?' she drawled as she withdrew her hand and held it tenderly to my slapped face. 'I'm sorry,' she whispered breathlessly. Within seconds I had lifted her Laura Ashley floral print around her waist, torn off her silk Janet Reger's, and balanced her precariously on the back of the wicker lounger.

'Frankie...' she murmured, her fingers exploring my face. I held her by the hips and entered her with passion, ignoring her pleas for me to be gentle. Then I kissed her hard to muffle her cries as she held onto me, unable to let go without falling off her perch. She soon took up the pace and thrust her hips to meet me. I lifted her onto the rug in front of the fire and we shuddered and moaned to a noisy conclusion.

After catching my breath, I hastily rearranged my clothing and helped her to her feet. 'Go back in before they miss us. I'll go and check the hens.'

She flattened and patted her hair, the way they do, and with a doe-eyed smile walked away, trying to balance on shaking legs, her torn knickers stuffed in her apron pocket.

I ambled off into the gardens smiling, stage one of my plan accomplished. I had both of them on my side and everything was under control - or so I thought.

I sauntered down the path and sat on a bench, enjoying the combination of peace and post-coital bliss. I watched the hens scratching and pecking, and Charlie grazing amongst the fruit trees - heaven. After a few minutes Liza joined me and we sat on the bench, my arm around her shoulders, enjoying the view.

'So, how did you get on with Michael, love?'

'He's pleasant enough,' she said, 'but a bit boring. He will make me a new tooth though.'

'Good,' I said.

'Yes,' she continued. 'He has all my impressions and records. He did the original work.'

'Really?' I asked with genuine interest.

'Marcus paid him cash to use the hospital's facilities after he hit me in a row and damaged the root in my tooth. That's how I lost it in the first place.'

I held her closer and kissed her forehead. Marcus was already on my list so there was no need to get upset about this, was there?

'Sandy was in a good mood when she came in,' she added. 'It's as if the ice has melted.'

I smirked. Her mouth dropped open.

'You *have*, haven't you?' She looked shocked. I shrugged. 'You *have* - you've bodged her, haven't you?'

'Bodged?' I said, '*bodged?*'

'You know, rogered her - given her one.' And then she gave me a dirty smile.

'Don't be so crude, young lady. I think you mean making

love, don't you? And besides, a gentleman never tells.' But I gave her a wink.

'You're terrible,' Liza said, shaking her head and relaxing back into my arm. 'Mind you, it seems to have done her good.'

'It would do you good too, if only you would let it,' I said, with a raise of my eyebrows. Liza just shook her head again, smiled, and rested her cheek on my chest. We sat in silence for a few minutes more.

'Oh well, time for phase two of my plan. Come on, we'd better go.'

I led her in silence back to the kitchen. It smelt of baking; Sandy was at her best bustling and baking. She was humming as she worked. Michael was reading *The Times* and sipping tea from a Royal Albert cup.

'Frankie, Liza - will you both be staying for dinner?' Sandy was still beaming.

'Love to,' I said, with perhaps a little more enthusiasm than was warranted. 'In fact, while we are on the subject of staying, I have a favour to ask.'

'Ask away,' said Michael, raising an eyebrow.

'We have nowhere to stay and Liza has been having a terrible time. I wondered...'

'Yes, of course,' said Sandy, 'though I will have to give you separate bedrooms.'

Liza looked at us both in turn with open-mouthed indignation; she was about to challenge the inferred misconduct when I interrupted.

'Of course,' I joked, 'we wouldn't want to cause a scandal at the Women's Institute, would we?'

Sandy laughed along, as did Liza, though she did scowl at me when no one was looking.

'In fact,' I continued, 'we have a little bit more of a favour to ask - would you mind if we parked our caravan down by the pony paddock for a few days? We have a friend with us, you see - Jenny. You'll love her.'

Sandy looked a little dubious but brightened when I added, 'Liza can share with Jenny and, if it's not too inconvenient, I can stay in the summerhouse to be out of your way. We won't impose at all.'

'Nonsense,' chirped Sandy. 'You're welcome to impose. Do whatever you want.' She beamed, presumably at the thought of having me all to herself at the bottom of the garden. She was lovely in every way and, who knows, if she'd been a little less clingy and maybe a bit less married, I could have been the lord of the manor... but life's not all beer and skittles, is it?

We returned to the pub to collect Jenny. It was closed for the afternoon and Jenny was sitting in the car.

She climbed out when she saw us coming. 'About bloody time. My arse has gone to sleep.'

'Do you want me to rub it for you?' I enquired in a

patronising tone. She shot me a sickly smile and kicked me in the shin, but I was still on cloud nine after my interlude with Sandy, so I just winced, and took a deep breath. 'Temper, temper!'

Once back at Sandy's we set up the caravan for a long stay, with all the china unpacked - more for show than anything, though I do like beautiful things and I helped with genuine enthusiasm. Then I ran the two girls through what I expected of them - after all, they had volunteered to be my team, hadn't they?

'Stick with Michael,' I said. 'One of you needs to be with him as much as possible. I don't trust him and he is in this up too his...' I searched for an appropriate word.

'Teeth?' Liza filled the gap, with a chuckle.

Jenny threw me a suggestive smile. 'How far do you want us to go with this?'

'This is bloody serious!' I snapped. 'Ok? That knife was real. He could have killed you,' I reminded her - then I realised my mistake.

'What do you mean - knife?' Liza shouted straight at me, and then she turned to Jenny. 'What he's talking about? Tell me!' She was getting angry.

'You two have some catching up to do,' I said hurriedly, grabbing my jacket. I left them to it.

I found Sandy scattering corn to the hens. 'Hello, darling,' I said, surprising her by sneaking up behind her and putting my arms around her waist.

'Stop it,' she said. 'Michael might see.'

I kissed her on the cheek. 'Do you have a car I could use for a while?'

'Of course. Take my new car. Michael bought it for me at an auction. It's in the barn and the keys are in it. 'Frankie,' she called as I walked away, 'will you be back for dinner?'

'Supper,' I replied, with a meaningful wink.

The barn was full of useful stuff. I rooted through the gardener's tools, pocketed a few choice items, and then sped off in her shiny little Suzuki Samurai. Good God, they were uncomfortable old things, weren't they? A clunky gearbox coupled to a wheezy little petrol engine and seats that felt as if they were folding you in two - a far cry from the luxury of Jenny's Shogun.

It started to drizzle and the squeaky little wipers just smeared the screen, making it worse. It looked like it would make a useful little tractor though - it had four-wheel drive and an electric winch mounted on the front for self-recovery. And, much as I moaned as it rattled along the lanes with the wind whistling through every gap in the flapping vinyl roof, I'd have liked it for my own plot. That was, if I still had one.

I parked up amongst the trees on the ridge behind my plot and covered the windows with sacking borrowed from Sandy's barn to stop reflections glinting off the glass. Then I tried to break up the vehicle's outline with a few fallen branches and piled last autumn's fallen leaves on the bonnet and roof. With a bit of luck that would be enough to stop its shining red paint, white soft-top, and rhino graphics giving me away.

I tried to get a view of what was happening at the grange, but my binoculars weren't really powerful enough, and besides I could only see the chimney tops. Then I made my way down the ridge and crossed the field at its foot, keeping close to the hedge, with my drab green wax jacket zipped up high and my hat brim pulled low. I wasn't sure I was even in the right place to uncover Marcus's devious plan, but when my feet had been dragged through gravel on the night I was abducted and then my head had hit the low archway, as it had several times before, where else could it be?

I made it unseen over the B road and into a field to the east of my plot, then walked steadily, head down, stopping only to cut a thumb stick from the hedge with the folding pruning-saw I'd borrowed from the barn. That way, at a distance, I could pass for a rambler enjoying the countryside.

Thankfully the rain kept coming, keeping any inquisitive people indoors and reducing the visibility from wet windows. At the point where my hedge joined the stream there was a fallen oak tree that had somehow kept growing. Its yard-thick trunk and sprouting branches provided great cover. I picked a comfortable spot and settled in to watch and wait.

First I scanned my plot. It was much as I had left it, except for a little tracked earthmover that had cleared the foundation of the old cottage. My little zoomster was there;

so my naturist friend June *had* passed my message on to Terry about getting it back to my place for me. I would have to make it up to her some time - not that my old car would do me any good right now, as pallets of dressed building stone blocked my gates from the inside. They must have been brought down from the big house along the tracks and bridle paths; which would explain the muddy ruts across the grass. I scanned the hedges; there was a new gap where the bridge crossed the stream. I couldn't see anything more because of the contours of the land.

It was a miserable day. The rain dripped off the brim of my hat with a rhythmic plop, plop, onto the front of my jacket. I dozed for a while and woke up with a start. That screaming face was getting further and further away, except this time it was Jenny screaming, not Liza - weird, but then aren't all dreams?

I was stiff and cold, so I took advantage of the growing gloom to move, though first I scanned my plot with the binoculars once more. Nothing - just a couple of rabbits playing and nibbling beneath the feeders, probably enjoying fresh shoots that'd sprung up from fallen grain. They were a sure sign there were no people about.

I headed back to my wrecked caravan. Most of the things that had been thrown outside were now back inside and the door was shut. The caravan had been pushed up close to the side of one of the field shelters and that had kept most of the weather out of the broken windows. Then I walked in the tracks left by the earthmover down to the stream and inspected the new bridge. Steel girders had been concreted in on each bank for support and railway sleepers in a herringbone pattern provided the deck. It was a good solid job - all the joints in the steel welded, the sleepers bolted in place, a coat of creosote for the wood, with red oxide primer coating the metal work - obviously built to last. I crossed it, jumping and stamping like one of the Billy Goats Gruff to test its strength; stupid really, but I felt more confident when no troll appeared from beneath.

The smooth leather soles of my new boots let me down on the ascent of the far bank and I slipped and slithered in the mud, falling to my knees and cursing. I streaked my face with mud from my dirty hands, commando-style, so anyone watching would think I meant to do it - yes, I'm childish, I know. I sneaked closer to the house and found a vantage point under some young ash saplings planted to fill a gap in the hedge; someone had obviously been keeping up maintenance on the place.

I lay and looked at the house with my binoculars. Lights were springing on here and there. I couldn't see much but when the yard lights came on, things got a little better. A brown Jeep Cherokee pulling into the yard - the one I had seen Jenny in at her agents - had activated them. A shapely looking woman with bubbly blonde curls and a maid's uniform stepped out. I was too far away to make out any facial features but she seemed oddly familiar. Then a door opened and Marcus hurried out to meet her, his military gait instantly recognisable. So was this his bit on the side? He was shouting at her and pointing back at the house. Then he raised his hand as if to slap her and she ran in terror through the open door. If this was his new lover, he was certainly bringing her up to speed.

I kept watching. The place was guarded, occasionally patrolled by two goons with walkie-talkies and torches. I watched them until I found the pattern in their routine and then peeled across the field and into the stables.

There were stalls inside; each one had a stable door that opened into the yard. Running across the back of the stalls was a corridor, big enough to remove a beast from a stall and move it to another without going outside. In the middle of the stable block was a larger open space that was enclosed by two tall pairs of wooden doors. When the doors were open it was possible to drive a lorry through the stone archway and into the yard. When they were closed the area inside provided a link, through side doors, between the two halves of the stables.

Some of the stalls on the other side of the archway had been removed to make a storage space; the rest was partitioned off for Liza's workshops. A narrow external covered staircase led to the roof space, which included several small rooms and a row of dormer windows. This space had, aeons ago, been used to house serfs who worked on the estate but now provided offices for Marcus's business endeavours. This upper floor was laid out in a similar way to the stalls in the stables below, with a long corridor above the corridor behind the stalls and a small room above each stall. Each stall was separated from the corridor behind by a wall topped with iron railings that went straight up to the oak beams above. A wide door, in the back wall, separated each stall from the corridor. Opening this would leave the stall's occupant no choice but to head for the central archway - or it could be opened right back to make the corridor accessible in either direction. The doors were barred on the corridor side, so entering any of the stalls would do me no good, as they were individual cells where I could easily be trapped.

I headed for the stone staircase as underneath, in the shadows, a door led directly into the corridor. It was locked, and so was the one at the top of the stairs. This was significant, as I'd never known them to be locked before, even when the house was empty and the stables were used to store building materials and scrap metal.

I disturbed a dog that growled and barked in a dark corner of the yard, so I scampered back to the hedges and the cover of darkness before the security men returned. When the commotion subsided I plodded back to the Suzuki and returned to Sandy's. A bit of home-cooked food and company would be welcome and I could dry my damp clothes by the Aga.

Chapter 19

I pulled into Sandy's drive and parked up back in the barn, locking the Suzuki and pocketing the keys to ensure continuous access to transport. Then I stalked down to the caravan, to the sounds of a full-scale row going on inside, I couldn't believe they were still at it - was this round two, or maybe three?

'Why didn't you tell me? You inconsiderate, self-centred bitch! You just swan around with your head in the fucking clouds. You're a dreamer - just like your stupid fucking husband!' Liza was certainly angry. She could also hold her own better than I could in a row with Jenny.

'I thought that you'd been through enough. I was trying to protect you. So much for my good deed!' Jenny yelled back.

'What good deed was that? Shagging in the back of a clapped-out van?' A neat parry from Liza.

As much as I love a good row, I decided to head for the kitchen and relative peace, and leave them to sort their own problems out, before the plates started to fly. So what happened to them sticking close to Michael? Teamwork is a wonderful thing, isn't it?

I walked straight into the kitchen; I was on top form now. 'Hello, Sandy.' I smiled and kissed her forehead as she turned to greet me. She was sitting by the Aga, embroidery frame in hand. 'Is Michael at home?'

'Yes,' she said. 'He's in his study working on some papers for court.'

I didn't like the sound of that, but what could I do? I decided to move my plan forward as fast as I could. I ate supper - some kind of flan-type thing that barely touched the sides. Then I grumbled a bit at the meagre rations and retired to the summerhouse, stopping off to see what was happening in the caravan on the way.

It was in darkness. Muted voices and music were just audible as I strained my ear at the door. Some things are best left, aren't they? So I decided to call it a day and get some sleep.

The next day I did my Sexton Blake act again, but this time I borrowed Sandy's Jack Russell terrier, Tina, and decided to be a bit bolder in my approach. I parked by the building works for the new doctors' surgery in the village, and approached the house from the southwest.

It was raining again so I used my turned-up collar and hat as a disguise, as before. I kept the brim low and used my thumb stick to keep my footing on the slippery bridle paths, which had been churned up around the grange by recent traffic. Tina was an excellent ratter and defender of chickens; I have seen her get the better of a fox that had a fifty-yard head start. She was a loyal, faithful animal, and generally as obedient as terriers get, but she was a crap detective. Lying in wait just wasn't her thing - she wanted to dig at rabbit holes and chase sticks. So all I managed was a good walk around the edge of the fields and back over to my wrecked caravan.

I shut her inside and told her to stay, hoping she wouldn't choose to escape through the broken windows. I also gave her half the pork pie I had smuggled from Sandy's kitchen. By the time I had got back to my hiding-place behind the fallen oak tree she was waiting for me. I managed a few minutes of spying and found out very little apart from the fact that there seemed to be a fair few people about, and that the brown Jeep was still there. Then I gave it up as a bad job and went back to Sandy's.

Sandy was in the lounge for a change, wearing a silk kimono and toe post sandals while reclining on the antique buttoned-leather and sipping sherry. When I came in she was flicking through a glossy magazine - *Country Living.* She tossed it casually onto the low table between us. The woman on the cover had an ash blond flick, framed by wild flowers, and the captions below the title heralded an article about bringing back Brimstone butterflies as well as an interview with the now legendary Mike Harding, comedian and folk singer extraordinaire. Life in the fast lane, I thought, with a sigh. I had to sit and catch my breath at the hectic scene.

'What have you been up to then, Frankie?' she enquired.

'Getting wet and arguing with your stupid dog.'

'It was nice of you to take her out. She enjoys a good walk.'

'It was, wasn't it?' I replied, unable to contain my frustration at my lack of progress. 'Where is everyone?'

'Michael has gone with Jenny and Liza to the Merry Hill Shopping Centre.'

Well, I thought, *whether it's money from my stash or his, he's still paying - so enjoy it, girls.* I hoped that they were keeping their end of the deal.

'They will be gone for hours,' Sandy continued. 'They're buying swimwear for the pool tomorrow. The weather is supposed to pick up. Then he's taking them on to a restaurant for dinner.'

I could do with a swim myself, I thought, imagining them laughing and splashing. It was a daydream that was destined to be short-lived. Sandy had risen and was slipping her silk kimono to the foot-thick Axminster carpet. Then she shuffled off in her scanties, swinging her hips and sliding her sandals on the floor.

'I'll run you a hot bath,' she said over her shoulder.

I stood, swallowed her sherry, and drooled after her. At least one of us knew how to follow orders - unlike the girls and that stupid mutt.

I focused on Sandy's shapely derrière as we made our way through the house. That may sound sexist, lecherous even, but actually I just didn't want to get lost. I get confused in large buildings and tend to break into a cold sweat if I'm deprived of the sight of the great outdoors for any length of time. Focusing on something helps me to relax - and nothing holds your attention quite like a beautiful woman, does it?

We climbed to a rather large bedroom at the top of the house. The smaller adjoining one been converted to an en-suite, with a large roll-topped cast-iron bath in the centre of its polished wooden floor. Sandy turned on the taps and water thundered into the deep bath, into which she poured a lavish dose of menthol Badedas.

'I could get used to this, you know, love,' I told her, brightening as I stripped. 'Why don't you kick Michael into touch? And I'll move in.' I laughed then sank onto the edge of the four-poster and watched her through the open door, swirling the bubbles with her hands before slipping her miniscule garments off and climbing into the bath.

'Come on in, Frankie.' She beckoned me to the tub with a crooked index finger, smirking. 'I'll scrub your back.'

'Only my back?' I replied with a grin as I slipped a little too enthusiastically into the deep water to join her, splashing the polished floor. My God, don't women like their baths hot - how do they stand it?

After a few minutes I was lobster-like but becoming acclimatised and enjoying the warmth and the company. It had been a long time since I'd soaked in a bath. I flopped back, resting my head on the edge, with Sandy doing her best to get me going with her inquiring toes.

'Go and get the sherry, love,' I told her. 'We can have a drink in bed.'

She climbed out and went to get it, trailing bubbles behind her.

So, the will-she-won't-she phase of our relationship was over and we were relaxed enough to make a few assumptions. It wasn't long before we were settling on the bed together, sipping at the sherry and chatting. Apparently Michael was away a lot these days, and I was always welcome.

'I'm glad to hear it,' I said.

I finished my drink and lay back in the middle of the bed with my eyes closed. Sandy worked on me, trying to get me interested, which of course I was - I was enjoying the attention. She threw one leg over my chest and wriggled her hips. I kept my eyes closed and tried my utmost to ignore her.

And that's how we spent the afternoon. We began with her holding onto the corner posts, astride my face. Then she moved down, giving me room to breathe, and impaled herself in a few eager thrusts. We finished with her kneeling and gripping the headboard and me gripping her hips from behind. Finally we dozed for an hour or two.

The idyll ended when I heard something outside, upon which I dressed hurriedly and ran back to the lounge, sherry and glasses in hand. I had to try several doors on the way and was beginning to panic at the sound of car doors slamming and the front door opening. I made it just in time, throwing myself into an easy chair and, in the first gloom of evening, doing my best to look as if I had been there for hours.

Michael came in first, looking suspiciously from me to the silk kimono on the floor and asking where Sarah was. 'Taking a bath and a nap,' I told him. He went off upstairs to check on her. Liza and Jenny had gone straight to the kitchen. I could hear them laughing through the open door, and then the sound of a slap on bare skin.

'Ouch, you bitch,' I heard Liza yelp. 'That hurt.'

Jenny was laughing again. 'Sorry, I couldn't stop myself. You've got such a smackable bum.' More laughter followed.

Naked girls trying on bikinis - *mmm*, the thought was appealing, but my mind was made up. So before they could finish whatever they were doing and come in, I had slipped out of the room, through the front door, and off into the night.

My plan had always been a simple one - to find out as much as I could about the comings and goings at the hall and, if I could, sneak in and have a nosey around. Then, before the deadline Marcus had set, I would simply walk in, armed with whatever information I'd found, and offer my services as per our arrangement - like Daniel going into the lion's den.

It was fairly obvious that I was going to find out more from the inside-out than I had from the outside-in. My exterior snooping was primarily to find a safe getaway route should the need arise - in my experience even the cleverest plans seldom work.

I parked back up on the ridge, stopping to listen to the weather forecast on the radio, then camouflaged the car and worked my way back round to my vantage point under the hedge. I lay still and watched for what seemed like hours until one by one the lights faded from the windows. When I'd judged the timing of the security patrols I sprinted to the stables, keeping close to the wall to avoid making too much noise on the gravel. I managed to keep just inside the blind spot of the sensors on the security lights and found the door at the top of the stairs unlocked.

I stepped furtively in and closed the door behind me, slipping the bolt against anyone who might follow. With my back against the door I closed my eyes and took deep breaths to steady my nerves and to let my eyes become accustomed to the almost complete darkness in the long low corridor. I broke into a sweat at the close proximity of the walls and ceiling, so I fished around in my pockets and found the tiny torch from Michael's tool kit. It had an advertising slogan printed on one side. I twisted its top to produce a fine beam of light. The corridor seemed to go on for miles, though I knew it was only a couple of hundred feet or so.

I felt a little dizzy, and the floor seemed as if it was coming up to meet me, but I pressed on. I made the most of my resolve and nosed around in the few offices near the door, but no evidence jumped out at me. I didn't even know what I was looking for. I tried the inner door that led into the old half of the house - locked - and then slipped back down the stone stairs and to the door below. There was no internal route between the first floor and the stables so this was my most concealed point of entry, and it was still locked. I collected the shovel that always stood near the ancient stone drinking trough next to the archway, and used it as a lever to open the door. After taking up the strain I counted to three under my breath and then jerked the handle. The old rim lock gave way with a crack. I narrowly missed dropping the shovel onto the stone floor.

A dog barked somewhere behind me so I slipped inside, taking the shovel with me, and slid the inner bolts shut. Again, I leant back against the door, eyes shut, once more trying to regain my composure and my night vision. After a minute or two the security men crunched up to the door and tried it. I heard mumbled words as matches flared and cigarettes were lit, and then the voices receded slowly into the darkness.

I opened my eyes. I was still clutching the shovel with white knuckles, so I leant it against the door. Then, using my little torch, shielding its beam with my hand, I looked around. I was in the first section of Liza's workshop. Everything seemed comfortable and familiar, just as when I had been there last. Test castings for a commemorative horse brass were still lying where Liza had left them, in a neat row on the workbench. Next to them was a half-finished headboard. She had been recovering it for a friend, I remembered; her presence surrounded me and gave me confidence as I pressed on.

I passed Liza's carpentry room and came out into the large open storage area, where I turned my torch off and trusted my knowledge of the room to guide me. That turned out to be a mistake; I walked straight into a long low car and fell onto the bonnet with a thud. After rolling onto the floor I lay still, my heart thumping, but no alarms or voices sounded, and no dogs barked, so I risked my torch.

The place was crammed with sports cars: a Ferrari - no, two Ferraris - a Lamborghini, an old Mercedes with gull wing doors, an E-type Jaguar and a couple I didn't recognise. But these weren't the pristine museum or showroom models you would have expected from an investment syndicate. One was a burnt-out wreck; another had rolled onto its roof in a collision and had blood stains on its tan leather seats. Others had windows smashed and parts stripped - in short, expensive scrap.

I moved on to the stables before my courage ran out and found stalls occupied by lame and aged horses. I switched the torch on again and met the wall-eyed stare of a painted pony. I dropped the torch in fear as its milky eyes fixed me and it startled me with a loud whinny. Panicking, I hurried to the door, throwing open the bolts and falling over the shovel with a clatter. My feet crunched on gravel. The yard was instantly flooded with light and shouts echoed all round me. I just kept on running, heading as fast as I could to my hiding place under the bushes, where I lay still and watched the commotion.

It gave me a real sense of the number of people in the house, as they all came rushing out. Marcus appeared and began bellowing orders. I counted five suited goons plus the two security men and four women, including the blonde from the Jeep. As well as these, there were several faces at the windows; I assumed they were syndicate members. Two of the ladies in the yard, apparently answering Marcus's calls, were dressed in an odd mixture of night attire and high heels - maybe, I speculated, they were there for the syndicate's entertainment?

The women eventually went back in and the men stood to receive further orders from Marcus. Then they searched around, shouting and banging for a while, before slowly drifting back inside.

As the night wore on into the small hours, doors opened and two of the ladies and three men left in a Bentley, followed closely by two of the goons in a Range Rover - again, syndicate members perhaps? It all got a bit boring after that so I decided to have a nap and see what comings and goings would transpire with the dawn.

And that's when my plan started to unravel.

Chapter 20

It was early morning; the sun poured over the edge of the hills to fill the world with its warming glow. I was woken by something tapping on the back of my head; I brushed the spot with my hand and then just ignored it. The sunlight made the insides of my eyelids glow.

Then the tapping came again, harder - hard enough to make me move.

'Not so fast, idiot.' I heard a deep, low chuckle that I recognised at once - Julian!

A hand grabbed my collar. I was dragged upright and then hauled along the bridle path towards the house, my feet barely touched the ground. I took a few wild swings and kicks, made no contact, and then felt another crack across the head with what turned out to be the twin barrels of a shotgun. I looked down the barrels for a moment and decided, despite my plan to hit Julian at the first opportunity, that I would give him a temporary reprieve.

'Look who I found lurking in the bushes, boss,' Julian bellowed when we reached the house. Voices sounded and footsteps hurried towards us.

'So you've decided to come after all,' said Marcus. 'Thank you, Julian. You can leave us now.'

Julian kicked me in the back of the leg, behind my knee, and sent me sprawling. I bit my tongue and I didn't hit him, though I could tell he was secretly quaking at the prospect.

'Hello, Marcus,' I stammered. 'Here I am, as arranged.'

'Quite. So what were you doing hiding under a hedge?' He looked me up and down as he spoke with a resigned expression that said *All par for the course with this scruff.*

'Just taking a nap. I arrived early and didn't want to disturb you.'

'So that wasn't you causing a commotion in the middle of the night?' he asked, with a raised eyebrow.

I shook my head a little too vigorously to be entirely convincing.

'No matter, you're here now, Frankie, so we might as well make use of you.' He walked away, turning to beckon me like an errant dog. 'Come along.'

I followed, head down. He led me straight to Liza's workshop.

'Let's get down to business, shall we?' he said. 'I suppose you're wondering what I want from you.'

I nodded, tongue-tied as always in the presence of an authority figure.

'As you know, Liza's absence means she is unable to fulfil

her commitments at the moment, and she may be incapacitated for some time to come.' He added the last bit with that habitual sneer of his; I clenched my fists in my pockets but kept shtum. He carried on. 'So that's what I want you to do. Keep up appearances.' I gave him a puzzled look. He responded with an exasperated shake of the head. 'Finish her outstanding jobs, fend off visitors to the workshop, and so on - just until our scheme comes to fruition. Do you think you can manage that?' He asked the question with patronising sarcasm. 'Good,' he said, not waiting for an answer. 'I'll leave Julian with you in case you change your mind. *Ciao.*' And with that he swivelled on his heels and marched away.

My old Gran used to say that anything that seems too good to be true usually is, and this was one of those occasions. I could see how keeping Liza's commitments would create the impression of normality - all the more so with me on the case - but was it worth a big bag of cash, plus the deeds to my plot? Answer: *No.* There had to be a catch, so my new task was to find out what it was.

Julian kept watch outside the door, occasionally chatting to the other goons on his walkie-talkie, arranging cover while he went off for a smoke, or whatever it was he did. I started by tidying up, sweeping the floor and workbenches, and then looking in the diary to see what jobs were due when.

I was getting pretty hungry so I asked Julian what time breakfast would be. 'Leave it with me,' he said and after what seemed like hours, though it was in all fairness only minutes, a woman in a black-and-white, waitress-cum-maid uniform came tottering over the gravel. She was doing her best to look dignified while trying to avoid twisting her ankles in her high heels. She had a nice shape, though with the sun behind her I couldn't see her face, so I just watched and waited. When she arrived I opened the door with a flourish and gestured her inside. Then I turned and heeled it shut in Julian's face before he had time to follow. She placed a tray on the bench just inside the door - a teapot, milk jug, toast rack, and a plate with a silver cover.

I tore my eyes away from her curves and walked over to turn on the gas for the forge. It ignited with a pop. 'Thank you, love,' I called, without looking back.

'Aren't you even going to say hello, Frankie?'

I turned with a start. *Lydia!* I was shocked, to say the least. 'What are you doing here?' I blurted out.

'The same as you, Frankie - just earning my keep.'

'Of course you are.' I gave her a mocking sneer - I'd been practising it, but I doubt it was a patch on Marcus's.'

'Don't be like that, Frankie. There are lots of things you don't know.' I noticed a softness in her expression that I had never seen before as I nodded agreement; I was definitely at a loss. At that moment Julian opened the door and looked in with a head motion that said 'out'; Lydia wobbled away on her heels. Obviously her duties didn't usually include providing for those in serfdom in the stables or she would get more suitable shoes. It certainly didn't seem like she had her feet under the table. It was more like she was enslaved like me - otherwise, Julian might have shown her a little more respect. Before he went out again Julian leaned in, took the cover off my plate, and nicked one of my sausages - but that's not when I hit him.

I investigated my surroundings. I found that the door that led into the big archway and the stables beyond was secured from the other side. The windows were opaque and barred with ancient ironwork against intruders. I was effectively a prisoner. Mind you, with the tools in the workshop I could have broken out pretty much anywhere I chose, even through the walls. The easy route would have been up into the rooms above, as all that separated me from them were the oak floorboards, and in places you could see light coming through them from the corridor above. I could even have kicked open the stable doors that had been screwed shut, as they had no use in the space that was now Liza's workshops. But if I did, what would I do? Escape? After going to such great lengths to get in? I decided to keep my head down, bide my time and see what I could suss out.

I had another look through the books, trying to find something to help pass the time. There were a few upholstery jobs, which frankly I'm rubbish at. I can scrape along as a reasonable labourer to assist Liza, but that's about it. Fortunately she appeared to have cut and sewn the fabrics for a few pieces of furniture, so all I had to do was fit it and nail it into place well enough to pass inspection until it left the workshop.

The metalwork and woodwork jobs I was a bit better at, so decided as much as possible to focus on them. When I was working with Liza I usually complained about how much she relied on me, telling her how she couldn't cope without me. But isn't it funny how quickly you realise how much you need someone when they aren't there?

A few days went by in this fashion without me learning much more. I was supplied with a camp bed and allowed supervised toilet visits and ablutions, courtesy of the charming Julian, as well as refreshments provided by the delightful Lydia, who appeared more tempting by the day. She was my one link to the bigger picture so I made it my primary mission to find a way to talk to her.

My chance came, eventually, when Julian for some reason wasn't there. I don't know where or why he wasn't - it wasn't my place to be informed about such things and much as I pressed his replacement, Tommy, for info he kept mum. Tommy was a more likeable bloke, with a boxer's profile, heavy brow, and shaven head. I learned that he trained with Julian and was a keen semi-pro boxer, so I decided not to hit him, not if I didn't have to. Julian, heavyweight or not, remained top of my list.

'He's a big lad, isn't he?' I quipped as I worked.

'Who, Julian?' replied Tommy.

I nodded.

'Yes,' Tommy agreed, 'and a bad-tempered bastard. It's the drugs.'

'Drugs?'

'Yes, all sorts - steroids, amphetamines and those growth hormone enhancers. GHB?'

I shook my head, lost.

'I'd keep out of his way if I were you.'

I grimaced. 'That's just what I was planning to do.'

Tommy brought in a little transistor radio and we listened to a local station, Beacon Radio 303, and sang along to the latest hits. It reminded me of happy days with Liza. I could picture her clawing the air and hissing along to 'Love cats' by The Cure; and as gaoler/gaolee relationships go it was pretty amicable. Tommy had noticed me giving Lydia the glad eye and teased me about it. He reckoned I ought to get Marcus to throw her into my deal for a few nights, as she was 'one of his tarts'. This unpleasant news was still music to my ears, as it proved she really was in the same boat as me and maybe could be called upon to become my one and only ally in the place.

One afternoon I was working at finishing the run of commemorative brasses for the Heavy Horse Society. I made a sand mould with one of the little wooden patterns Liza had skilfully carved in one of the boxes she had equally carefully dovetailed, and then melted a small amount of brass in a crucible over the forge. I could have gone faster, making, say, half a dozen or more at a time, but I was doing them one by one as I only had the upholstery left to do, and I needed to spin things out as long as I could.

Lydia had started by delivering breakfast then collecting the breakfast things at lunchtime and so on, but after a few days we developed a new routine, which meant her waiting while I finished each meal. We took the opportunity to indulge in slightly flirtatious small talk while Tommy stood outside and turned a blind eye.

On this particular day I was taking my time over lunch - a new habit, in contrast to my usual practice of wolfing down everything in sight.

'Here, love,' I said. 'I made this for you.' I gave her a ring I had cast in brass with a little horseshoe motif.

'It's lovely,' she said, trying it on.

To be honest, it wasn't. It was an amateurish mess, but chocolates and flowers were out of the question, weren't they? I'd resisted a heavy come-on, as I knew this just wasn't the way to go with Lydia. In fact, with my knowledge of her history with Jenny, I couldn't be altogether sure I wasn't barking up the wrong tree entirely.

She seemed genuinely pleased by the ring. Perhaps she saw it as a small act of friendship and normality in a world that had gone crazy. Who knows?

'I'll have to get *you* something now,' she said, holding her hand out for a better look and beaming.

'I could always use some supper,' I replied with a wink. 'It's a long time between dinner and breakfast.'

'I'll see what I can do,' she said, a trifle suggestively, and then she kissed me on the cheek.

I had never got on with Lydia that well. When she'd first been introduced to me as Jenny's partner, she'd seemed snobby and standoffish, but lately she'd grown on me. She was really a pleasant woman; it seemed the initial coldness she had shown me was just born of her fear of my closeness to Jenny. There was a soft, almost frail, gentility to her words and actions that made it impossible for me to believe that she could be on the inside of this scam, so I decided to ask her about it, though it was a subject we had avoided so far.

'So what brings you here then?' I asked, then qualified the question by adding, 'Are you mixed up in all this?' She seemed reluctant to answer, so I decided to push her a little. 'Jenny said you'd dumped her for some bloke. Was it Marcus?'

That did it. The claws came out. 'She *did*, did she? The deceitful bitch. It was *Jenny* who dumped *me*.'

'That's not how I heard it,' I goaded her, and she loosened up and told me her version of the way things had gone.

'We were working at a bar in Cyprus, in Paphos, down by the castle on the harbour.'

'Where the posh folks moor their yachts, I suppose?'

'Yes,' she continued. 'That's how I first got to know it, on sailing holidays with my parents years ago. It's a lovely place and we did a bit of everything - cooking, cleaning and, of course, entertaining; we virtually ran the place for the old Cyprian couple who owned it.'

'Sounds idyllic,' I said. 'So what happened?'

'They sold up, behind our backs. I don't think we could have afforded to buy it anyway, but it would have been nice to have been asked, after all our hard work, wouldn't it?' I nodded and encouraged her to continue. 'Well, that was when Marcus entered the picture, him and his snooty wife. I knew her from school - you know the sort, always looking at you but just to check if you are looking at her, you know?' Again I nodded. 'Well, Jenny and her hit it off like a house on fire - all night parties, drugs, drink, she just went wild.'

'Wait a minute,' I said, holding my head and pacing the room to try and clear my thoughts. 'You mean they knew each other in Cyprus? Before Jenny came back here?'

'Yes.'

'Jenny and Liza - you're sure?'

'Yes, Frankie, positive.'

Remember when I said I felt like I had been had? A mug? This was where it all fitted together! 'Carry on, love, tell me everything,' I implored.

She warmed to her task and filled in the details. 'Well, I was getting pretty fed up of it all. We were supposed to be together and then I found them in bed. I was horrified but Jenny just laughed and asked me to join them.'

'You mean, *in bed*, in bed?' I said with a serious look.

'What else would I mean?'

'But I thought you two were an item?'

'So did I,' came her reply. 'Until that bitch came along

and spoiled everything. It broke my heart.' She slumped onto the bench and sniffed, fighting back the tears.

'I'm sorry, love,' I said and took her hands in mine.

'It's ok,' she replied. 'It's the drugs - they turn people into monsters. I hate them.'

That made two of us. I'd had my own share of dealing with the after-effects of illicit drugs. She leant her head on my shoulder.

'It's not your fault, Frankie.'

Her forgiveness made me feel guilty for the passion I'd often shared with Jenny while they were together. It all made sense now; I'd been a fool, hadn't I? I bet *you* knew all along, didn't you? Well, I was in too deep to turn back now and, despite everything, they were still my friends. I loved them both. And what is more natural than the two people you love, loving each other? So why then had they deceived me? To protect me? To save my feelings? It was all I could think of - and if it was true they had certainly gone a funny way about doing it, leaving me here in slavery and them living it up in Sandy's pool. I was still lost but just as determined.

'So why are you here, then?' I asked.

'I slept with Marcus out of spite, and he got me to courier his drugs. I got caught and he bailed me out and brought me here. The police are looking for me so I have no choice but to stay.' Her eyes were wet and her voice was thick with emotion. 'He makes me do whatever he says.'

I sat next to her and put my arm around her shoulders. 'So when did you come back to England?'

'Ages ago. I was back before Jenny.'

'And you've been working here all that time?' I asked, and she nodded. 'So it was you who locked the window in Liza's room the night she fell?'

She pushed my arm away and nodded again, then she stood up, avoiding my gaze. 'I have to go,' she whispered tearfully. She picked up the tray and hurried out through the door.

I worked on in sullen silence for an hour or two. I was gathering damsels in distress faster than Sir Galahad and there wasn't a suit of armour in sight.

Eventually, Tommy put his head round the door. 'What's up, Frankie? You look like someone shot your puppy.'

'Close, Tom.'

'Listen, mate,' he continued, 'I'm off. My mate Shane is covering tonight. He's all right, so don't worry. Here, I'll leave you this.' He handed me his little transistor radio.

'Cheers, mate.'

I smiled, we shook hands, and he left.

I turned the radio up as loud as its little speakers would go and worked on, my blood boiling at all the treachery. My anger was making me clumsy with the castings, which made me even more irritable. As I pulled the little wooden pattern from the compacted sand I slipped and ruined the mould. I slammed my fist into the sand, then went and sat on the bench where Lydia had been. It was all a mess and I felt hopeless. My plan was in tatters and my reasons for being there were in serious doubt. I needed inspiration and could find none.

At that moment the door rattled open and Lydia stepped in, a bottle of brandy in one hand and Swiss chocolates in the other. Her uniform was gone, replaced by a dressing gown and slippers.

'I hope you don't mind, Frankie. I need some company.'

'Of course not, love.' I beamed and took her hand. Then I led her through the doorway and bolted it, locking us in my little prison. 'Wait here,' I said. 'I've got something to finish.'

And off I went, pumping up the forge with the old leather bellows and melting brass, then knocking out the mould and dropping the hot metal hissing into the water vat beside the forge. When I had finished I went back to Lydia and kissed her, not on the cheek, but on the lips, and she kissed me back, her tongue finding mine. The irony of it struck me - Jenny's two 'ex's' alone together - but what could be more natural than people who were loved, loving each other?

I slipped the dressing gown off Lydia's shoulders as she leant back against the workbench, exposing the bare skin beneath. I kissed her face, her neck, her chest, then I sank to my knees so that her breasts were at face level and gave her nipples a playful nip that made her gasp. I then carried on down her belly, running the tip of my tongue around the rim of her navel and still further down, until she threw her head back and uttered a faint moan - a cue to continue if ever I heard one. She grabbed my hair and stood on tiptoes, thrusting her hips against my probing tongue.

I pushed her back onto the bench and stood over her as she lay back, smiling up at me. She sighed and reached for me and I lifted her calves to my shoulders. Then, placing my palm on her pubis and with my fingers spread on the firm flatness of her belly, I slipped my thumb gently between her labia and massaged her close to climax before entering her.

Later we sipped brandy, ate chocolates, and slept on the floor, huddled together under my open sleeping bag, enjoying the warmth of the forge.

Next morning Julian kicked the door open. 'Get some clothes on, slut - you're wanted!' He dragged Lydia out by a handful of her lovely blonde hair while she struggled to keep her dressing gown closed.

Believe it or not, that's still not when I hit him.

Chapter 21

With Julian back, my daily routine reverted to what it had been before, Lydia bringing in my tray and plonking it down in silence while my oafish guardian leered at her. He'd taken to groping her as she bent to open the door or slapping her bottom as she walked away; he also made suggestive comments that often left tears in her eyes.

One day Lydia arrived a little early while Julian was off smoking, or whatever he went to do, and Shane was covering for him. He let her in with a courteous nod and then gave me a wink when she stepped inside, after which he pulled the door shut behind her.

'Lydia,' I exclaimed, throwing my arms around her, 'let me get you out of here. We have to go - now!' I should add, mind you, that I had no idea how this feat was to accomplished.

'No,' she said, 'it will be ok.'

'Do you really think so, love?'

'Yes,' she said, brightening. 'It won't be much longer. It'll all be over soon now.' I shook my head, puzzled, and she hastened to explain. 'Marcus has promised to sort everything out. He can get the charges dropped. They're going to give me my own little cottage. It's being rebuilt now, across the field, on the other side of the stream. You can come and stay with me if you like.'

Despite the irony, I put on my best smile. 'Sure, I'd love to,' I told her. 'You'd better go before he gets back. I'm going to try and persuade him to let me see you again.'

'I'd like that. Good luck, Frankie.' She kissed me hurriedly. I don't know how, but I found my hand unexpectedly on her thigh. She pushed it away and straightened her skirt. 'Cheeky.' She winked and walked away, her head held high and with a bit more bounce in her step than I had seen for a while.

Once she was gone, I tried to concentrate on finding my way out of this mess. I needed to see Jenny and Liza *now* to try and make some sense of this. Everyone had an angle - something to gain or something to give - except me. I suppose the best thing you can do in situations like that is work with what you've got, so I kept my head down and plodded on. I decided to make a truce with Julian. I couldn't hope to beat him in a fight - I was at too great a disadvantage, what with my problems with bright lights, enclosed spaces, corridors, labels, authority figures, and crowds. Being pleasant to unappealing strangers didn't come naturally to me but, like I said, you have to work with what you've got...

The pattern continued, Lydia playing serving-wench and stoically enduring Julian's unwelcome attentions. There was *one* small difference, however - *me*. Usually the door was half open, providing a welcome draught of fresh air to offset, a little, the heat of the forge and to provide Julian with a means of keeping an eye on me. One lunchtime, as Lydia walked away with the tray, I decided to use it to try and get Julian on my side as we both gazed after her through the open door. 'She's gorgeous, isn't she?'

'She certainly is,' said Julian, with a little whistle past the match he was chewing.

'And she's great in the sack,' I told him. 'A real animal. You know when kids write in the dirt on lorries?'

He turned with a look of interest. 'Yes?'

'Well - she is.'

'Is what?'

'That dirty,' I replied with a laugh.

The big thug's shoulders bobbed as he chuckled along with me.

'Yes,' I assured him, 'she's up for anything, that one.'

'I might pick her yet,' he grunted with a last leer at her as she disappeared into the house.

'You could do worse,' I added, pretending to know what he was talking about.

I returned to trying to work out how to set the temperature and timer on Liza's pottery kiln for another job in her books. You know when I said I could cope with keeping up with most stuff except for the upholstery? Well,

I lied. I'm even worse with pottery - I haven't got a clue, though don't tell Liza that…

I gave up on the kiln and decided to stretch the work on the brasses out as long as I could. 'You have to give it to Marcus,' I shouted to Julian over the roar of the forge, 'he's got some fantastic birds.'

Julian took the bait. 'When this is all over Marcus says I can have my pick of the lot as a bonus,' Julian answered. 'I was going to go for your Gypo - she's got a lovely chubby ass.' He described a curvy outline in the air with his huge hands. 'But I might change me mind yet.'

I nodded approvingly. 'Yes, mate, you'd be better off with Lydia. She knows the score, that one. Why have a bird that spits when you can have one that swallows?'

Julian slapped his thigh and roared with laughter. 'You is all reet, ya know, Frankie.' He gave me a broad smile.

I carried on messing about doing my best to look busy until the tea tray arrived. Julian eyed Lydia with a beady stare, taking in every stitch of her clothing and every inch of her lithe form. I beckoned her closer and pulled her towards me, holding her tightly round the waist and kissing her passionately.

'Don't,' she said, flicking her eyes at Julian.

'Don't worry, love, he's ok.'

She looked doubtful and pecked me back before leaving with her tray.

'So is she part of *your* deal, then?' Julian asked after she had gone.

'No, mate, I just helped myself.'

'How do you do it, man? The women here all do what Marcus say; I never see any of 'em give it away.'

'Well, you've either got it or you haven't,' I joked. He laughed again.

I opened a bag of clay and messed with lumps of the stuff. It was no use, I didn't know where to start. I decided to make a few extra brasses to fill in the time. As dinner grew closer, I went over and leant on the door-frame.

'I'm hungry.'

'She'll be here soon, man,' Julian said.

'No, I don't mean that, you pillock - *hungry*. You know.' He was lost. I decided to try a different tack. 'I tell you what, how about we make a deal?'

'It depends what the deal is, Frankie.'

That was better than a flat 'no' so I pressed on. 'You help me out, and I help you out.' He was leaning into the conversation, looking interested. 'Why wait for Marcus to let you have her? I can help you out. You can have her any time you like, as long as you don't mind it a bit rough,' I added with a wink.

'That's just how I like it,' he muttered, with another deep chuckle. I give him a blow-by-blow account of my recent encounter with Lydia. I know I said a gentleman never tells, but I've never been accused of being a gentleman.

'So what's the deal, then?' asked Julian and I filled him in.

I had my chance. I could distract Julian and, while he had his hands full, leg it. There was no point in me staying any longer after all. The big man swallowed it whole and we shook on it. When Lydia came with the supper, I pulled her inside and closed the door. Julian grinned, content to leave us together for a few minutes as arranged.

'That Julian gives me the creeps,' said Lydia. 'He raped one of the girls in the house!'

'Really, love?'

'Yes, she was new and she'd got drunk to face going with some seedy bloke Marcus wanted to impress. While she was sleeping it off that bastard tied her to the bed.'

'What did Marcus do?'

'Nothing,' she answered. 'He just demoted him and sent him out here to guard you.'

'Don't worry, love. You're safe here with me. I have a plan. We can be together tomorrow night - Julian is off and I've arranged everything.'

She looked pensive. 'I don't know, Frankie. What if we get caught again? I don't want to get beaten and raped like that poor girl. He made a real mess of her. It's my worst nightmare.' There were tears in her eyes.

'We won't get caught, love,' I told her in a rush. 'Trust me, it's all arranged. Just wear some flat shoes when you come over with the dinner, so you don't make too much noise on the gravel.'

She sniffed and nodded consent. Shortly afterwards she left, shooting me a last nervous smile.

So, Marcus had something over us all - Lydia was a drug smuggler, I was an armed robber, and Julian was a rapist. I knew that I'd been set up, and probably Lydia had been too, maybe even Julian. I wondered what secrets the other 'staff' had to hide.

The next day went much as planned. Marcus sent a lovely redhead over from the house to ask about the horse brasses, as someone had been on the phone panicking about them.

'I'll have them ready in the morning,' I said, with a charming smile, and as she left I threw half a dozen of them back in the crucible to melt. I'd already made them all twice over and was scraping the barrel for something to fill the time. At dinner Julian let Lydia in and then made himself scarce as arranged. We chatted and drank the wine she'd brought.

I slipped the pill Julian had supplied into her glass and she reacted much as he'd said she would, becoming all floppy and agreeable. I kept up the pretence, kissing her and teasing her to give it time to work, then I slipped my hand in her knickers and felt the relaxed state the drug had induced in her muscles - she was ready for anything.

I carried her over to my sleeping bag on the floor and playfully tied her hands to the legs of the kiln. She squirmed and moaned; her pupils gave me the dilated look of total submission that I was waiting for. So, wracked with guilt, I opened the door and whistled Julian.

I know what you're thinking, and yes, I am a heartless bastard, abusing the trust of the 'weak and needy'. But so fucking what! I needed a way out and this was it. You have to work with what you've got, remember?

'She's all yours, mate,' I said. 'I'll have my turn later.'

He grinned and stood over her, taking off his shirt and dropping his trousers. Then he pulled the belt from the loops and lashed her across her exposed thighs.

'You've got it coming, bitch!' he hissed at her and, despite her drugged state, she started screaming.

'Don't worry, mate - I'll shut her up.' I knelt next to her and placed my hand over her mouth as she kicked and struggled. Julian laughed and dropped his boxer shorts with an evil leer.

I stood and watched; her kicks were barely registering on his muscular frame. He grinned as he grabbed her ankles and flipped her over, face down, then he began to lower himself to his knees between her legs. She kicked him hard and he turned to me, shouting. 'Hold the bitch still, will you - I thought you were going to shut her up?'

And *that* is when I hit him.

I dragged my fist from the water vat in a glittering arc.

My homemade brass knuckles made contact with his ribs with a crunch. He buckled and finished the journey to his knees with a groan. I held his head back by his braided hair and smashed my armoured fist into his face. Then, as his eyes rolled trying to focus on me, I hit him once more to make sure he was out of the game, the third and last time. I let go and his unconscious form flopped to the floor with a thud.

'Weak and needy,' I mouthed as I dropped the lump of cold brass onto his chest.

I gathered up the now semi-conscious Lydia, tugging the slipknot free from the kiln, bundled her into my sleeping bag, and slung it over my shoulder. Then I stepped outside and set off into the night.

Chapter 22

It was raining hard as I stepped outside and, forgetting myself, I stepped a little too far from the wall. The security lights came on with a clunk, their halogen brilliance dazzling me. I made it to the hedge and stumbled along as fast as I could, trying to shut my eyes for a second or two as I fought to regain my night vision. I heard a dog barking behind us but I didn't dare look back at the blinding lights - I just put my head down and kept going.

I came to the spot with the ash saplings, the spot where Julian had captured me, and crawled under the hedge and out the other side. I had to drag the sleeping bag through and over a few roots. Lydia moaned pitifully from inside. 'Not far now, love,' I whispered sympathetically as I humped her back over my shoulder and ran on.

I now had the cover of the hedge and my night vision was improving, though the rain was coming down steadily and the muddy ground was starting to squelch under my boots. I startled some night-feeding mammal, a badger I think, and it scuttled off, startling me in turn. A moment later I stumbled and dropped Lydia. She cried out, but I couldn't quite make out what she said. I didn't bother to wait for her to make a second attempt to speak; I just dragged her up onto my shoulder again and carried on.

We made good time until we got to the slope down to the stream and disaster struck. I lost my footing in the mud on the steep bank - *again*. I tried to hang on to Lydia as we rolled down to the bridge, narrowly missing the water - well, at least *I* missed it. Lydia wasn't so lucky. With a sickening thud the sleeping bag hit the edge of the steel frame and then rolled with a splash into the stream, which was swollen by the heavy summer rain. I scrambled in after it and managed to drag it up the far bank. Lydia wasn't making a sound. I was a wreck, gibbering nonsense and sobbing, as I stumbled on through the rain.

My plan had been to head for the ridge and my camouflaged Suzuki, if it was still there. Thinking on my feet - or, rather, on my knees in the mud - I decided on my wrecked caravan instead. After heaving Lydia in through a broken window, I unzipped the dripping bag and uncovered her on the moonlit floor.

The rain was still tipping down, beating on the roof like peas on a drum, and she wasn't moving. She lay naked, wet and cold, with a deep gash on her forehead above her hair line. The water and blood had mixed together and plastered her hair to her face; I did my best to wipe it away from her eyes and held my head to her chest, hoping to hear her heart beat. But I couldn't hear anything over the noise of the rain. I tried to see if her breath was moving her chest, but the flickering shadows of the hazels blown by the wind were playing tricks, and I was getting in more and more of a panic.

I decided to cover her over with the few scraps that came to hand, and to leave her. You're shocked? But what else could I do? I scrambled up the ridge and back to my hidden transport. I tried the key. The engine hesitated for a moment. I tried again, and again. The starter motor was getting more sluggish with every attempt. I started screaming at it, 'Come on, *come on!*' I had no chance; the battery was dead. Some idiot had left the radio on.

Now, I could have bump-started it, if I'd had someone to push, but pushing a vehicle with chunky off-road tyres on rough ground, in the dark and wet, on my own, just wasn't going to work.

In the distance I could see a glow around the house as more lights came on and then the beams of headlights pierced the darkness. Desperate now, I scrambled out and unreeled the cable from the winch. It was powered by a separate battery, which, I discovered later, had a cut-off switch to start the engine in an emergency. I dragged it downhill as far as it would reach and wrapped it round a thickish young tree, clipping it back onto itself. I didn't know if the tree would stand the strain but I was at the end of the cable and had no other choice; my mind was too befuddled to come up with a better plan. I took the handbrake off, put the gear lever in neutral, and stood back with the cable remote control in my hand. It was slow at first. Everything seemed to be creaking under the strain, including me. But as it overcame the friction of the tyres, dragging sideways through the soil and leaves, the front of the car slowly swung round and pointed downhill. A few more turns of the winch drum and it was off.

I had to leap out of the way as it nearly flattened me. 'Shit!' It just careered down the ridge, smashing bushes and bracken as it went. 'Shit, shit, shit!'

Then, with a jerk and a thud, the cable came to its end, running backwards under the car and out between the back wheels. The sapling buckled under the impact.

I ran and jumped onto the back of the car and bounced from side to side, hoping to break the already badly-damaged trunk of the young tree - but it held firm. I took out my pocket saw and went back, cutting through the trunk as far as I dared. As it started to twist and splinter I ran and jumped into the back as the car started its bumping, pounding, descent. I scrambled into the cab, slammed it into gear and slipped my foot off the clutch. The engine spluttered into life with a jerk that banged my chin on the steering wheel, drawing blood. I dipped the clutch and revved the engine, then I changed back into a more suitable gear for the speed and released the clutch to gain control before crossing the open field. I was praying I hadn't been seen as I careered through a gap in the hedge and out onto the road.

But what next? My gateway was blocked on the inside with immovable pallets of stone. I pulled up against the hedge, my caravan tantalisingly close on the other side. Leaving the engine running, I scrambled through, cutting and scratching myself in my desperation. I could hear the sound of dogs running loose and people shouting - they were getting nearer. I dragged Lydia's limp form through the window. She moaned again as she landed in a heap on the ground. Thank God, she was still alive!

I dragged the poor girl through the hedge by her ankles and dumped her in the back of the Suzuki before speeding off into the night. As I roared away, I could see headlights in my rear-view mirror; they were closing fast, so I took a hard right and smashed through a field gate. Then I headed back up and over the ridge with the lights turned off before heading left and back out onto the road. Then I floored it and, with the engine screaming and everything else rattling and grinding, I sped along the narrow country lanes in a final bid for safety. I was sobbing and crying out to Lydia as we went. 'Hold on, love - *please don't die!*'

If I'd been stopped by some eagle-eyed peeler at that point, all blue lights and bells, God knows how I'd have explained myself, with a half-dead woman, naked and bleeding and with her hands tied, in the back. I was also covered in Julian's blood, as well as caked in mud, and Sandy's little Suzuki was half wrecked and dragging a small tree snaking and bouncing in its wake.

Shortly afterwards, the battered little car limped back into Sandy's drive. I stashed it discreetly in the barn to protect us all from prying eyes and carried Lydia, covered with my jacket, into the summerhouse. I lay her on the lounger, locked the doors, and drew the curtains. She was cold and deathly white. I started massaging her limbs to bring some warmth and life back. She was breathing - that was good - and moaning - not so good maybe. How much of her stupor was due to the pill, and how much to the bang on the head, I'd no idea.

The bleeding from her head had almost stopped and the blood had crusted in her matted hair. I was tempted to cover her and let her sleep it off, but then I remembered overdose scenes in old films and decided to try and keep her awake.

I stripped my own rags off and carried her into the shower, where I propped her up and scrubbed her clean. Then I carried her, wrapped in a fluffy gown with a towel bound turban-like around her head, back to the lounger and covered her with blankets. I lit the fire, gave her sips of tepid water, and held her head, rocking her like a baby and humming songs to comfort her.

What the fuck had I done? My stupid plan had almost killed her! It was all too much for me. I was on the side of truth and justice, fighting the bad guys like the sheriff in the white hat in those old Saturday morning picture shows. Now it had all gone tits-up and I felt no better than one of the bad guys.

I rocked her until we both fell into a fitful sleep. I woke in the early hours to the sound of birds singing and Lydia stumbling out of the bathroom.

'What happened, Frankie?' she asked blearily.

'What do you remember, love?' I replied, rushing to steady her.

'We were drinking and talking, and then Julian was grabbing me and I was screaming, and then... and then... *nothing.*'

I breathed an inward sigh of relief. 'He came in when I popped out to the loo and tried to attack you, so I fought him off and we ran.' She held her hand to her head. 'You slipped in the dark and banged your head,' I explained helpfully.

She slumped down in a chair. 'I see,' she said, surprisingly calmly. Then she vomited over the polished wood floor.

I carried her back to the lounger and covered her up, trying to remember my schoolboy first aid - what are the symptoms of concussion? Then I had perhaps the best plan I'd come up with so far. I ran to the house and woke Sandy and Michael.

Sandy tried to grill me about where I'd been, I ignored her and took Michael to one side and mumbled a hasty explanation; he collected a black leather case and disappeared up to the summerhouse. I got Sandy working on breakfast and tea, to keep her occupied, and then followed Michael.

Lydia was naked on the lounger with Michael feeling every joint of every limb, squeezing and prodding as doctors do. He got her sticking her tongue out and saying 'ah'; he even looked down her ears with a little lens. He took her blood pressure, pulse, and temperature, then he flicked on a little torch - the same as the one I had stolen with his tools - and shone it in her eyes, though I didn't realise the significance of that until much later.

'She seems fine. Lots of superficial cuts and bruises, and perhaps the mildest of concussions; something we will have to keep an eye on. And she could do with a few stitches in that,' he said, pointing to her head. 'A nasty gash. I'll run her into the hospital if you like.'

'No,' I said. 'Can't you do it?'

'Well, I can,' he replied, 'but I would rather someone more suitably qualified took a look at her.'

'No, Michael, we trust you.'

He shrugged and pulled out a few things from his bag. 'I'll give her a local anaesthetic.'

'Hold on Michael, I need a word.' I grabbed his arm and dragged him outside. 'She's had a dose of GHB,' I explained.

'The date rape drug? She hasn't been... has she?' he asked, ashen faced. Then he started ranting. 'You've gone too far this time, Frankie!'

'It wasn't me-'

'Then who the hell-'

'Your bloody syndicate, that's who,' I white-lied to him. 'But don't worry, I saved her. All I need to know is this - will it clash with your injection?'

'I don't think so,' he said, 'but I can always run her into the hospital-'

'No,' I said, 'forget the anaesthetic. Just fix her up, please.'

And he did. She squirmed a bit at the pain of having stitches with no anaesthetic, while I held her still, but she was soon sleeping soundly. I gave Sandy some crap about her being hurt in a riding accident, which I'm sure she didn't believe, but - bless her - she rallied to the flag and nursed poor Lydia like a pro. I left her bustling and went to find Jenny and Liza.

Chapter 23

I walked over to the caravan and tried the door. It was open so I went straight in and put the kettle on with a clang.

'Good morning, ladies,' I chirped as they disengaged from a warm embrace. Jenny was looking a bit worried and Liza obviously blushing. I nodded towards the bed and caught Jenny's eye. 'Got room for a little 'un? I don't take up much space and I'm knackered.'

'Fuck off, Frankie,' came Jenny's defensive reply.

'Don't be like that, love,' I said, drawing the little stool up to the side of their bed. They might have been a bit surprised, but I wasn't - not any more. 'You ought to keep the door locked; you never know who might walk in.'

'Go away and leave us alone,' said Jenny, reaching for a discarded t-shirt.

'Don't be so mean,' I replied. 'Don't forget, what's mine is yours, and what's yours is mine.'

She gave me a disgruntled look and turned to Liza. I had my back to them now, rattling cups, but I saw them mouthing and gesturing in the mirrors.

'Where've you been then, Frankie?' demanded Liza, attempting to change the subject.

'On the nest, if I know him,' said Jenny. 'Shacked up with some tart, doing God knows what, God knows where.'

I laughed. 'Funny you should say that, love. That's exactly where I've been, and it's not only the big fella who knows her - you both do, as intimately as I do. Well, at least one of you does.' I continued to watch them in the mirrors and did my best to hear what they were whispering as I waited for the kettle to boil.

Jenny got up and started to close the wardrobe doors across the bedroom space.

'A bit late for modesty, don't you think?' I commented drily as I handed them cups of tea, deliberately forgetting the saucers, just to annoy Jenny. Well, she always told me that in relationships, tolerance was important, and so I decided to teach her some.

I grabbed the small bag of white powder from beside the bed as Jenny pushed the doors back, then walked outside with my tea, waiting to see what they would do. There was a brief silence then I could hear the pair of them dressing hurriedly, with hushed mumbles and rapid whispers. They stumbled through the door after me, with buttons done up wrong, t-shirts inside out, no socks, and hair quickly tied back.

'I've never seen either of you quite so eager to see me.' I was beaming and dangling the bag of powder carelessly in my left hand, revelling in the rare feeling of having the upper hand over not just one woman, but two.

'Stop being a fucking smart aleck and tell me what the hell is going on,' said Jenny.

'That's better.' I held the moment as long as I could. 'The Jenny I know and love is back with us at last.' I put down my cup and then, with a sweeping bow, offered my free hand to Liza to help her delicately down from the step where she stood just behind Jenny. She descended and gave me a nervous smile. 'Nice tooth!' I told her, inspecting Michael's work.

'Thanks,' she said, with a shy look at her feet.

Jenny revved up for the next round of verbal assault and made a grab for the bag, while Liza remained dumbstruck. I silenced her with my finger to her lips, holding the bag away at arm's length.

'Summerhouse, one o'clock sharp - be there,' I said and turned curtly away, ignoring the storm of abuse being hurled at me from behind.

My next stop was to assess the damage to Sandy's car. She would kill me when she clapped eyes on it - or maybe enjoy trying. I smirked as I walked around it. Michael could always buy her another one with the profits from his syndicate.

It was in a bit of a state, to be honest, with every panel battered and dented and the soft top ripped from end-to-end. I started at the top by removing and folding the roof; then I disentangled the winch cable and rewound it. After that I washed and cleaned the whole thing as best I could. I even pushed out a few of the softer dents with my hands, from inside the panels. 'Good as new,' I thought aloud, as Michael strolled up behind me.

'My God, Frankie! What have you done to it?' he exclaimed, circling the car.

'Don't worry, I haven't finished yet. Anyway, you can always claim another from the insurance when it's over.' He muttered something I didn't hear, but I couldn't be bothered to ask him to repeat it. 'I've got something to discuss with you, Michael. I'll find you later. In the meantime, keep Sandy occupied and as far away from the summerhouse as you can.'

He sighed, nodded, and walked back the way he had come.

Sorting out the car took most of the morning. I spent the rest of it in the utility room perched on the dryer in the nip, with all my worldly goods going round in circles just like that bloke - in *that* ad - though not so well paid. That left me time to collect tea and toast from the kitchen and to prepare Lydia for the onslaught to come. I did this by waking her, shoving her back in the shower, and giving her a t-shirt, jogging trousers, and slippers I'd stolen from Sandy's clean laundry. They were about the same size, which was handy. I decided *not* to tell her anything about Jenny and Liza; as they say, first impressions count, and I wanted to sit back and watch their expressions.

Apprehension registered on Lydia's face when, finally, we heard heels clicking towards the open doors of the summerhouse. As Jenny and Liza came inside, the shift from smiles to silent fury was almost too fast to comprehend. It was one of those claws-out-backs-up moments.

'Tea, ladies?' I interjected, arranging the cups. 'Sit down, we need to talk.' Oddly, I enjoyed saying that. It was something I was more used to hearing directed at me. The girls darted anxious glances at the bag of white powder, which I had left carelessly on the tea tray.

It all went moderately well for a few minutes, with the usual 'hellos' and 'how-are-yous' getting trotted out. It was clear no one really cared for an honest answer to the health enquiries. Lydia had been drugged, assaulted, knocked unconscious, dragged around in a sack half the night - literally through a hedge backwards - before undergoing minor surgery with no anaesthetic; and she just said, 'Fine, thanks.' They were mentally circling each other, judging moves, shooting each other guarded looks; the air was charged with tension. I sat in silent apprehension, watching like a spectator witnessing Kasparov win his first world title.

Cups clinked shakily on saucers and pale lips kissed gilt rims, but we were getting nowhere. *Sod this*, I thought, and I went for the kill. 'So what happened in Cyprus then, ladies? And what have you all got to do with this syndicate scam? Come on, cough up!'

I crossed the room and locked the doors, pocketing the key for good effect. Then I stood behind Lydia's chair, trying to balance the odds psychologically - and to be honest I was still on her side, though whether it was because of the recent proof of at least some truth in her words or my memories of the nights we had shared in the glow of the forge, I don't know.

They opted to tell me everything, all of them, at the same time. Their voices rose in volume, tempo and pitch until my ears were ringing. Gradually I began to work things out. It seemed that basically Lydia was telling the truth and that Liza was far deeper into the whole drugs thing than she had ever admitted. She and Marcus had pooled resources to import a huge consignment of drugs straight from South America - a one-off deal to set them up forever and cut out the middlemen in Cyprus. It had all gone wrong when the ship carrying the drugs had sunk in a freak storm in the Atlantic hurricane season - I remembered my radio burbling isobars on that fateful night all those months ago. She had agreed when Marcus proposed a big insurance scam to clear their mutual debts so they could part company and she could begin life anew with Jenny.

It was only her unexpectedly meeting Jenny in my caravan that had moved events on at this pace. Apparently they had both wanted to tell me - of course they had - but the right moment never came. I nodded, smiled, and decided that before my eardrums suffered permanent damage I should leave them to sort themselves out. Sweet little Lydia appeared capable of fending for herself. I tipped the powder out in a heap amongst the dirty cups on the tray, poured the last of the tea over it, and unlocked the door. Then I went outside to sit on the bench in front of the summerhouse. They were still shouting at the top of their voices. 'That shit is all you two care about!' screamed Lydia. This was followed by the crash of breaking china, though whether clumsy or irate fingers were responsible, I couldn't tell. The coven broke up after that and Jenny stormed past me en route for the caravan, with Lydia trotting in her wake.

I went back inside and found Liza stony-faced and gazing into space. When I called her name gently from the open door, giving myself room for a quick getaway, she turned to me with tears springing in her eyes - I melted at once and crossed to her, ready to provide her with the proverbial shoulder to cry on, to be her port in a storm. How wrong I was; she flew at me - literally! The first punch bloodied my nose. The second glanced off my cheek. I struggled to get her under control and managed to pin her down to the lounger by her wrists.

'You bastard, Frankie!' she spat at me as I straddled her.

'What have I done?'

She squirmed and carried on at full volume. 'You brought that cow back! You've ruined *everything*! Jenny will go back with her for sure!'

'If she does, you've got no one to blame but yourself, you self-centred bitch!' I shouted back at her. I relaxed my grip and she punched me in the face again. I lost my temper and slapped her. 'You got me into this fucking mess, love!' I ranted, grabbing her arms again. 'I've been through hell because of you.'

She started to sob, her fury spent, so I cautiously relaxed my grip again and lay down next to her. We stared at the pine-panelled ceiling in silence for a few minutes.

'Why did we run, if you were in on it?' I asked at last.

'I got frightened. I knew it was an insurance scam but when he started talking about life insurance I thought they were going to kill me.' She sniffed back a tear.

'And what about Jenny?' I asked.

'When the debts were paid we were going to keep the bar in Cyprus and live together, but now Lydia's back and everything's ruined.' She started to sob again and I held her close. Her tears were soaking my shirt and warming my chest.

'It can't be that bad, love,' I told her. 'Let's go and find them and see what's going on.'

'No!' she snapped, drying her eyes on the back of her hand. 'Lock the doors again and draw the curtains. I want to leave them to it. I'm not going to interfere any more. If it's over, it's over.'

I locked up and switched the stereo on, just letting whatever LP was on the turntable play. I glanced at the label; Genesis - *Invisible Touch*. Trying to block out the whirlwind of thoughts in my head, I rejoined Liza on the lounger and held her head against my chest. She sniffed a few more times then turned to face me and kissed me.

'Thank you, Frankie.'

'What for?'

'Everything. I'm sorry for dragging you into all this. You're a good friend.'

'I am, aren't I?'

She gave me one of her playful slaps and I kissed her back, first softly and then with more passion. I was waiting for her to push me away, but the push didn't come. And I'm not sure why - maybe she was getting her retaliation in first, copying my tactics, or maybe it was the overwhelming emotions of the day, but the moment I had waited for since that flat-tyre-on-the-bridle-path day had come.

She led me by the hand to the bathroom. We stripped and shared a long hot shower. She turned to face the wall and I applied the rich bubbles to her smooth skin. As she closed her eyes, I let my hands wander. I pressed myself against her buttocks, first gently and then with growing enthusiasm; she gasped and bit her lip as I found my mark. We were soon working together, she grinding her hips back to meet my eager movements. My enthusiasm grew and my thrusts lifted her feet from the floor. I paused and she turned to face me. I lifted her and she wrapped her legs around my waist, leaning back against the wall as the hot water pounded us from above and the haunting lyrics of 'In too deep' played softly in the background.

I suppose you're wondering, was it worth the wait? I thought the same while drying at a leisurely pace. Now don't get me wrong - it was good, as good as sex can get - but how much better could it have been if I'd still felt that impelling tug of love that had been my focus for so long? It was time to face it, I'd been deluding myself. I'd been a mug, been had. I loved her, but she didn't love me. And that is what makes sex into something more, isn't it?

'Don't think that this changes anything between us,' Liza called from the living room. 'We're still only friends. I've made my choice.'

'I know, love,' I answered with a sigh, *and besides,* I told myself under my breath, *I've had enough of all this drama and emotional roller-coaster stuff - I'm off!* I'd decided it was time to do my usual disappearing act. They could sort themselves out, and I would be miles away by this time tomorrow. One of nature's born survivors, me - and I didn't need any of them, or this mess, any more.

I strolled back into the living room. She was rubbing her nose on the back of her hand and massaging her gums with her fingertips; she must have found some powder that had escaped the cold tea. I found my jacket and put my few possessions in a pillowcase as she returned to the bathroom, combing her wet hair and taking advantage of the toiletries in the cabinet.

'So what *is* the scam then?' I asked.

She filled me in. The plan was to sucker rich people with dodgy cash that needed laundering into investing in their syndicates - race horses, fast cars, pedigree cattle, and clubs - anything. They'd been selling off the investments and pocketing the cash.

'That'll never work,' I said. 'They'll come after you *both.*'

'That's the clever bit,' she replied. 'They plan to fill the stables with decrepit horses and scrap cars, all their assets, and then burn the lot. They will be claiming from the insurance for the real stuff, and paying back the investors with some of the insurance money.'

'So he plans to burn the animals to death?' I asked.

'I suppose so. I hadn't really thought about it.'

And they called me heartless! And her a vegetarian!

'This way Marcus will be able to rebuild the old part of the house. I thought it was a good plan when he first explained it,' she added as we walked out into the garden.

Ah, but as you know, in my experience plans always go wrong.

'Come on, love,' I said, leading the way. 'You call burning the place down, with everything in it, a good plan?'

'As long as I'm not in there, I don't care,' she replied flippantly. 'Besides, what can we do about it anyway?'

I just shook my head. 'Let's see how things are in the caravan, love.'

My intention was to retrieve the bag of cash, pinch Sandy's car, and drive off into the sunset. Well, if no one else seemed to care, why should I?

Chapter 24

We strolled casually through the garden, keeping a little further apart than we usually would. With my natural gift for looking guilty as sin, even when I'm innocent, we must have had *sex* written all over us. As we got closer to the caravan we could hear screaming from inside.

'Shit! They're killing each other!' I broke into a trot. Liza kept pace and we raced to the caravan. I burst inside, just ahead of Liza.

Lydia was face down on the floor, screaming for help, her hands bound behind her back. The place was a shambles, with broken glass and smashed china all over the floor. I knelt by her. The wound in her scalp had opened up again and blood was running into her eyes; her hands were purple. Some callous soul had inserted a small bar into the dressing-gown cord they had bound her with and used it as a lever, twisting her bonds tourniquet-tight.

I struggled with the knots in a panic, shouting, 'Who did this? Tell me!'

Liza pushed me off and sliced through the cord with a knife from the contents of the kitchen drawers that were spilled over the floor. Lydia cried out with the pain of the lifeblood rushing back into her fingers. I shook her.

'Where is she? Where's Jenny?

'They took her,' she sobbed. I realised I was still shaking her - and stopped.

'Who?'

'Two men, one with a stick and a limp - big men. They said you would know where and they'll be waiting for you.'

I picked up the cut cord and the bar. Someone was apparently hell-bent on seeing that Lydia never played the piano again. The *bar* - it was the torch I'd dropped in the barn! Its dental supplies logo had brought them straight here. After all, how many dentists were there in the syndicate?

'Run to the house and get Michael,' I shouted at Liza. She fell to her knees and began shaking and sobbing uncontrollably. This was the last straw for her.

'It's all my fault!' she cried out, snot and tears mingling as they ran down her face. 'I've ruined everything.'

She was inconsolable, but there was no time to comfort her now. 'Pull yourself together, you stupid bitch, and get Michael - fast!'

'It's all my fault,' she kept repeating, over and over. 'I'm sorry, I'm sorry.'

I took her by the shoulders and shook her hard. 'Come on, Liza! They're getting away!'

'It's too late! 'It's all my fault!' You don't understand, you don't understand.' She grabbed me and clung on. 'You don't understand what I've done.'

She was dead right there; I didn't have a clue. She might as well have been speaking mandarin Chinese. Whatever the case, I was quite sure that hanging onto me and screaming nonsense in my face wasn't going to improve my comprehension. I pushed her off, then stood up and ran for the house. Michael must have heard the commotion and was coming out of the back door.

'Get up to the caravan quick,' I shouted as I ran.

'What do you want me to do?'

'I don't know,' I answered. 'Just go - do whatever you think best.'

I rushed into the house, pushing Sandy aside, and found my way to Michael's study, where I locked the door and picked up the phone. It had to happen sooner or later, didn't it? 'Uncle John? It's me - Frankie. I'm in trouble again.' A dry laugh sounded on the other end. 'They've got Jenny - help us, *please*!' The laughing stopped.

Within a couple of minutes I was thrashing Sandy's car around the lanes back to Liza's house.

Liza had said they were going to burn their investments in the old part of the house - and *Jenny* was one of them. Liza's sobs had helped me slot the last piece of the puzzle into place. I recalled her anxiety over the conversation she had heard the night she fell from the roof. Life insurance needs lives - correction - bodies!

I had no idea what I was going to do. I just hoped I could do *something*. My plans never work anyway, so I decided just to adlib. God knew what I'd have to face - Jerry and Johnny probably, plus the balance of the goons at the house, with all their guns and dogs. All I had to counter that was my disappointment and my anger. I sped up the drive, ignoring the security man's attempt to flag me down and forcing him to jump out of my path as I careered for the stables.

I screeched to a halt and leapt out shouting. 'Jenny? Jenny! Where are you?' I started kicking stable doors open, then hurried into the workshops. The place seemed to be deserted. There was a wheel from one of the investment cars mounted on the spinning lathe and there were shards of silvery metal everywhere. The centres of another two magnesium-alloy wheels, reduced to stubs by the lathe, were lying in a pile of similar shards on the floor.

A trail of powder from a fertiliser sack had been mingled with the metallic shards on the floor; a wad of cotton cushion-filling and split tubes of superglue were lying where they met. The mixture of metal shards and coarse fertiliser powder spilled out down the corridor towards the stables. I ran along the corridor and found the floor thickly carpeted with fresh straw. I could also smell hexane solvent from the furniture restoration in the air; its fumes were already making my head spin.

The animals in the stalls were kicking up a fuss so I opened the stall doors and pinned them back in order to release the frightened creatures. The corridor filled quickly with terrified beasts. I reached the last stall and picked up a fork used for mucking out in order to goad the last horses into coming out. Only then did it dawn on me that the main archway doors were shut and that I was now stuck behind a wall of panicking animals.

A bull shouldered his way through the press, heading straight for me. I scrambled up onto the dividing wall between the corridor and the stalls, hanging onto the iron railings above and bracing myself with my legs parted against the bars. I rammed the tines of the fork between the floorboards above and started to lever and twist, breaking a small hole. I was sweating, my muscles burning, as I worked to make it big enough to squeeze through. At last I managed to haul myself through it and emerged onto the upper floor. Once through, I ran for the door to the stone staircase. The dizziness of the confinement and the solvent fumes was overtaking me with every step. Somewhere in my confused mind I could hear a voice shouting, a waking dream - I tried to shut it out and ran on.

As I reached the outer door I realised the voice was real. 'Frankie!' it shouted. It was Jenny. I ran back as far as I dared. She shouted again. I forced my shaking legs on and tried the door that separated me from her; it was locked with a huge bolt and padlock.

'Hold on, love!' I shouted. 'Don't worry - I'll get you out.'

I headed for the stairs, descended the stone steps two at a time, and ran out into the yard; then I staggered to the barred doors that filled the archway. The hefty locking bar was padlocked into place and I couldn't move it, so I pulled the winch cable once more from Sandy's car. The hook on the end made it too thick to slip between the bar and the doors. I ran back into the workshop and found a knife, which I used to cut seat belt webbing from the car. Then I lashed it round the bar and tied my best knot - was it left over right and under, or right over left? - I couldn't remember, so I set about looping the ends under and over as many times as I could then hooked on the cable and switched on the winch to reel it in.

The winch strained and the car started to move, its wheels dragging on the gravel. I jumped in and started the engine; I tried reversing but the doors held. As a last resort I drove straight for the doors and pounded them with the flimsy bull bars until the mounting bolts of the locking bar finally started to give - then I slipped into reverse again. All four wheels were spinning as I hurtled backwards. The cable came to its end with a jerk and the doors burst open, releasing a stampede of frightened animals into the yard.

I fought my way through them, getting knocked to the ground and scrambling to my feet a couple of times on the way, heading back to the workshop. There I started emptying tools from trays onto the floor, all the time shaking and shouting. 'Hold on, love! I'm coming!' Then I found what I was looking for - a large crowbar.

I turned to run back to Jenny as the cyanoacrylate-soaked cotton burst into flames, fanned by the air from the doors I had kicked open. My schoolboy knowledge of chemistry, reinforced by news clips and American films, flashed back to me - the exothermic properties of the glue meant that mixing it with cotton caused combustion. Someone who knew their stuff had planned a fire, using the materials available in the workshops and stables - a plan that would convince the fire scene investigators that it was an accident. The magnesium had been stabilised for a while by the quickly-evaporating hexane, buying them time to leave. Adding the nitrates from the fertiliser made the mix for old-fashioned flashgun powder or, I thought with a start, a DIY bomb! The word catalysed me to action as the mix ignited with white-heat brightness. I panicked and, with a crucible, scooped water from the vat for cooling metal next to the forge and flung it onto the flames.

It's a pity my school chemistry hadn't familiarised me with the word pyrophoricity. A sudden whoosh of flames knocked me off my feet and left me blinking and momentarily blinded. My skin felt tight and tingled with pain.

I dropped the crucible and scrabbled desperately to find the door, where I rolled outside onto the gravel, gasping for air. As I regained my vision I saw four suited goons, two with shotguns, running towards me.

I leapt to my feet and retrieved the crowbar from the floor just inside the open door, all the time battling against the heat. Then I turned to face the goons bearing down on me. A fifth hobbled on a stick to catch up.

Shit, only a fool like me would turn up to a gunfight with a crowbar. There was no way I could fight them all off, especially not in the state I was in. But running, my favourite ploy in situations like this, just wasn't an option. I hefted the crowbar in both hands and tried to look more menacing than I felt.

If my plan was to bludgeon my way out of it with just a crowbar - well, like all my plans, it didn't work. But, as things turned out, it didn't need to. My salvation was announced by a dark grey plume that billowed from the archway and came in the unlikeliest and most unheroic form - a transit van with its horn blaring and roof beacons flashing orange into the smoke.

Johnny never knew what hit him; he did the last fifty yards sprawled on the bonnet of the van. The others scattered like skittles as the van hit them. A gun almost levelled at me went off with an ineffectual bang into the gravel. The van skidded to a halt. I read *John McCormack - Plant Hire and Surfacing* in foot-high letters down its side. The front doors flew open and Dennis and Fred charged headlong at the dazed goons; they were actually smiling.

I tottered on my feet for a couple of seconds then, still clutching the bar, I threw myself up the stairs into the burning building. The long corridor was already filling with smoke and I knew that Jenny was imprisoned behind the door at the far end. Sparks and tongues of fire were already coming up though the floorboards and acrid choking fumes clawed at my eyes and throat. I could hear Jenny pounding the door, though weakly, and her cries were growing faint.

'Hold on, love!' I shouted. I was rooted to the spot with fear - desperate to help but quailing in terror. An explosion from below jerked me to my senses. I gripped the bar and ran, ran like I had never run before.

I got to the far end of the corridor and set about hammering and wrenching at the bolt. Somehow I smashed through the door and then half-dragged, half-carried Jenny back the length of the corridor. I stumbled and we half-fell down the steps, choking and gasping for air, onto the gravel below. The fight with the goons was still raging. Jenny's hair was smoking and her skirt was smouldering. I dragged her to the stone trough and splashed water over her with my hands. She didn't seem to be breathing so I held her nose, covered her mouth with mine, and blew into her lungs - air just as foul as that she had already inhaled. After a few puffs, thank god, it started to work. She coughed and spluttered with life and I clung to her.

Chapter 25

With Jenny breathing again, I sat back with a sigh and laughed wheezily. Was it relief? Or was it the false euphoria of the hexane fumes? I don't know, but for a moment I felt good. Then a vicious thud between my shoulder blades sent me sprawling over Jenny's limp body. I tried to cover her as blows rained down on us both. The blows kept coming and coming, but somehow I managed to focus and grabbed wildly out at the source of the attack. My hands closed on the head of a silver-topped walking cane - Johnny's cane - as it came down once more in the direction of Jenny's head. I twisted and pulled, wrenching the cane from the hand that wielded it. Our attacker was thrown off balance; I heard feet scattering gravel as he tried to regain his footing.

I rolled over Jenny as she lay gasping for air and scrambled to my feet, holding the cane club-like over my right shoulder, ready to strike. 'Come on, you bastard!' I yelled.

I focused on our assailant and saw that it was not Johnny, but Marcus. He must have picked up the cane after Johnny was mown down by the van. The shock of recognition made me hesitate, just for a moment. The next thing I knew Marcus was grinning as he executed a spinning kick that slammed into my ribs and sent me reeling. I quickly regained my balance and swung at him wildly. He just laughed as he stepped away.

I shook my head and tried to focus. Memories I'd struggled to forget since that fateful night on Fair Hill all those years ago - the night I'd taken Digger's car and ran - came flooding back. I was becoming a fighter again, the ugliest kind of fighter there is - a bare-knuckle boxer. The limp body of an eager young opponent lay at my feet as the lights dazzled me and the roars of an angry crowd filled my ears. Memories of Simon the boxing coach shouting at me to practise until I had committed each move to my muscle-memory swarmed into my brain. I could hear him as clear as day stressing the need for instinctive movement, with no space for thought between action and reaction. Box fast, box clever.

I let the cane drop and clutched at my ribs, trying to ignore the pain. Marcus paused, smiling, then removed his jacket and rolled up his sleeves. 'Come on then, Frankie,' he said. 'Let's see if you can fight me like a man.'

I drew myself up and stepped over Jenny. He came at me, whirling his hands in a fanning motion and making odd yelping noises. I took up my stance, my weight over my back foot, with my guard held high, my head down, bracing myself.

He landed a few ineffectual punches, together with a flurry of sharp kicks delivered with a flick of his ankle. I absorbed them all and eased my left foot back, searching from the corners of my eyes for a safe space where I could carry on the fight without hurting Jenny.

Marcus dropped his guard, thinking I was retreating, but without giving him warning I came back at him. I jabbed him once, twice. The first blow broke his defences; the second drew blood from his bottom lip. Seeing my opportunity, I let fly with a right hook, shifting all my weight onto my front foot for one killer blow - I contacted *nothing*. His elbow in my kidneys accelerated my momentum as I crashed into the gravel. He laughed and casually picked up the cane, then drew a sword blade from its length. If I had realised it was a sword-stick I might have held on to it.

'And now, Frankie, I'm going to kill you both.'

I scrambled to cover Jenny as he advanced upon her and raised the weapon. 'I'm sorry, Jen,' I blurted out. 'I love you.'

I closed my eyes. As I readied myself for the impact of the blade an echoing crack sounded nearby and - *nothing happened*. No searing pain, no numbing thud followed by the trickle of warm blood - nothing. I opened my eyes as a heavy crunch in the gravel broke the silence. My astonished gaze met Marcus's face, which was now level with mine. He was kneeling, ghostly white, with his mouth gaping. Blood was seeping out in a huge circle on his chest. Then a second crack sounded and he slumped in a crooked heap with his limbs at awkward angles. I slowly lifted my head. Liza stood there, trembling and pale-faced, with the revolver from my van smoking in her outstretched hands.

A chorus of *nee-nahs* and *wah-wahs*, and the deeper bellow of a fire engine's horn was drawing close to the house. The firemen arrived first, smashing in doors in the parts of the building yet to be reached by the flames and pumping foam into the stables.

A ragged and dazed collection of refugees appeared in the yard, including, supported between two firemen, a very sorry-looking Julian. Then the ambulances arrived and their crews hastened to the rescue. Jenny was stretchered, her face covered by an oxygen mask, into the back of one, and Liza was sat down on a folding chair fetched from another. A fire officer in a white helmet kicked the gun away from her feet; I watched as he stood looking down at it and talking on a walkie-talkie. The ambulance crew were checking Liza's pulse and asking her name as they wrapped her in a blanket to keep out the chill of the first wave of shock.

Jenny's ambulance was filled with shouts from its frantic crew and beeps from brightly lit machines as the doors were slammed shut. It spat gravel from spinning tyres as it accelerated away, its sirens and lights adding to the chaos.

I didn't see what happened next as I was already running, stumbling through the smoke and back along the hedgerow. Well, what could I do? Hospitals make me nervous and prisons are just a maze of corridors, which you know I can't stand.

Dennis and Fred picked me up on the main road. I spotted the van through the trees and waved them to a standstill. They were swapping tales of valour, in blow-by-blow detail. I huddled in the back, like a sleeping hamster, and let them take me back to Sandy's.

'You would 'a had that fucker in a straight fight, Frankie,' Fred said, consolingly.

He may have been right but, you know, fighting just isn't my thing. I found that out in a clearing between caravans on a windswept hill in Westmorland a long time ago. Violence has consequences - life-changing consequences, and now any kind of fighting frightens me out of my wits. And here I was, once again, running from the scene. When we arrived at Sandy's I pulled myself together for one last effort.

The house was empty, so I bundled clothes from Sandy's wardrobe and dresser into a suitcase and threw it in the caravan. Then I raided the kitchen to stock up the fridge and cupboards and to replace the broken china. I cleared the caravan up hurriedly and swept the shards and splinters out of the door with a broom from the summerhouse, where I'd stocked up with towels and linen for the beds. Then I collected Lydia from where she slumbered on the summerhouse lounger and made her comfortable on the back seat of Jenny's car, while I hitched up the caravan and finally moved off.

I took us to a farm I know close to Bewdley. The first thing I did when we got there was to call the hospital, pretending to be a worried brother enquiring about his sister, who had recently been admitted after being caught up in a fire. Jenny was going to be ok. That done, we decided to stay a few days while the dust settled. I called Uncle John - Digger to you - and he came over for a chat.

He was chauffeured over in his Jaguar, with Dennis and

Fred in the front seats. He stepped out with a smile. 'You'll never believe what's happened, Frankie,' he said with a smile. 'Some low-life broke into the yard while we were in Appleby and stole one of my vans. The police found it, wrecked.' He shook his head. 'But I got your suit back,' he added, with a wink. 'In fact I have all your stuff in the back of the car. Oh, and by the way, Molly sent her thanks for the cash.'

'I hope she spent it wisely,' I said.

'Oh, she did that. Her bloke got out of jail and they buggered off to Spain for a long holiday,' he said as he walked back to the car.

'What about little Molly?' I asked.

'She was dumped on me. I was told to get her "bloody-selfish father" to look after her until she got back.' He opened the back door. 'A girl needs her father to keep her on the straight and narrow, or anything might happen.'

I knew he was alluding to his disappointment in Jenny and her descent into a lifestyle his Victorian sense of morality thought unnatural. She was, after all, his best friend's daughter, whom he'd taken under his wing after her parents died in a motorway accident.

Little Molly stepped out of the Jaguar, my horrible suit jacket draped around her shoulders. She ran to me and threw her arms round me. Then Digger left me with a handshake, a smile, and a pat on the back. No debts owed, no favours to repay, *nothing*.

Molly, Lydia, and I ate dinner together that night and, despite everything, we laughed and chatted. Like I said, I'm easily dispirited, a quitter – but, on the bright side, I don't stay down for long.

Then I hitched up once more and we moved on. 'Don't worry!' I said as the gatepost grazed the caravan's shining side, 'that'll polish out.'

Lydia shook her head in disbelief. I glanced in the rear-view mirror as I listened to Molly chirping excitedly in the back.

'Where we going, Frankie?'

'Don't you mean *Dad?*' Lydia corrected her.

'Ok, *Auntie* Lydia,' Molly intoned, rolling her eyes. 'Where are we going - *Dad*?'

I grinned at her. 'I know a little place in South Devon. They have music and a pool, and the owner has a lovely flock of Faverolles.'

Molly rolled her eyes again. 'You and your flipping chickens, Frankie... Sorry, I mean, Dad. Are you coming with us, Lydia?'

Lydia looked at me and I looked back at her.

'Sure,' she said at last. 'I would love to.'

I laughed and patted her knee. 'You know, Lydia, I could quite easily fall for a girl like you. Have you got anyone special waiting at home?'

It has to be said - I fall in love far too easily. She was still laughing as we pulled out onto the main road and headed south.

I still feel guilty and ashamed for leaving the other two like that. It wakes me up in the small hours, but the feeling won't last forever. They say Liza will get off with a light sentence as she was under a lot of stress, not responsible for her actions, and I can agree with that. Jenny will survive to sing again. She's as tough as old boots, that one. Perhaps I was hoping they would stay on at the big house when things cooled down. I could go back to my plot, and we could all live happily ever after. But life's not like that, is it?

To Be Continued

Part two:

Thinking About Breathing.

I'd been away for a while, at Her Majesty's pleasure if you must know, and arrived home to find a family member had been killed and left us all on the brink of financial ruin. The police said it was an accident, but I thought otherwise. It had to be murder and I was determined to prove it - even if I died trying

FRANKIE FULWOOD

ABOUT THE AUTHOR

I'm Frankie—half Gypsy, half Gorgie—and these are my stories. I've been kicked and punched, kidnapped and beaten, shot and stabbed; not to mention being treated like a mug by more thoughtless birds than I care to remember. I've mixed with toffs and rogues, hard men and philosophers, and seen some of the most beautiful and horrifying things a man can see. I haven't always done the right thing and maybe I was never the bloke to take home to meet your mum, but I have always been loyal to my friends and a sucker for a pretty face.

I grew up with the great Gypsy tradition of tall tales told around a camp fire, sparkling eyes in eager faces as the storyteller captivated his or her audience. There were always cheers for the good guys and boos for the baddies as smoke and flames rose into the evening sky. So, these are my tales. I tell them to you as the great Romani voices of the past told theirs to me—but be warned! I have never been one to let the truth stand in the way of a good yarn...

22009613R00172

Printed in Poland
by Amazon Fulfillment
Poland Sp. z o.o., Wrocław